THE NAME OF THE GAME

A pink-faced tech manned a control panel just inside the shuttle hatch corridor. He wore a red T-shirt with the GalacTech logo over his left breast. Tight blond curls cut close to his head reminded Leo of a lamb's pelt; perhaps it was an effect of his obvious youth. The tech smiled at Van Atta, and cocked his head in a plea for introduction. "Is this the new teacher you were telling us about?"

"Indeed. Leo Graf, this is Tony—he'll be among your first trainees. Tony is a welder and joiner, second grade—working on first, eh, Tony? Shake hands with Mr. Graf."

Van Atta was smirking. Leo had the impression that if he hadn't been in free fall, he would have been bouncing on his heels.

Tony pulled himself obediently over the control panel. He wore red shorts—

Leo blinked, and caught his breath in shock. The boy had no legs. Emerging from his shorts was a second set of arms.

"The name of the game, Leo," said Van Atta, "is bioengineering. . . ."

Baen Books by Lois McMaster Bujold

The Vorkosigan Saga:

LOIS McMASTER BUJOLD

FALLING FREE

A Baen Books Original

Baen Publishing Enterprises
P.O. Box 1403
Riverdale, NY 10471

ISBN: 0-671-57812-X

Cover art by Pat Turner

First printing, April 1988
Fifth printing, June 1999

Distributed by Simon & Schuster
1230 Avenue of the Americas
New York, NY 10020

Printed in the United States of America

For Dad.

The author would like to thank three gentlemen for helping improve the ratio of science to fiction in this story: Dr. Henry Bielstein, for information on space physiology and medicine; James A. McMaster, welding engineer; and Wallace A. Voreck, explosives technology consultant. Much that is technically correct I owe to them; any errors are my own.

My debt exceeds words to the late Dr. Robert C. McMaster, physicist, engineer, teacher and inventor, for help beyond technical, beyond measure. The errors are still my own, but I'm working on them.

—Lois McMaster Bujold
May 1987

Chapter 1

The shining rim of the planet Rodeo wheeled dizzily past the observation port of the orbital transfer station. A woman whom Leo Graf recognized as one of his fellow disembarking passengers from the Jump ship stared eagerly out for a few minutes, then turned away, blinking and swallowing, to sit rather abruptly on one of the bright cushioned lounge chairs. Her eyes closed, opened, caught Leo's; she shrugged in embarrassment. Leo smiled sympathetically. Immune himself to the assorted nauseas of space travel, he moved to take her place at the crystal viewport.

Scanty cloud cover swirled in the thin atmosphere far below, barely veiling what seemed excessive quantities of red desert sand. Rodeo was a marginal world, home only to GalacTech mining and drilling operations and their support facilities. But what was he doing here? Leo wondered anew. Underground operations were hardly his field of expertise.

The planet slid from view with the rotation of the station. Leo moved to another port for a view back toward the hub of the station's wheel, noting the stress points and wondering when they'd last been x-rayed for secretly propagating flaws. Centrifugal g-forces here at the rim where this passenger lounge

1

was situated seemed to be running at about half Earth-standard, a little light perhaps. Deliberately stress-reduced, trouble anticipated in the structure?

But he was here for training, they'd said at GalacTech headquarters on Earth, to teach quality control procedures in free fall welding and construction. To whom? Why here, at the end of nowhere? 'The Cay Project' was a singularly uninformative title for his assignment.

"Leo Graf?"

Leo turned. "Yes?"

The speaker was tall and dark-haired, perhaps thirty, perhaps forty. He wore conservative-fashionable civilian clothes, but a quiet lapel pin marked him as a company man. Best sedentary executive type, Leo decided. The hand he held out for Leo to shake was evenly tanned but soft. "I'm Bruce Van Atta."

Leo's thick hand was pale but flecked with brown spots. Crowding forty, sandy and square, Leo wore comfortable red company coveralls by long habit, partly to blend with the workers he supervised, mostly that he need never waste time and thought deciding what to put on in the morning. "Graf", read the label printed over his left breast pocket, eliminating all mystery.

"Welcome to Rodeo, the armpit of the universe," grinned Van Atta.

"Thank you," Leo smiled back automatically.

"I'm head of the Cay Project now; I'll be your boss," Van Atta amplified. "I requested you personally, y'know. You're going to help me get this division moving at last, jack it up and light a fire under it. You're like me, I know, got no patience with deadheads. It was a hell of a job to have dumped on me, trying to make *this* division profitable—but if I succeed, I'll be the Golden Boy."

"Requested me?" Cheering, to think that his reputation preceded him, but why couldn't one ever be requested by somebody at a garden spot? Ah, well. . . . "They told me at HQ that I was being sent out here to give an expanded version of my short course in non-destructive testing."

"Is that all they told you?" Van Atta asked in astonishment. At Leo's affirmative shrug, he threw back his head and laughed. "Security, I suppose," Van Atta went on when he'd stopped chuckling. "Are you in for a surprise. Well, well. I won't spoil it." Van Atta's sly grin was as irritating as a familiar poke in the ribs.

Too familiar—oh, hell, Leo thought, this guy *knows* me from somewhere. And he thinks I know him. . . . Leo's polite smile became fixed in mild panic. He had met thousands of GalacTech personnel in his eighteen-year career. Perhaps Van Atta would say something soon to narrow the possibilities.

"My instructions listed a Dr. Cay as titular head of the Cay Project," Leo probed. "Will I be meeting him?"

"Old data," said Van Atta. "Dr. Cay died last year—several years past the date he should have been forcibly retired, in my opinion, but he was a vice-president and major stockholder and thoroughly entrenched—but that's blood over the damned dam, eh? I replaced him." Van Atta shook his head. "But I can't wait to see the look on your face when you see—come along. I have a private shuttle waiting."

They had the six-man personnel shuttle to themselves, but for the pilot. The passenger seat molded itself to Leo's body during the brief periods of acceleration. Quite brief periods; clearly they were not braking for planetary re-entry. Rodeo turned beneath them, falling farther away.

"Where are we going?" Leo asked Van Atta, seated beside him.

"Ah," said Van Atta. "See that speck about thirty degrees above the horizon? Watch it. It's home base for the Cay Project."

The speck grew rapidly into a far-flung chaotic structure, all angles and projections, with confetti-colored lights spangling its sharp shadows. Leo's practiced eye picked out the clues to its function, the tanks, the ports, the greenhouse filters winking in the sunlight, the size of the solar panels versus the estimated volume of the structure.

"An orbital habitat?"

"You got it," said Van Atta.

"It's huge."

"Indeed. How many personnel would you guess it could handle?"

"Oh—fifteen hundred."

Van Atta's eyebrows rose, in slight disappointment, perhaps, at not being able to offer a correction. "Almost exactly. Four hundred-ninety-four rotating GalacTech personnel and a thousand permanent inhabitants."

Leo's lips echoed the word, permanent . . . "Speaking of rotation—how are you handling null-gee deconditioning in your people? I don't—" his eyes inventoried the enormous structure, "I don't even see an exercise wheel. No spinning gym?"

"There's a null-gee gym. The rotating personnel get a month downside after every three-month shift."

"Expensive."

"But we put the Habitat up there for less than a quarter of the cost of the same volume of living quarters in one-gee spinners."

"But surely you'll lose what you've saved in construction costs over time in personnel transportation and medical expenses," argued Leo. "The extra shuttle trips, the long leaves—every retiree who breaks an arm or a leg until the day he dies will be suing GalacTech for the cost of it plus mental anguish, whether he had significant bone demineralization or not."

"We've solved that problem too," said Van Atta. "Whether the solution is cost-effective—well, that's what you and I are here to try and prove."

The shuttle sidled delicately into alignment with a hatch on the side of the Habitat and seated itself with a reassuringly authoritative click. The pilot shut down his systems and unbuckled himself to float past Leo and Van Atta and check the hatch seals. "Ready for disembarking, Mr. Van Atta."

"Thank you, Grant."

Leo released his seat restraints, and stretched and relaxed in the pleasureable familiarity of weightlessness. Not for him the unfortunate nauseas of null-gee that sapped the efficiency of so many employees. Leo's body was ordinary enough, downside; here, where control and practice and wit counted more than strength, he was at last an athlete. Smiling a little to himself, he followed Van Atta from hand-grip to hand-grip and through the shuttle hatch.

A pink-faced tech manned a control panel just inside the shuttle hatch corridor. He wore a red T-shirt with the GalacTech logo over his left breast. Tight blond curls cut close to his head reminded Leo of a lamb's pelt; perhaps it was an effect of his obvious youth.

"Hello there, Tony," Van Atta greeted him with cheerful familiarity.

"Good afternoon, Mr. Van Atta," the youth replied deferentially. He smiled at Leo, and cocked his head at Van Atta in a pantomime plea for an introduction. "Is this the new teacher you were telling us about?"

"Indeed he is. Leo Graf, this is Tony—he'll be among your first trainees. He's one of the habitat's *permanent* residents," Van Atta added with peculiar emphasis. "Tony is a welder and joiner, second grade—working on first, eh, Tony? Shake hands with Mr. Graf."

Van Atta was smirking. Leo had the impression that if he hadn't been in free fall, he would have been bouncing on his heels.

Tony pulled himself obediently over the control panel. He wore red shorts—

Leo blinked, and caught his breath in shock. The boy had no legs. Emerging from his shorts were a second set of arms.

Functional arms, he was even now using his—his lower left hand, Leo supposed he'd have to call it—to anchor himself as he reached out to Leo. His smile was perfectly unselfconscious.

Leo had lost his own hand grip, and had to fumble to retrieve it, and stretch awkwardly to meet the proffered handshake. "How do you do," Leo managed to croak. It was almost impossible not to stare. Leo forced his gaze to focus on the young man's bright blue eyes.

"Hello, sir. I've been looking forward to meeting you." Tony's handshake was shy but sincere, his hand dry and strong.

"Um . . ." Leo stumbled, "um, what's your last name, uh, Tony?"

"Oh, Tony's just my nickname, sir. My full designation is TY-776-424-XG."

"I, uh—guess I'll call you Tony, then," Leo mur-

mured, increasingly stunned. Van Atta, most un-
helpfully, seemed to be thoroughly enjoying Leo's
discomforture.

"Everybody does," said Tony agreeably.

"Fetch Mr. Graf's bag, will you, Tony?" said Van
Atta. "Come on, Leo, I'll show you your quarters,
and then we can do the grand tour."

Leo followed his floating guide into the indicated
cross-corridor, glancing back over his shoulder in
renewed amazement as Tony launched himself accurately across the chamber and swung through the
shuttle hatch.

"That's," Leo swallowed, "that's the most extraordinary birth defect I've ever seen. Somebody had a
stroke of genius, to find him a job in free fall. He'd
be a cripple, downside."

"Birth defect." Van Atta's grin had grown twisted.
"Yeah, that's one way of describing it. I wish you
could have seen the look on your face, when he
popped up like that. I congratulate you on your
self-control. I about puked when I first saw one, and
I was prepared. You get used to the little chimps
pretty quick, though."

"There's more than one?"

Van Atta opened and closed his hands in a counting gesture. "An even one-thousand. The first generation of GalacTech's new super-workers. The name of
the game, Leo, is bioengineering. And I intend to
win."

Tony, with Leo's valise clutched in his lower right
hand, swooped between Leo and Van Atta in the
cylindrical corridor and braked to a halt in front of
them with three deft touches on the passing hand-
grips.

"Mr. Van Atta, can I introduce Mr. Graf to somebody on the way to Visitor's Wing? It won't be *much* out of the way—Hydroponics."

Van Atta's lips pursed, then arranged themselves in a kindly smile. "Why not? Hydroponics is on the itinerary for this afternoon anyway."

"Thank you, sir," cried Tony, and darted off with enthusiasm to open the air safety seal before them at the end of the corridor, and linger to close it again behind them on the other side.

Leo fastened his attention on his surroundings, as a less-rude alternative to surreptitiously studying the boy. The Habitat was indeed inexpensively constructed, mostly pre-fab units variously combined. Not the most aesthetically elegant design—a certain higgledy-piggledy randomness indicated an organic growth pattern since the Habitat's inception, units stuck on here and there to accomodate new needs. But its very dullness incorporated safety advantages Leo approved, the interchangeability of airseal systems for example.

They passed dormitory wings, food preparation and dining areas, a workshop for small repairs—Leo paused to gaze down its length, and had to hurry to catch up with his guide. Unlike most free-fall living spaces Leo had worked in, there was no effort here to maintain an arbitrary up-and-down to ease the visual psychology of the inhabitants. Most chambers were cylindrical in design, with work spaces and storage efficiently packing the walls and the center left free of obstruction for the passage of—well, one could hardly call them pedestrians.

En route they passed a couple of dozen of the— the four-handed people, the new model workers, Tony's folk, whatever they were called—did they have an official designation, Leo wondered? He stared covertly, breaking off his gaze whenever one looked back, which was often; they stared openly at him, and whispered among themselves.

He could see why Van Atta dubbed them chimps. They were thin-hipped, lacking the powerful gluteal locomotor muscles of people with legs. The lower set of arms tended to be more muscular than the uppers in both males and females, power-grippers, and thus appeared falsely short by comparison to the uppers; bow-legged, if he squinted them to a blur.

They were dressed mostly in the sort of comfortable, practical T-shirt and shorts that Tony wore, evidently color-coded, for Leo passed a cluster of them all in yellow hovering intently around a normal human in GalacTech coveralls who had a pump unit half-apart, lecturing on its function and repair. Leo thought of a flock of canaries, of flying squirrels, of monkeys, of spiders, of swift bright lizards of the sort that run straight up walls.

They made him want to scream, almost to weep; and yet it wasn't the arms, or the quick, too-many hands. He had almost reached Hydroponics before he was able to analyze his intense unease. It was their faces that bothered him so, Leo realized. They were the faces of children. . . .

A door marked "Hydroponics D" slid aside to reveal an antechamber and a large airy end chamber extending some fifteen meters beyond. Filtered windows on the sun side, and an array of mirrors on the dark side, filled the volume with brilliant light, softened by green plants that grew from a carefully-arranged set of grow tubes. The air was pungent with chemicals and vegetation.

A pair of the four-armed young women, both in blue, were at work in the antechamber. A plexiplastic grow tube three meters long was braced in place, and they floated along its length carefully transplanting tiny seedlings from a germination box into a spiral series of holes along the tube, one plant per hole, fixing them in place with flexible sealant around each tender stalk. The roots would grow inward, becoming a tangled mat to absorb the nutritive hydroponic mist pumped through the tube, and the leaves and stems would bush out in the sunlight and eventually bear whatever fruit was their genetic destiny. In this place, probably apples with antlers, thought Leo in mild hysteria, or potatoes with eyes that really winked at you.

The dark-haired girl paused to adjust a bundle under her arm. . . . Leo's mind ground to a complete halt. The bundle was a baby.

A live baby—of course it was alive, what did he expect? Leo gibbered inwardly. It peered around its—mother's?—torso to glower suspiciously at Leo-the-stranger, and tightened its four-handed clutch on home base, taking a squishy defensive grip on one of the girl's breasts as if in fear of competition. "Ackle," it remarked aggressively.

"Ow!" The dark-haired girl laughed, and spared a lower hand to pry the little fat fingers loose without missing a beat of her upper hands patting sealant in place around a stem. She finished with a quick squirt of fixative from a tube floating conveniently beside her, just out of the infant's reach.

The girl was slim, and elvish, and wonderfully weird to Leo's unaccustomed eyes. Her short, fine hair clung close to her head, framing her face, shaped to a point at the nape of her neck. It was so thick it reminded Leo of cat fur: one might stroke it, and be soothed.

The other girl was blonde, and babyless. She looked up first, and smiled. "Company, Claire."

The dark-haired girl's face lit with pleasure. Leo

flushed in the heat of it. "Tony!" she cried happily, and Leo realized he had merely received an accidental dose, as it were, of that beam of delight, as it swept over him to its true target.

The baby released three hands and waved them urgently. "Ah, ah!" The girl turned in air to face the visitors. "Ah, ah, *ah*!" the baby repeated.

"Oh, all *right*," she laughed. "You want to fly to Daddy, hm?" She unhooked a short tether from a sort of soft harness on the baby's torso to a belt around her own waist, and held the infant out. "Fly to Daddy, Andy? Fly to Daddy?"

The baby indicated enthusiasm for the proposal by waving all four hands vigorously about and squealing eagerly. She launched him toward Tony with considerably more velocity than Leo would have dared to impart. Tony, grinning cheerfully, caught him—handily, Leo thought in blitzed inanity.

"Fly to Mommy?" Tony inquired in turn. "Ah, ah," the baby agreed, and Tony hung him in air, gently pulling his arms out—like straightening out a starfish, Leo thought—and imparting a spin rolled him through the air for all the world like a wheel. The baby pulled his hands in, clenching his face in sympathetic effort, and spun faster, and gurgled with laughter at the success of his effort. Conservation of angular momentum, thought Leo. Naturally . . .

Claire tossed the infant back one more time to his father—mind-boggling, to think of that blond boy as a father of anything—and followed herself to brake to a halt hand-to-hand against Tony, who proffered an automatic helping grasp for that purpose. That they continued to hold hands was clearly more than a courteous anchoring.

"Claire, this is Mr. Graf," Tony did not so much

introduce as display him, like a prize. "He's going to be my advanced welding techniques teacher. Mr. Graf, this is Claire, and this is our son Andy." Andy had clambered headward on his father, and was wrapping one hand in Tony's blond hair and another around one ear, blinking owlishly at Leo. Tony gently rescued the ear and re-directed the clutch to the fabric of his red T-shirt. "Claire was picked to be the very first natural mother of us," Tony went on proudly.

"Me and four other girls," Claire corrected modestly.

"Claire used to be in Welding and Joining too, but she can't do Outside work any more," Tony explained. "She's been in Housekeeping, Nutrition Technology, and Hydroponics since Andy was born."

"Dr. Yei said I was a very important experiment, to see which sorts of productivity were least compromised by my taking care of Andy at the same time," explained Claire. "I sort of miss going Outside—it was exciting—but I like this, too. More variety."

GalacTech re-invents Women's Work? thought Leo bemusedly. Are we about to put an R&D group to work on the applications of fire, too? But oh, you are certainly an experiment. . . . His thought was unreflected in his bland, closed face. "Happy to meet you, Claire," he said gravely.

Claire nudged Tony, and nodded toward her blonde co-worker, who had drifted over to join the group.

"Oh—and this is Silver," Tony went on obediently. "She works in Hydroponics most of the time."

Silver nodded. Her medium-short hair drifted in soft platinum waves, and Leo wondered if it was the source of her nickname. She had the sort of strong facial bones that are sharp and unhappily awkward at thirteen, arrestingly elegant at thirty-five, now not quite halfway through their transition. Her blue gaze was cooler and less shy than the busy Claire's, who was already distracted by some new demand from Andy. Claire retrieved the baby and re-attached his safety line.

"Good afternoon, Mr. Van Atta," Silver added particularly. She pirouetted in air, with eyes that cried silently, Notice me! Leo noticed that all twenty of her manicured fingernails were lacquered pink.

Van Atta's answering smile was secretive and smug. "Afternoon, Silver. How's it going?"

"We have one more tube to plant after this one. We'll be finished ahead of shift change," Silver offered.

"Fine, fine," said Van Atta jovially. "Ah—do try to remember to arrange yourself right-side up when you're talking to a downsider, Sugarplum."

Silver inverted herself hastily to match Van Atta's orientation. Since the room was radially arranged, right-side-up was a purely Van Atta-centric direction, Leo noted dryly. Where *had* he met the man before?

"Well, carry on, girls." Van Atta led out, Leo following, Tony bringing up the rear regretfully, looking back over his shoulder.

Andy had returned his attention to his mother, his determined little hands foraging up her shirt, on which dark stains were spreading in autonomic response. Apparently that was one bit of ancient biology the company had not altered. The milk dispensers were certainly ideally pre-adapted to life in free fall, after all. And even diapers had a heroic history in the dawn of space travel, Leo had heard.

His brief amusement drained away, and he pushed off after Van Atta, silent and reflective. He held his judgment suspended, he reassured himself, not paralyzed. In the meantime, a closed mouth could not impede the inflow of data.

They paused at Van Atta's Habitat office. Van Atta switched on the lights and air circulation as they entered. From the stale smell Leo guessed the office was not often used; the executive probably spent most of his time more comfortably downside. A large viewport framed a spectacular view of Rodeo.

"I've come up in the world a bit since we last met," said Van Atta, matching his gaze. The upper atmosphere along Rodeo's rim was producing some gorgeous prismatic light effects at this angle of view. "In several senses. I don't mind returning the favor. The man at the top owes it to remember how he got there, I think. Noblesse oblige and all that." The tilt of Van Atta's eyebrow invited Leo to join him in self-congratulatory satisfaction.

Remember. Quite. Leo's blank memory was getting excruciatingly uncomfortable. He smiled and seized the pause while Van Atta activated his desk comconsole to turn away and make a slow, politely-waiting-type orbit of the room, as if idly examining its contents.

A little wall plaque bearing a humorous motto caught his eye. *On the sixth day God saw He couldn't do it all*, it read, *so He created ENGINEERS*. Leo snorted, mildly amused.

"I like that too," commented Van Atta, looking up to check the cause of his chuckle. "My ex-wife gave it to me. It was about the only thing the greedy bitch didn't take back when we split."

"Were you an—" Leo began, and swallowed the words, *engineer, then?* as he finally remembered, and then wondered how he could ever have forgotten. Leo had known Van Atta as an engineering subordinate at that time, though, not as an executive superior. Was this sleek go-getter the same idiot he had kicked impatiently upstairs to Administration just to get him out from underfoot on the Morita Station project—ten, twelve years ago now? Brucie-baby. Oh, yes. Oh, hell . . .

Van Atta's comconsole disgorged a couple of data disks, which he plucked off. "You put me on the fast track. I've always thought it must give you a sense of satisfaction, since you spend so much of your time training, to see one of your old students make good."

Van Atta was no more than five years younger than Leo. Leo suppressed profound irritation—he wasn't this paper-shuffler's ninety-year-old retired Sunday school teacher, damn it. He was a working engineer, hands-on, and not afraid to get them dirty, either. His technical work was as close to perfection as his relentless conscientiousness could push it, his safety record spoke for itself. . . . He let his anger go with a sigh. Wasn't it always so? He'd seen dozens of subordinates forge ahead, often men he'd trained himself. Yeah, and trust Van Atta to make it seem a weakness and not a point of pride.

Van Atta spun the data disks across the room at him. "There's your roster and your syllabus. Come on, and I'll show you some of the equipment you'll be working with. GalacTech's got two projects in the wind they're thinking of finally turning these Cay Project quaddies loose on."

"Quaddies?"

"The official nickname."

"It's not, um . . . pejorative?"

Van Atta stared, then snorted. "No. What you do not call them out loud, however, is 'mutants,' genetic paranoia being what it is after that Nuovo Brasilian military cloning fiasco. This whole project could have been carried out much more conveniently in Earth orbit, but for the assorted legal hysterias about human gene manipulation. Anyway, the projects. One to assemble Jump ships in orbit around Orient IV, and another building a deep space transfer facility at some nexus away the hell-and-gone beyond Tau Ceti called Kline Station—cold work, no habitable planets in the system and its sun is a cinder, but the local space harbors no less than six wormhole exits. Potentially very profitable. Lots of welding under the most difficult free-fall conditions—"

Leo's brief angst was swallowed in interest. It had always been the work itself, not the pay and perks, that held him in thrall. Screw executive privilege—didn't it mostly mean being stuck downside? He followed Van Atta out of the office back into the corridor where Tony still waited patiently with his luggage.

"I suppose it was the development of the uterine replicators that made it all possible," Van Atta opined while Leo stowed his gear in his new quarters. More than a mere sleep cubicle, the chamber included private sanitary facilities and a comconsole as well as comfortable-looking sleep restraints—no morning backache on this job, Leo thought with minor satisfaction. Headache was another problem.

"I'd heard something about those things," said Leo. "Another invention from Beta Colony, wasn't it?"

Van Atta nodded. "The outer worlds are getting too damn clever these days. Earth's going to lose its edge if it doesn't shape up."

Too true, Leo thought. Yet the history of innovation suggested this was an inevitable pattern. Management who had made huge capital investments in one system were naturally loathe to scrap it, and so the latecomers forged ahead—to the frustration of loyal engineers. . . . "I'd thought the use of uterine replicators was limited to obstetrical emergencies."

"Actually, the only limitation on their use is the fact that they're hideously expensive," said Van Atta. "It's probably only a matter of time before rich women everywhere start ducking their biological duties and cooking up their kids in 'em. But for GalacTech, it meant that human bioengineering experiments could at last be carried out without involving a lot of flaky foster-mothers to carry the implanted embryos. A neat, clean, controlled engineering approach. Better still, these quaddies are total constructs—that is, their genes are taken from so many sources, it's impossible to identify their genetic parents either. Saves quantities of legal grief."

"I'll bet," said Leo faintly.

"This whole thing was Dr. Cay's obsession, I gather. I never met him, but he must have been one of those, you know, charismatic types, to push through a project with this enormous lead time before any possible pay-off. The first batch is just turning twenty. The extra arms are the wildest part—"

"I've often wished I had four hands, in free fall," Leo murmured, trying not to sound too dubious out loud.

"—but most of the changes were this bunch of metabolic stuff. They never get motion-sick—something about re-wiring the vestibular system—and their muscles maintain tone with an exercise regimen of barely fifteen minutes a day, max—nothing like the hours you and I would have to put in during a long stint in null-gee. Their bones don't deteriorate at all.

They're even more radiation-resistant than us. Bone marrow and gonads can take four and five times the rems we can absorb before GalacTech grounds us— although the medical types are pushing for them to do their reproducing early in life, while all those expensive genes are still pristine. After that, it's all gravy for us; workers who never require downside leave; so healthy they'll go on and on, cutting high-cost turnover; they're even," Van Atta snickered, "self-replicating."

Leo secured the last of his scanty personal possessions. "Where . . . will they go when they, uh, retire?" he asked slowly.

Van Atta shrugged. "I suppose the company will have to work something out, when the time comes. Not my problem, fortunately; *I'll* be retired before then."

"What happens if they—quit, go elsewhere? Suppose somebody offers them higher pay? GalacTech will be out-of-pocket for all the R&D."

"Ah. I don't think you've quite grasped the beauty of this set-up. They don't quit. They aren't employees. They're capital equipment. They aren't paid in money—though I wish *my* salary was equal to what GalacTech is spending yearly to maintain 'em. But that will get better as the last replicator cohort gets older and more self-sufficient. They stopped producing new ones about five years ago, see, in anticipation of turning that job over to the quaddies themselves." Van Atta licked his lips and raised his eyebrows, as if in enjoyment of a salacious joke. Leo could not regret missing its point.

Leo turned, curling in air and crossing his arms. "Spacer's Union is going to call it slave labor, you know," he said at last.

"The Union's going to call it worse names than

that. Their productivity is going to look sick," growled Van Atta. "Loaded language bullshit. These little chimps have cradle to grave security. GalacTech couldn't be treating them better if they were made of solid platinum. You and I should have so good a deal, Leo."

"Ah," said Leo, and no more.

Chapter 2

The observation bubble on the side of the Cay Habitat had a televiewer, Leo discovered to his delight, and furthermore it was unoccupied at the moment. His own quarters lacked a viewport. He slipped within. His schedule allowed this one free day, to recover from trip fatigue and Jump lag before his course was to begin. A good night's sleep in free fall had already improved his tone of mind vastly over yesterday, after Van Atta's—Leo could only dub it "disorientation tour."

The curve of Rodeo's horizon bisected the view from the bubble, and beyond it the vast sweep of stars. Just now one of Rodeo's little mice moons crept across the panorama. A glint above the horizon caught Leo's eye.

He adjusted the televiewer for a close-up. A GalacTech shuttle was bringing up one of the giant cargo pods, refined petrochemicals or bulk plastics bound for petroleum-depleted Earth perhaps. A collection of similar pods floated in orbit. Leo counted. One, two, three . . . six, and the one arriving made seven. Two or three little manned pushers were already starting to bundle the pods, to be locked together and attached to one of the big orbit-breaking thruster units.

Once grouped and attached to their thruster, the pods would be aimed toward the distant wormhole exit point that gave access to Rodeo local space. Velocity and direction imparted, the thruster would detach and return to Rodeo orbit for the next load. The unmanned pod bundle would continue on its slow, cheap way to its target, one of a long train stretching from Rodeo to the anomoly in space that was the Jump point.

Once there, the cargo pods would be captured and decelerated by a similar thruster, and positioned for the Jump. Then the Superjumpers would take over, cargo carriers as specially designed as the thrusters for their task. The monster cargo jumpers were hardly more than a pair of Necklin field generator rods in their protective housings so positioned as to be fitted around a constellation of pod bundles, a bracketing pair of normal space thruster arms, and a small control chamber for the jump pilot and his neurological headset. Without their balancing pod bundles attached the Superjumpers reminded Leo of some exceptionally weird and attenuated long-legged insects.

Each Jump pilot, neurologically wired to his ship to navigate the wavering realities of wormhole space, made two hops a day, inbound to Rodeo with empty pod bundles and back out again with cargo, followed by a day off; two months on duty followed by a month's unpaid but compulsory gravity leave, usually financially augmented with shuttle duties. Jumps were more wearing on pilots than null-gee was. The pilots of the fast passenger ships like the one Leo had ridden in on yesterday called the Superjumper pilots puddle-jumpers and merry-go-round riders. The cargo pilots just called the passenger pilots snobs.

Leo grinned, and considered that train of wealth gliding through space. No doubt about it, the Cay Habitat, fascinating as it was, was just the tail of the dog to the whole of GalacTech's Rodeo operation. That single thruster-load of pods being bundled now could maintain a whole town full of stockholding widows and orphans in style for a year, and it was just one of an apparently endless string. Base production was like an inverted pyramid, those at the bottom apex supporting a broadening mountain of ten-percenters, a fact which usually gave Leo more secret pride than irritation.

"Mr. Graf?" an alto voice interrupted his thoughts. "I'm Dr. Sondra Yei. I head up the psychology and training department for the Cay Habitat."

The woman hovering in the door wore pale green company coveralls. Pleasantly ugly, pushing middle-aged, she had the bright mongolian eyes, broad nose and lips and coffee-and-cream skin of her mixed racial heritage. She pushed herself through the aperture with the concise relaxed movements of one accustomed to free fall.

"Ah, yes, they told me you'd be wanting to talk to me." Leo courteously waited for her to anchor herself before attempting to shake hands.

Leo gestured at the televiewer. "Got a nice view of the orbital cargo marshalling here. Seems to me that might be another job for your quaddies."

"Indeed. They've been doing it for almost a year now." Yei smiled satisfaction. "So, you don't find adjusting to the quaddies too difficult? So your psyche profile suggested. Good."

"Oh, the quaddies are all right." Leo stopped short of expanding on his unease. He was not sure he could put it into words anyway. "I was just surprised, at first."

"Understandable. You don't think you'll have trouble teaching them, then?"

Leo smiled. "They can't possibly be worse than the crew of roustabouts I trained at Jupiter Orbital #4."

"I didn't mean trouble *from* them." Yei smiled again. "You will find they are very intelligent and attentive students. Quick. Quite literally, good children. And that's what I want to talk about." She paused, as if marshalling her thoughts like the distant cargo pushers.

"The GalacTech teachers and trainers occupy a parental role here for the Habitat family. Although parentless, the quaddies themselves must someday— indeed, are already becoming parents. From the beginning we've been at pains to assure they were provided with role models of stable adult responsibility. But they *are* still children. They will be watching you closely. I want you to be aware, and take care. They'll be learning more than welding from you. They'll also be picking up your other patterns of behavior. In short, if you have any bad habits—and we all have some—they must be parked downside for the duration of your stay. In other words," Yei went on, "watch yourself. Watch your language." An involuntary grin crinkled her eyes. "For example, one of our creche personnel once used the cliche 'spit in your eye' in some context or other . . . not only did the quaddies think it was hilarious, but it started an epidemic of spitting among the five-year-olds that took weeks to suppress. Now, you'll be working with much older children, but the principle remains. For instance—ah—did you bring any personal reading or viewing matter with you? Vid dramas, newsdiscs, whatever."

"I'm not much of a reader," said Leo. "I brought my course material."

"Technical information doesn't concern me. What we've been having a problem with lately is, um, fiction."

Leo raised an eyebrow, and grinned. "Pornography? I'm not sure I'd worry about that. When I was a kid we passed around—"

"No, no, not pornography. I'm not sure the quaddies would understand about pornography anyway. Sexuality is an open topic here, part of their social training. Biology. I'm far more concerned about fiction that clothes false or dangerous values in attractive colors, or biased histories."

Leo wrinkled his forehead, increasingly dismayed. "Haven't you taught these kids any history? Or let them have stories . . . ?"

"Of course we have. The quaddies are well-supplied with both. It's simply a matter of correct emphasis. For example—a typical downsider history of, say, the settlement of Orient IV usually gives about fifteen pages to the year of the Brothers' War, a temporary if bizarre social aberration—and about two to the actual hundred or so years of settlement and building-up of the planet. Our text gives one paragraph to the war. But the building of the Witgow trans-trench monorail tunnel, with its subsequent beneficial economic effects to both sides, gets five pages. In short, we emphasize the common instead of the rare, building rather than destruction, the normal at the expense of the abnormal. So that the quaddies may never get the idea that the abnormal is somehow expected of them. If you'd like to read the texts, I think you'll get the idea very quickly."

"I—yeah, I think I'd better," Leo murmured. The degree of censorship imposed upon the quaddies implied by Yei's brief description made his skin crawl—and yet, the idea of a text that devoted whole sections to great engineering works made him want to stand up and cheer. He contained his confusion in a bland smile. "I really didn't bring anything on board," he offered placatingly.

She led him off for a tour of the dormitories, and the supervised creches of the younger quaddies.

The little ones amazed Leo. There seemed to be so many—maybe it was just because they moved so fast. Thirty or so five-year-olds bounced around the free fall gym like a barrage of demented ping pong balls when their creche mother, a plump pleasant downsider woman they called Mama Nilla, assisted by a couple of quaddie teenage girls, first let them out of their reading class. But then she clapped her hands, and put on some music, and they fell to and demonstrated a game, or a dance, Leo was not sure which, with many sidelong looks at him and much giggling. It involved creating a sort of duo-decahedron in mid-air, like a human pyramid only more complex, hand to hand to hand changing its formation in time to music. Cries of dismay went up when an individual slipped up and spoiled the group's formation. When perfection was achieved, everybody won. Leo couldn't help liking that game. Dr. Yei, watching Leo laugh when the young quaddies swarmed around him afterwards, seemed to purr with contentment.

But at the end of the tour she studied him with a little smile quirking her mouth. "Mr. Graf, you're still disturbed. You sure you're not harboring just a little of the old Frankenstein complex about all this? It's all right to admit it to me—in fact, I want you to talk about it."

"It's not that," said Leo slowly. "It's just . . . well,

I can't really object to your trying to make them as group-centered as possible, given that they'll be living all their lives on crowded space stations. They're disciplined to a high degree for their ages, also good—"

"Vital to their survival, rather, in a space environment!"

"Yes . . . but what about—about their self-defense?"

"You'll have to define that term for me, Mr. Graf. Defense from what?"

"Well, it seems to me you've succeeded in raising about a thousand technical-whiz—doormats. Nice kids, but aren't they a little—feminized?" He was getting in deeper and deeper; her smile had quirked to a frown. "I mean—they just seem ripe for exploitation by—by somebody. Was this whole social experiment your idea? It seems like a woman's dream of a perfect society. Everybody's so *well behaved*." He was uncomfortably conscious of having expressed his thought badly, but surely she must see the validity. . . .

She took a deep breath, and lowered her voice. Her smile had become fixed. "Let me set you straight, Mr. Graf. I did not invent the quaddies. I was assigned here six years ago. It's the GalacTech specs that call for *maximum socialization*. But I did inherit them. And I care about them. It's not your job—or your business—to understand about their legal status, but it concerns me greatly. Their safety lies in their socialization.

"You seem to be free of the common prejudices against the products of genetic engineering, but there are many who are not. There are planetary jurisdictions where this degree of genetic manipulation of humans would even be illegal. Let those people— just once—perceive the quaddies as a threat, and—" she clamped her lips on further confidences, and retreated onto her authority. "Let me put it this way, Mr. Graf. The power to approve—or disapprove—training personnel for the Cay Project is mine. Mr. Van Atta may have called you in, but I can have you removed. And I will do so without hesitation if you fail in speech or behavior to abide by psych department guidelines. I don't think I can put it any more clearly than that."

"No, you're—quite clear," Leo said.

"I'm sorry," she said sincerely. "But until you've been on the Habitat a while, you really must refrain from making snap judgments."

I'm a testing engineer, lady, thought Leo. *It's my job to make judgments all day long.* But he did not speak the thought aloud. They managed to part on a note of only slightly strained cordiality.

The entertainment vid was titled "Animals, Animals, Animals." Silver set the re-run for the "Cats" sequence for the third time.

"Again?" Claire, sharing the vid viewing chamber with her, said faintly.

"Just one more time," Silver pleaded. Her lips parted in fascination as the black Persian appeared over the vid plate, but out of deference to Claire she turned down the music and narration. The creature was crouched lapping milk from a bowl, stuck to its floor by downside gravity. The little white droplets flying off its pink tongue arced back into the dish as though magnetized.

"I wish I could have a cat. They look so soft . . ." Silver's left lower hand reached out to pantomime-pat the life-sized image. No tactile reward, only the colored light of the holovid licking without sensation over her skin. She let her hand fall through the cat, and sighed. "Look, you can pick it up just like a baby." The vid shrank to show the cat's downsider owner carting it off in her arms. Both looked smug.

"Well, maybe they'll let you have a baby soon," offered Claire.

"It's not the same thing," said Silver. She could not help glancing a little enviously at Andy, though, curled up asleep in midair near his mother. "I wonder if I'll ever get a chance to go downside?"

"Ugh," said Claire. "Who'd want to? It looks so uncomfortable. Dangerous, too."

"Downsiders manage. Besides, everything interesting seems to—to come from planets." Everyone interesting, too, her thought added. She considered Mr. Van Atta's former teacher, Mr. Graf, met on her last working shift yesterday in Hydroponics. Yet another legged Somebody who got to go places and make things happen. He'd actually been born on old Earth, Mr. Van Atta said.

There came a muffled tap on the door of the soundproof bubble, and Silver keyed her remote control to open the door. Siggy, in the yellow shirt and shorts of Airsystems Maintenance, stuck his head through. "All clear, Silver."

"All right, come on."

Siggy slipped inside. She keyed the door shut again, and Siggy turned over, reached into the tool pouch on his belt, jimmied open a wall plate, and jammed the door's mechanism. He left the wall plate open in case of urgent need for re-access, such as Dr. Yei knocking on the door to inquire brightly, What were they doing? Silver by this time had the back cover off the holovid. Siggy reached delicately past her to clip his home-made electronic scrambler across the power lead cable. Anyone monitoring their viewing through it would get static.

"This is a great idea," said Siggy enthusiastically.

Claire looked more doubtful. "Are you sure we won't get into a whole lot of trouble if we're caught?"

"I don't see why," said Silver. "Mr. Van Atta disconnects the smoke alarm in his quarters whenever he has a jubajoint."

"I thought downsiders weren't allowed to smoke on board," said Siggy, startled.

"Mr. Van Atta says it's a privilege of rank," said Silver. *I wish I had rank.* . . .

"Has he ever given you one of his jubas?" asked Claire in a tone of gruesome fascination.

"Once," said Silver.

"Wow," said Siggy, grinning in admiration. "What was it like?"

Silver made a face. "Not much. It tasted kind of nasty. Made my eyes red. I really couldn't see the point to it. Maybe downsiders have some biochemical reaction we don't get. I asked Mr. Van Atta, but he just laughed at me."

"Oh," said Siggy, and switched his interest to the holovid display. All three quaddies settled around it. An anticipatory silence fell in the chamber as the music swelled and the bold red title letters rotated before their eyes—"The Prisoner of Zenda."

The scene opened on an authentically-detailed street scene from the dawn of civilization, before space travel or even electricity. A quartet of glossy horses, harness jingling, drew an elaborate box on wheels across the ground.

"Can't you get any more of the 'Ninja of the Twin Stars' series?" complained Siggy. "This is more of your darned dirtball stuff. I want something realistic, like that chase scene through the asteroid belt . . ." His hands pursued each other as he made nasal sound effects indicating machinery undergoing high acceleration.

"Shut up and look at all the animals," said Silver. "So many—and it's not even a zoo. The place is littered with them."

"Littered is right," giggled Claire. "They're not wearing diapers, you know. Think about that."

Siggy sniffed. "Earth must have been a really disgusting place to live, back in the old days. No wonder people grew legs. Anything, to prop them up in the air away from—"

Silver switched the vid off with a snap. "If you can't think of anything else to talk about," she said dangerously, "I'll go back to my dorm. *With* my vid. And you all can go back to watching 'Cleaning and Maintenance Techniques for Food Service Areas.'"

"Sorry." Siggy curled his four arms around himself in a submissive ball, and tried to look contrite. Claire refrained from further comment.

"Huh." Silver switched the vid back on, and continued watching in rapt and uninterrupted silence. When the railway scenes began, even Siggy stopped squirming.

Leo was well launched into his first class lecture.

"Now, here is a typical length of electron beam weld . . ." he fiddled with the controls of his holovid display. A ghost image in bright blue light, the computer-generated x-ray inspection record of the original object, sprang into being in the center of the room. "Spread out, kids, so you can all get a good look at it."

The quaddies arranged themselves around the display in a spherical shell of attentiveness, automatically extending helping hands to neighbors to absorb and trade momentum so that all achieved a tolerable hover. Dr. Yei, sitting in—if you could call it that— floated unobtrusively in the background. Monitoring him for his political purity, Leo supposed, not that it mattered. He did not propose to alter his lecture one jot for her presence.

Leo rotated the image so that each student could see it from every angle. "Now let's magnify this part. You see the deep-V cross section from the high-energy-density beam, familiar from your basic welding courses, right? Note the small round porosities here . . ." the magnification jumped again. "Would you say this weld is defective or not?" He almost added, *Raise your hand*, before realizing what a particularly unintelligible directive that was here. Several of the red-clad students solved the dilemma for him by crossing their upper arms formally across their chests instead, looking properly hesitant. Leo nodded toward Tony.

"Those are gas bubbles, aren't they sir? It must be defective."

Leo smiled thanks for the desired straight line. "They are indeed gas porosities. Oddly enough, though, when we crunch the numbers through, they do not appear to be defects. Let us run the computer scan down this length, with an eye to the digital read-out. As you see," the numbers flickered at a corner of the display as the cross-section moved dizzyingly, "at no point do more than two porosities appear in a cross-section, and at all points the voids occupy less than five percent of the section. Also, spherical cavities like these are the least damaging of all potential shapes of discontinuities, the least likely to propagate cracks in service. A non-critical defect is called a *discontinuity*." Leo paused politely while two dozen heads bent in unison to highlight this pleasingly unambiguous fact on the autotranscription of their light boards, braced between lower hands for a portable recording surface. "When I add that this weld was in a fairly low-pressure liquid storage tank, and not, for example, in a thruster propulsion chamber with its massively greater stresses, the slipperiness of this definition becomes clearer. For in a thruster the particular degree of defect that shows up here *would* have been critical."

"Now," he switched the holovid display to one in red light. "This is a holovid of the same weld from data bits mapped by an ultrasonic pulse reflective scan. Looks quite different, doesn't it? Can anyone identify *this* discontinuity?" He zoomed in on a bright area.

Several sets of arms crossed again. Leo nodded toward another student, a striking boy with aquiline nose, brilliant black eyes, wiry muscles, and dark mahogany skin contrasting elegantly with his red T-shirt and shorts. "Yes, Pramod?"

"It's an unbonded lamination."

"Right!" Leo tapped his holovid controls. "But check down this scan—where have all our little bubbles gone? Anybody think they magically closed between tests? Thank you," he said to their knowing grins, "I'm glad you don't think that. Now let's put both maps together." Red and blue melded to purple at overlapping points as the computer integrated the two displays.

"And *now* we see the little bugger," said Leo, zooming in again. "These two porosities, plus this lamination, all in the same plane. You can see the fatal crack starting to propagate already, on this rotation—" The holovid turned, and Leo emphasized the crack with a bright pink light. "That, children, is a defect."

They oohed in gratifying fascination. Leo grinned and plunged on. "Now, here's the point. Both these test scans were valid pictures—as far as they went.

But neither one was complete, neither alone sufficient. The maps were not the territories. You have to know that x-radiography is excellent for revealing voids and inclusions, but poor at finding cracks except at certain chance alignments, and ultrasound is optimum for just those laminar discontinuities x-rays are most likely to miss. Both maps, intelligently integrated, yielded a judgment."

"Now," Leo smiled a bit grimly, and replaced the gaudy image with another, monochrome green this time. "Look at this. What do you see?" He nodded at Tony again.

"A laser weld, sir."

"So it would appear. Your identification is quite understandable—and quite wrong. I want you all to memorize this piece of work. Look well. Because it may be the most evil object you ever encounter."

They looked wildly impressed, but totally bewildered. He commanded their absolute silence and utmost attention.

"*That*," he pointed for emphasis, his voice growing heavy with scorn, "is a falsified inspection record. Worse, it's one of a series. A certain subcontractor of GalacTech supplying thruster propulsion chambers for Jump ships found its profit margin endangered by a high volume of its work being rejected—after it had been placed in the systems. So instead of tearing the work apart and doing it over right, they chose to lean on the quality control inspectors. We will never know for certain if the chief inspector refused a bribe or not, because he wasn't around to tell us. He was found accidentally very dead due to an apparent power suit malfunction, attributed to his own errors made when attempting to don it while drunk. The autopsy found a high percentage of alcohol in his bloodstream. It was only much later that it was pointed out that the percentage was so high, he oughtn't to have been able to walk, let alone suit up.

"The assistant inspector *did* accept the bribe. The welds passed the computer certification all right— because it was the same damn good weld, replicated over and over and inserted into the data bank in place of real inspections, which for the most part were never even made. Twenty propulsion chambers were put on-line. Twenty time-bombs.

"It wasn't until the second one blew up eighteen months later that the whole story was finally uncovered. This isn't hearsay; I was on the probable-cause investigating team. It was I who found it, by the oldest test in the world, eye-and-brain inspection. When I sat there in that station chair, running those hundreds of holovid records through one by one, and first recognized the piece when I saw it again—and again—and again—for the computer only recognized that the series was free of defects—and I *realized* what those bastards had done . . ." His hands were shaking, as they always did at this point of the lecture, as the old memories flickered back. Leo clenched them by his sides.

"The judgment of the map was falsified in these electronic dream images. But the universal laws of physics yielded a judgment of blood that was absolutely real. Eighty-six people died altogether. *That*," Leo pointed again, "was not merely fraud, it was coldest, cruelest murder."

He gathered his breath. "This is the most important thing I will ever say to you. The human mind is the ultimate testing device. You can take all the notes you want on the technical data, anything you forget you can look up again, but this must be engraved on your hearts in letters of fire.

"There is *nothing, nothing, nothing* more important to me in the men and women I train than their absolute personal integrity. Whether you function as welders or inspectors, the laws of physics are implacable lie-detectors. You may fool men. You will never fool the metal. That's all."

He let his breath out, and regained his good humor, looking around. The quaddie students were taking it with proper seriousness, good, no class cut-ups making sick jokes in the back row. In fact, they were looking rather shocked, staring at him with terrified awe.

"So," he clapped his hands together and rubbed them cheerfully, to break the spell, "now let's go over to the shop and take a beam welder apart, and see if we can find everything that can possibly go wrong with it. . . ."

They filed out obediently ahead of him, chattering among themselves again. Yei was waiting by the door aperture as Leo followed his class. She gave him a brief smile.

"An impressive presentation, Mr. Graf. You become quite articulate when you talk about your work. Yesterday I thought you must be the strong silent type."

Leo flushed faintly, and shrugged. "It's not so hard, when you have something interesting to talk about."

"I would not have guessed welding engineering to be so entertaining a subject. You are a gifted enthusiast."

"I hope your quaddies were equally impressed. It's a great thing, when I can get somebody fired up. It's the greatest work in the world."

"I begin to think so. Your story . . ." she hesitated. "Your fraud story had great impact. They've never heard anything like it. Indeed, I never heard about that one."

"It was years ago."

"Really quite disturbing, all the same." Her face bore a look of introspection. "I hope not overly so."

"Well, I hope it's very disturbing. It's a true story. I was there." He eyed her. "Someday, they may be there. Criminally negligent, if I fail to prepare them."

"Ah." She smiled shortly.

The last of his students had vanished up the corridor. "Well, I better catch up with them. Will you be sitting in on my whole course? Come on along, I'll make a welder of you yet."

She shook her head ruefully. "You actually make it sound attractive. But I'm afraid I have a full-time job. I have to turn you loose." She gave him a short nod. "You'll do all right, Mr. Graf."

Chapter 3

Andy stuck out his tongue, extruding the blob of creamed rice Claire had just spooned into his mouth. "Beh," he remarked. The blob, spurned as food, apparently exerted new fascination as a plaything, for he caught it between his upper right and lower left hands as it slowly rotated off. "Eh!" he protested as his new satellite was reduced to a mere smear.

"Oh, Andy," Claire muttered in frustration, and removed the smear from his hands with a vigorous swipe from a rather soiled high-capillarity towel. "Come on, baby, you've got to try this. Dr. Yei says it's *good* for you!"

"Maybe he's full," Tony offered helpfully.

The nutritional experiment was taking place in Claire's private quarters, awarded her upon the birth of Andy and shared with the baby. She often missed her old dormitory mates, but reflected ruefully that the company had been right; her popularity and Andy's fascination would probably not have survived too many night feedings, diaper changes, gas attacks, mysterious diarrheas and fevers, or other infant nocturnal miseries.

Of late she'd missed Tony, too. In the last six weeks she'd hardly seen him, his new welding in-

39

structor was keeping him so busy. The pace of life seemed to be picking up all over the Habitat. There were days when there scarcely seemed to be time to draw breath.

"Maybe he doesn't like it," suggested Tony. "Have you tried mixing it with that other goo?"

"Everybody's an expert," sighed Claire. "Except me . . . He ate some yesterday, anyway."

"How does it taste?"

"I don't know, I never tried it."

"Hm." Tony plucked the spoon from her hand and twirled it in the opened seal-a-cup, picked up a blob, and popped it in his mouth.

"Hey—!" began Claire indignantly.

"Beh!" Tony choked. "Give me that towel." He rid himself of his sample. "No wonder he spits it out. It's Gag Station."

Claire grabbed the spoon back, muttered "Huh!", and floated over to her kitchenette to push it through the hand-holes to the water dispenser and give it a steaming rinse. "Germs!" she snapped accusingly at Tony.

"You try it!"

She sniffed the food cup in renewed doubt. "I'll take your word for it."

Andy in the meantime had captured his lower right hand with his uppers and was gnawing on it.

"You're not supposed to have meat yet," Claire sighed, straightening him back out. Andy inhaled, preparing for complaint, but let it go in a mere "Aah," as the door slid open revealing a new object of interest.

"How's it going, Claire?" asked Dr. Yei. Her thick useless downsider legs trailed relaxed from her hips as she pulled herself into the cabin.

Claire brightened. She liked Dr. Yei; things always seemed to calm down a bit when she was around. "Andy won't eat the creamed rice. He liked the strained banana well enough."

"Well, next feeding try introducing the oatmeal instead," said Dr. Yei. She floated over to Andy, held out her hand; he captured it with his uppers. She peeled off his hands, held her hand down farther; he grasped at it with his lowers, and giggled. "His lower body coordination is coming along nicely. Bet it will nearly match the upper by his first birthday."

"And that fourth tooth broke through day before yesterday," said Claire, pointing it out.

"Nature's way of telling you it's time to eat creamed rice," Dr. Yei lectured the baby with mock seriousness. He clamped to her arm, beady eyes intent upon her gold loop earrings, nutrition quite forgotten. "Don't fret too much, Claire. There's always this tendency to push things with the first child, just to reassure yourself it can all be done. It will be more relaxed with the second. I guarantee all babies master creamed rice before they're twenty no matter *what* you do."

Claire laughed, secretly relieved. "It's just that Mr. Van Atta was asking about his progress."

"Ah." Dr. Yei's lips twitched in a rather compressed smile. "I see." She defended her earring from a determined assault by placing Andy in air just beyond reach. A frustrated paroxysm of swimming-motions gave him only an unwanted spin. He opened his mouth to howl protest; Dr. Yei surrendered instantly, but bought time by holding out just her fingertips.

Andy again headed earring-ward, hand over hand over hand. "Yeah, go for it, baby," Tony cheered him on.

"Well," Dr. Yei turned her attention to Claire. "I actually stopped by to pass on some good news. The company is so pleased with the way things have turned out with Andy, they've decided to move up the date for you to start your second pregnancy."

Tony's face split in a delighted grin, beyond Dr. Yei's shoulder. His upper hands clasped in a gesture of victory. Claire made embarrassed-suppression motions at him, but couldn't help grinning back.

"Wow," said Claire, warm with pleasure. So, the company thought she was doing *that* well. There had been down days when she'd thought no one noticed how hard she'd been trying. "How much up?"

"Your monthly cycles are still being suppressed by the breast feeding, right? You have an appointment at the infirmary tomorrow morning. Dr. Minchenko will give you some medicine to start them up again. You can start trying on the second cycle."

"Oh my goodness. That soon." Claire paused, watching the wriggling Andy and remembering how the first pregnancy had drained her energy. "I guess I can handle it. But whatever happened to that two-and-a-quarter-year ideal spacing you were talking about?"

Dr. Yei bit her words off carefully. "There is a Project-wide push to increase productivity. In all areas." Dr. Yei, always straightforward in Claire's experience, smiled falsely. She glanced at Tony, hovering happily, and pursed her lips.

"I'm glad you're here, Tony, because I have some good news for you too. Your welding instructor Mr. Graf has rated you tops in his class. So you've been picked as gang foreman to go out on the first Cay Project contract GalacTech has landed. You and your co-workers will be shipping out in about a month to a place called Kline Station. It's on the far end of the wormhole nexus, beyond Earth, and it's a long ride, so Mr. Graf will be going along to complete your training en route, and double as engineering supervisor."

Tony surged across the room in excitement. "At last! Real work! But—" he paused, stricken. Claire, one thought ahead of him, felt her face becoming mask-like. "But how's Claire supposed to start a baby next month if I'm on my way to where?"

"Dr. Minchenko will freeze a couple of sperm samples before you go," suggested Claire. "Won't he . . . ?"

"Ah—hm," said Dr. Yei. "Well, actually, that wasn't in the plans. Your next baby is scheduled to be fathered by Rudy, in Microsystems Installation."

"Oh, no!" gasped Claire.

Dr. Yei studied both their faces, and arranged her mouth in a severe frown. "Rudy is a very nice boy. He would be very hurt by that reaction, I'm sure. This can't be a surprise, Claire, after all our talks."

"Yes, but—I was hoping, since Tony and I did so well, they'd let us—I was going to ask Dr. Cay!"

"Who is no longer with us," Dr. Yei sighed. "And so you've gone and let yourselves become pair-bonded. I warned you not to do that, didn't I?"

Claire hung her head. Tony's face was mask-like, now.

"Claire, Tony, I know this seems hard. But you in the first generations have a special burden. You are the first step in a very detailed long-range plan for GalacTech, spanning literally generations. Your actions have a multiplier effect all out of proportion—Look, this isn't by any means the end of the world for you two. Claire has a long reproductive career scheduled. It's quite probable you'll be getting back together again someday. And you, Tony—you're tops.

GalacTech's not going to waste you, either. There will be other girls—"

"I don't want other girls," said Tony stonily. "Only Claire."

Dr. Yei paused, went on. "I shouldn't be telling you this yet, but Sinda in Nutrition is next for you. I've always thought she was an extraordinarily pretty girl."

"She has a laugh like a hacksaw."

Dr. Yei blew out her breath impatiently. "We'll discuss it later. At length. Right now I *have* to talk with Claire." She thrust him firmly out the door and keyed it shut on his frown and muffled objections.

Dr. Yei turned back to Claire and fixed her with a stern gaze. "Claire—did you and Tony continue to have sexual relations after you became pregnant?"

"Dr. Minchenko said it wouldn't hurt the baby."

"Dr. Minchenko knew?"

"I don't know . . . I just asked him, like, in a general way." Claire studied her hands guiltily. "Did you expect us to stop?"

"Well, yes!"

"You didn't tell us to."

"You didn't ask. In fact, you were quite careful not to bring up the subject, now that I think back—oh, how could I have been so blind-sided?"

"But downsiders do it all the time," Claire defended herself.

"How do you know what downsiders do?"

"Silver says Mr. Van Atta—" Claire stopped abruptly.

Dr. Yei's attention sharpened, knife-like and uncomfortable. "What do you know about Silver and Mr. Van Atta?"

"Well—everything, I guess. I mean, we all wanted

to know how downsiders did it." Claire paused. "Downsiders are *strange*," she added.

After a paralyzed moment, Dr. Yei buried her suffused face in her hands and sniggered helplessly. "And so Silver's been supplying you with detailed information?"

"Well, yes." Claire regarded the psychologist with wary fascination.

Dr. Yei stifled her chortles, a strange light growing in her eyes, part humor, part irritation. "I suppose—I suppose you'd better pass the word to Tony not to let on. I'm afraid Mr. Van Atta would become a little upset if he realized his personal activities had a second-hand audience."

"All right," Claire agreed doubtfully. "But—you always wanted to know all about me and Tony."

"That's different. We were trying to help you."

"Well, we and Silver are trying to help each other."

"You're not supposed to help yourselves." The sting of Dr. Yei's criticism was blunted by her suppressed smile. "You're supposed to wait until you're served." Yei paused. "Just how many of you are privy to this, ah, Silver-mine of information, anyway? Just you and Tony, I trust?"

"Well, and my dormitory mates. I take Andy over there in my off hours and we all play with him. I used to have my sleep restraints opposite Silver's until I moved out. She's my best friend. Silver's so—so brave, I guess—she'll try things I'd never dare." Claire sighed envy.

"Eight girls," Yei muttered. "Oh, lord Krishna . . . I trust none of them have been inspired to emulation yet?"

Claire, not wishing to lie, said nothing. She didn't need to; the psychologist, watching her face, winced.

Yei turned indecisively in air. "I've got to have a

talk with Silver. I should have done it when I first suspected—but I thought the man had the wit not to contaminate the experiment—asleep on my feet. Look, Claire, I want to talk with you more about your new assignment. I'm here to try and make it as easy and pleasant as possible—you know I'll help, right? I'll get back to you as soon as I can."

Yei peeled Andy off her neck where he was now attempting to taste her earring and handed him back to Claire, and exited the airseal door muttering something about "containing the damage . . ."

Claire, alone, held her baby close. Her troubled uncertainty turned like a lump of metal under her heart. She had tried so hard to be good. . . .

Leo squinted approvingly against the harsh light and dense shadows of the vacuum as a pair of his space-suited students horsed the locking ring accurately into place on the end of its flex tube. Between the two of them their eight gloved hands made short work of the task.

"Now Pramod, Bobbi, bring up the beam welder and the recorder and put them in their starting position. Julian, you run the optical laser alignment program and lock them on."

A dozen of the four-armed figures, their names and numbers printed in large clear figures on the front of each helmet and across the backs of their silvery work suits, bobbed about. Their suit jets puffed as they jockeyed for a better view.

"Now, in these high-energy-density partial penetration welds," Leo lectured into his spacesuits's audio pick-up, "the electron beam must not be allowed to achieve a penetrating steady-state. This beam can punch through half a meter of steel. Even one spiking event and your, say, nuclear pressure vessel or your propulsion chamber can lose its structural integrity. Now, the pulser that Pramod is checking right now—" Leo made his voice heavy with hint; Pramod jerked, and hastily began punching up the system readout on his machine, "utilizes the natural oscillation of the point of beam impingement within the weld cavity to set up a pulsing schedule that maintains its frequency, eliminating the spiking problem. *Always* double check its function before you start."

The locking ring was firmly welded to its flex tube and duly examined for flaws by eye, hologram scan, eddy current, the examination and comparison of the simultaneous x-ray emission recording, and the classic kick-and-jerk test. Leo prepared to move his students on to the next task.

"Tony, you bring the beam welder over—TURN IT OFF FIRST!" Feedback squeal lanced through everyone's earphones, and Leo modulated his voice from his first urgent panicked bellow. The beam had in fact been off, but the controls live; one accidental bump, as Tony swung the machine around, and— Leo's eye traced the hypothetical slice through the nearby wing of the Habitat, and he shuddered.

"Get your head out of your ass, Tony! I saw a man cut in half by one of his friends once by just that careless trick."

"Sorry . . . thought it would save time . . . sorry . . ." Tony mumbled.

"You know better." Leo calmed, as his heart stopped palpitating. "In this hard vacuum that beam won't stop till it hits the third moon, or whatever it might encounter in between." He almost continued, stopped himself; no, not over the public comm channel. Later.

Later, as his students unsuited in the equipment locker, laughing and joking as they cleaned and stored their work suits, Leo drifted over to the silent and pale Tony. Surely I didn't bark at him *that* hard, Leo thought to himself. Figured he was more resilient . . . "Stop and see me when you're finished here," said Leo quietly.

Tony flinched guiltily. "Yes, sir."

After his fellows had all swooped out, eager for their end-of-shift meal, Tony hung in air, both sets of arms crossed protectively across his torso. Leo floated near, and spoke in a grave tone.

"Where were you, out there today?"

"Sorry, sir. It won't happen again."

"It's been happening all week. You got something on your mind, boy?"

Tony shook his head. "Nothing—nothing to do with you, sir."

Meaning, nothing to do with work, Leo interpreted that. All right, so. "If it's taking your mind off your work, it does have something to do with me. Want to talk about it? You got girl trouble? Little Andy all right? You have a fight with somebody?"

Tony's blue eyes searched Leo's face in sudden uncertainty, then he grew closed and inward once again. "No, sir."

"You worried about going out on that contract? I guess it will be the first time away from home for you kids, at that."

"It's not that," denied Tony. He paused, watching Leo again. "Sir—are there a great many other companies out there besides ours?"

"Not a great many, for deep interstellar work," Leo replied, a little baffled by this new turn in the conversation. "We're the biggest, of course, though there's maybe a half dozen others that can give us some real competition. In the heavily populated systems, like Tau Ceti or Escobar or Orient or of course Earth, there's always a lot of little companies operating on a smaller scale. Super-specialists, or entrepreneurial mavericks, this and that. The outer worlds are coming on strong lately."

"So—so if you ever quit GalacTech, you could get another job in space."

"Oh, sure. I've even had offers—but our company does the most of the sort of work I want to do, so there's no reason to go elsewhere. And I've got a lot of seniority accumulated by now, and all that goes with it. I'll probably be with GalacTech till I retire, if I don't die in harness." *Probably from a heart attack brought on by watching one of my students try to accidentally kill himself.* Leo did not speak the thought aloud; Tony seemed chastized enough. But still abstracted.

"Sir . . . tell me about *money*."

"Money?" Leo raised his brows. "What's to tell? The stuff of life."

"I've never seen any—I'd understood it was sort of coded value-markers to, to facilitate trade, and keep count."

"That's right."

"How do you get it?"

"Well—most people work for it. They, ah, trade their labor for it. Or if they own or manufacture or grow something, they can sell it. I work."

"And GalacTech gives you *money*?"

"Uh, yes."

"If I asked, would the company give me money?"

"Ah . . ." Leo became conscious of skating on very thin ice. His private opinion of the Cay Project had perhaps better remain just that, while he ate the company's bread. His job was to teach safe quality welding procedures, not—foment union demands, or whatever this conversation was sliding toward. "Whatever would you spend it on, up here? GalacTech gives you everything you need. Now, when I'm downside, or not on a company installation, I have to buy my own food, clothing, travel and what-not. Besides," Leo reached for a less queasily specious argument, "up till now, you haven't actually done any work for GalacTech, although it's done plenty for you. Wait till you've actually been out on a contract and done some real producing. Then maybe it might be time to talk about money." Leo smiled, feeling hypocritical, but at least loyal.

"Oh." Tony seemed to fold inward on some secret disappointment. His blue eyes flicked up, probing Leo again. "When one of the company Jump ships leaves Rodeo—where does it go first?"

"Depends on where it's wanted, I guess. Some run straight all the way to Earth. If there's cargo or people to divide up for other destinations, the first stop is usually Orient Station."

"GalacTech doesn't own Orient Station, does it?"

"No, it's owned by the government of Orient IV. Although GalacTech leases a good quarter of it."

"How long does it take to get to Orient Station from Rodeo?"

"Oh, usually about a week. You'll probably be stopping there yourself quite soon, if only to pick up extra equipment and supplies, when you're sent out on your first construction contract."

The boy was looking more outer-directed now, perhaps thinking about his first interstellar trip. That was better. Leo relaxed slightly.

"I'll be looking forward to that, sir."

"Right. If you don't cut your foot, er, hand off meanwhile, eh?"

Tony ducked his head and grinned. "I'll try not to, sir."

And what was that all about? Leo wondered, watching Tony sail out the door. Surely the boy could not be thinking of trying to strike out on his own? Tony had not the least conception of what a freak he would seem, beyond his familiar Habitat. If he would only open up a little more . . .

Leo shrank from the thought of confronting him. Every downsider staff member in the Habitat seemed to feel they had a right to the quaddies' personal thoughts. There wasn't a lockable door anywhere in the quaddies' living quarters. They had all the privacy of ants under glass.

He shook off the critical thought, but could not shake off his queasiness. All his life he had placed his faith in his own technical integrity—if he followed that star, his feet would not stumble. It was ingrained habit by now, he had brought that technical integrity to the teaching of Tony's work gang almost automatically. And yet . . . this time, it did not seem to be quite enough. As if he had memorized the answer, only to discover the question had been changed.

Yet what more could be demanded of him? What more could he be expected to give? What, after all, could one man do?

A spasm of vague fear made him blink, the hard-edged stars in the viewport smeared, as the looming shadow of the dilemma clouded on the horizon of his conscience. *More* . . .

He shivered, and turned his back to the vastness. It could swallow a man, surely.

Ti, the freight shuttle co-pilot, had his eyes closed. Perhaps that was natural at times like this, Silver thought, studying his face from a distance of ten centimeters. At this range her eyes could no longer superimpose their stereoscopic images, so his twinned face overlapped itself. If she squinted just right, she could make him appear to have three eyes. Men really were rather alien. Yet the metal contact implanted in his forehead, echoed at both temples, did not have that effect, seeming more a decoration or a mark of rank. She blinked one eye closed, then the other, causing his face to shift back and forth in her vision.

Ti opened his eyes a moment, and Silver quickly flinched into action. She smiled, half-closed her own eyes, picked up the rhythm of her flexing hips. "Oooh," she murmured, as Van Atta had taught her. *Let's hear some feedback, honey*, Van Atta had demanded, so she'd hit on a collection of noises that seemed to please him. They worked on the pilot, too, when she remembered to make them.

Ti's eyes squeezed shut, his lips parting as his breath came faster, and Silver's face relaxed into pensive stillness once again, grateful for the privacy. Anyway, Ti's gaze didn't make her as uncomfortable as Mr. Van Atta's, that always seemed to suggest that she ought to be doing something else, or more, or differently.

The pilot's forehead was damp with sweat, plastering down one curl of brown hair around the shiny plug. Mechanical mutant, biological mutant, equally touched by differing technologies; perhaps that was why Ti had first seen her as approachable, being an odd man out himself. Both freaks together. On the other hand, maybe the Jump pilot just wasn't very fussy.

He shivered, gasped convulsively, clutched her tightly to his body. Actually, he looked—rather vulnerable. Mr. Van Atta never looked vulnerable at this moment. Silver was not sure just what it was he did look like.

What's he getting out of this that I'm not? Silver wondered. What's wrong with me? Maybe she really was, as Van Atta had once accused, frigid—an unpleasant word, it reminded her of machinery, and the trash dumps locked outside the Habitat—so she had learned to make noises for him, and twitch pleasingly, and he had commended her for loosening up.

Silver reminded herself that she had another reason for keeping her eyes open. She glanced again past the pilot's head. The observation window of the darkened control booth where they trysted overlooked the freight loading bay. The staging area between the bay's control booth and the entrance to the freight shuttle's hatch remained dimly lit and empty of movement. *Hurry up Tony, Claire*, Silver thought worriedly. *I can't keep this guy occupied all shift.*

"Wow," breathed Ti, coming out of his trance and opening his eyes and grinning. "When they designed you folks for free fall they thought of *everything*." He released his own clutch on the wings of Silver's shoulderblades to slide his hands down her back, around her hips, and along her lower arms, ending with an approving pat on her hands locked around his muscular downsider flanks. "*Truly* functional."

"How *do* downsiders keep from, um, bouncing apart?" Silver inquired curiously, taking practical advantage of having cornered an apparent expert on the subject.

His grin widened. "Gravity keeps us together."

"How strange. I always thought of gravity as something you had to fight all the time."

"No, only half the time. The other half, it works for you," he assured her.

He undocked from her body rather gracefully— perhaps it was all that piloting experience showing through—and planted a kiss in the hollow of her throat. "Pretty lady."

Silver blushed a little, grateful for the dim lighting. Ti turned his attention momentarily to a necessary clean-up chore. A quick whistle of air, and the spermicide-permeated condom was gone down the waste chute. Silver suppressed a faint twinge of regret. It was just too bad Ti wasn't one of them. Too bad she was such a long way down the roster of those scheduled for motherhood. Too bad . . .

"Did you find out from your doctor fellow if we really need those?" Ti asked her.

"I couldn't exactly ask Dr. Minchenko directly," Silver replied. "But I gather he thinks any conceptus between a downsider and one of us would abort spontaneously, pretty early on—but nobody knows for sure. Could be a baby might make it to birth with lower limbs that were neither arms nor legs, but just some mess in between." *And they probably wouldn't let me keep it.* . . . "Anyway, it saves chasing body fluids around the room with a hand vac."

"Too true. Well, I'm certainly not ready to be a daddy."

How incomprehensible, thought Silver, for a man that old. Ti must be at least twenty-five, much older than Tony, who was nearly the eldest of them all. She was careful to float facing the window, so that the pilot had his back to it. *Come on, Tony, do it if you're going to.* . . .

A cool draft from the ventilators raised goose bumps on all her arms, and Silver shivered.

"Chilly?" Ti asked solicitously, and rubbed his hands up and down her arms rapidly to warm them by friction, then retrieved her blue shirt and shorts from the side of the room where they had drifted. Silver shrugged into them gratefully. The pilot dressed too, and Silver watched with covert fascination as he fastened his shoes. Such inflexible, heavy coverings, but then feet were inflexible, heavy things in their own right. She hoped he'd be careful how he swung them around. Shod, his feet reminded her of mallets.

Ti, smiling, unhooked his flight bag from a wall rack where he had stowed it when they'd retreated to the control booth half an hour earlier. "Gotcha something."

Silver perked up, and her four hands clasped each other hopefully. "Oh! Were you able to find any more book-discs by the same lady?"

"Yes, here you go—" Ti produced some thin squares of plastic from the inner reaches of his flight bag. "Three titles, all new."

Silver pounced on them and read their labels eagerly. Rainbow Illustrated Romances: *Sir Randan's Folly*, *Love in the Gazebo*, *Sir Randan and the Bartered Bride*, all by Valeria Virga. "Oh, wonderful!" She wrapped her upper right arm around Ti's neck and gave him a quite spontaneous and vigorous kiss.

He shook his head in mock despair. "I don't know how you can read that dreck. I think the author is a committee, anyway."

"It's *great*!" Silver defended her beloved literature indignantly. "It's so, so full of color, and strange places and times—a lot of them are set on old Earth, way back when *everybody* was still downside—they're amazing. People kept animals all around them—these enormous creatures called horses actually used to carry them around on their backs. I suppose the gravity tired people out. And these rich people, like—like company executives, I guess—called 'lords' and 'nobles' lived in the most fantastic habitats, stuck to the surface of the planet—and there was *nothing* about all this in the history *we* were taught!" Her indignation peaked.

"That stuff's not history, though," he objected. "It's fiction."

"It's nothing like the fiction they give us, either. Oh, it's all right for the little kids—I used to love *The Little Compressor That Could*—we made our creche-mother read it over and over. And the Bobby BX-99 series was all right . . . *Bobby BX-99 Solves the Excess Humidity Mystery* . . . *Bobby BX-99 and the Plant Virus* . . . it was then I asked to specialize in Hydroponics. But downsiders are ever so much more interesting to read about. It's so—so—when I'm reading this," she clutched the little plastic squares tightly, "it's like they're real, and I'm not." Silver sighed hugely.

Although perhaps Mr. Van Atta *was* a bit like Sir Randan . . . high of status, commanding, short-tempered. . . . Silver wondered briefly why short temper in Sir Randan always seemed so exciting and attractive, full of fascinating consequences. When Mr. Van Atta became angry, it merely made her sick to her stomach. Perhaps downsider women had more courage.

Ti shrugged baffled amusement. "Whatever turns you on, I guess. Can't see the harm in it. But I brought something better for you, this trip—" he rummaged in his flight bag again, and shook out a froth of ivory fabric, intricate lace and ribbony satin. "I figured you could wear a regular woman's blouse all right. It's got flowers in the pattern, thought you'd like that, being in hydroponics and all."

"Oh . . ." One of Valeria Virga's heroines might have been at home in such a garment. Silver reached for it, drew her hand back. "But—but I can't take it."

"Why not? You take the book-discs. It wasn't *that* expensive."

Silver, who felt she was beginning to have a fairly clear idea of how money worked from her reading, shook her head. "It's not that. It's, well—you know, I don't think Dr. Yei would approve of our meeting like this. Neither would—would a lot of other people." Actually, Silver was fairly sure that "disapprove" would barely begin to cover the consequences should her secret transactions with Ti be found out.

"Prudes," scoffed Ti. "You're not going to let them start telling you what to do *now*, are you?" But his scorn was tinged with anxiety.

"I'm not going to start telling them what I *am* doing either," said Silver pointedly. "Are you?"

"God, no," he waved his hands in horrified negation.

"So, we are in agreement. Unfortunately, that," she pointed regretfully at the blouse, "is something I can't hide. I couldn't wear it without someone demanding that I explain where I got it."

"Oh," he said, in the blunted tone of one struck by incontrovertable fact. "Yeah, I—guess I should have thought of that. Do you suppose you could put it away for a time? I've only been taking my gravity leaves on the Rodeo side because all the shuttle bonus berths at Orient IV get nailed by the senior guys. Well, and you can log a lot more hours here faster, with all the freight hauling. But I'll have my shuttle commander's rating and be back to permanent Jump status in just a few more cycles."

"It can't be shared, either," said Silver. "You see, the thing about the books and the vid dramas and things, besides being small and easy to hide, is that they can be passed all around the group without being used up. Nobody gets left out. So I can get, um, a lot of cooperation when I want to, say—get away for a little time by myself?" A toss of her head indicated the privacy they were presently enjoying.

"Ah," gulped Ti. He paused. "I—hadn't realized you were passing the stuff around."

"Not share?" said Silver. "That would be *really* wrong." She stared at him in mild offense, and pushed the blouse back toward him on the surge of the emotion, quickly, before she weakened. She almost explained further, then thought better of it.

Best Ti didn't know about the uproar when one of the book-discs, accidently left in a viewer, had been found by one of the Habitat's downsider staff and turned over to Dr. Yei. The search—barely alerted, they had scrambled successfully to hide the rest of the contraband library, but the fierce intensity of the search had been warning enough to Silver of how serious was her offense in the eyes of her authorities. There had been two more surprise inspections since, even though no more discs had been found. She could take a hint.

Mr. Van Atta himself had taken her aside—her! —and urged her to spy out the leak for him among her comrades. She had started to confess, stopped just in time, as his rising rage tightened her throat with fear. "I'm going to crucify the little sneak when I get my hands on him," Van Atta had snarled. Maybe Ti would not find Mr. Van Atta and Dr. Yei and all their staffs ranked together so intimidating— but she dared not risk losing her one sure source of downsider delights. Ti at least was willing to barter for what was in effect a bit of Silver's labor, the one invisible commodity not accounted for in any inventory; who knew, another pilot might want *things* of some kind, far more difficult to smuggle out of the Habitat unnoticed.

A long-awaited movement in the loading area caught

her eye. And you thought you were risking trouble
for a few books, Silver thought to herself. Wait'll *this*
shit gets on the loose. . . .

"Thank you anyway," said Silver hastily, and
grabbed Ti around the neck for a prolonged thank-
you kiss. He closed his eyes—wonderful reflex,
that—and Silver rolled hers toward the view out the
control booth window. Tony, Claire, and Andy were
just disappearing into the shuttle hatch flex tube.

There, thought Silver, that's it. I've done what I
can—the rest is up to you. Good luck, double-luck.
And more sharply, *I wish I was going with you.*

"Oof! Look at the time!" Ti broke off their embrace. "I've got to get this checklist completed before Captain Durrance gets back. Guess you're right
about the shirt," he stuffed it unceremoniously back
into his flight bag, "what *do* you want me to bring
you next time?"

"Siggy in Airsystems Maintenance asked me if there
were any more holovids in the *Ninja of the Twin
Stars* series," Silver said promptly. "He's up to Number 7, but he's missing 4 and 5."

"Ah," said Ti "now that was decent entertainment.
Did you watch them yourself?"

"Yes," Silver wrinkled her nose, "but I'm not sure—
the people in them did such horrible things to one
another—they are fiction, you say?"

"Well, yes."

"That's a relief."

"Yes, but what would you like for yourself?" he
persisted. "I'm not risking reprimand to gratify Siggy,
whoever he is. Siggy doesn't have your," he sighed
in remembered pleasure, "dear double-jointed hips."

Silver fanned out the three new book cards in her
lower right hand. "More, please, sir."

"If it's dreck you want," he captured each of her

hands in turn and kissed their palms, "it's dreck you shall have. Uh, oh, here comes my fearless captain." Ti hastily straightened his shuttle pilot's uniform, turned up the light level, and picked up his report panel as an airseal door at the far end of the loading bay swished open. "He hates being saddled with junior Jumpers. Tadpoles, he calls us. I think he's uncomfortable because on my Jumpship, I'd outrank him. Still, better not give the old guy something to pick on . . ."

Silver made the book cards disappear into her work bag and took up the pose of an idle bystander as Captain Durrance, the shuttle commander, floated into the control booth.

"Snap it up, Ti, we've had a change of itinerary," said Captain Durrance.

"Yes, sir. What's up?"

"We're wanted downside."

"Hell," Ti swore mildly. "What a pain. I had a hot date lined—er," his eye fell on Silver, "was supposed to meet a friend for dinner tonight at the Transfer Station."

"Fine," said Captain Durrance, ironically unsympathetic. "File a complaint with Employee Relations, your work schedule is interfering with your love life. Maybe they can arrange that you not have a work schedule."

Ti took the hint, and moved hastily out to continue his duties as a Habitat technician arrived to take over the loading bay control booth.

Silver made herself small in a corner, frozen in horror and confusion. At the Transfer Station, Tony and Claire had planned to stow away on a Jump ship for Orient IV, get beyond the reach of GalacTech, find work when they got there; a horribly risky plan, in Silver's estimation, a measure of their desperation. Claire had been terrified, but at last persuaded by Tony's plan of carefully thought-out stages. At least, the first stages had been carefully thought-out; they had seemed to get vaguer, farther away from Rodeo and home. They had not planned on a downside detour in any version.

Tony and Claire had surely hidden themselves by now in the shuttle's cargo bay. There was no way for Silver to warn them—should she betray them to save them? The ensuing uproar was guaranteed to be ghastly—her dismay wrapped like a steel band around her chest, constricting breathing, constricting speech.

She watched on the control booth's vid display in miserable paralysis as the shuttle kicked away from the Habitat and began to drop toward Rodeo's swirling atmosphere.

Chapter 4

The dim cargo bay seemed to groan all around Claire as deceleration strained its structure. Buffeting, accompanied by a hissing whistle, vibrated through the shuttle's metal skin.

"What's wrong?" gasped Claire. She released an anchoring hand upon the plastic crate behind which they had hidden to double her grasp of Andy and hold him closer. "Are we sideswiping something? What's that funny noise?"

Tony hurriedly licked a finger and held it out. "No draft to speak of." He swallowed, testing his eustachican tubes. "We're not depressurizing." Yet the whistle was rising.

Two mechanical ka-chunks, one after the other, that were nothing at all like the familiar thump and click of a hatch seal seating itself properly, shot terror through Claire. The deceleration went on and on, much too long, confused by a strange new vector of thrust that seemed to emanate from the shuttle's ventral side. The side of the cargo bay to which the crates were anchored seemed to push against her. She nervously put her back to it, and cushioned Andy upon her belly.

The baby's eyes were round, his mouth an echoing

"o" of bewilderment. *No, please, don't start crying!* She dared not release the cry locked in her own throat; it would set him off like a siren. "Patty cake, patty cake, baker's man," Claire choked. "Microwave a cake as fast as you can . . ." She tickled his cheek, flicking her eyes at Tony in mute appeal.

Tony's face was white. "Claire—I think this shuttle's going downside! I bet those bangs were the airfoils deploying."

"Oh, no! Can't be. Silver checked the schedule—"

"It looks like Silver made a big mistake."

"I checked it too. This shuttle was supposed to be picking up a load of stuff at the Transfer Station, *then* going downside."

"Then you *both* made a big mistake." Tony's voice was harsh and shaking, anger masking fear.

Oh, help, don't yell at me—if I don't stay calm, neither will Andy—this wasn't my idea. . . .

Tony rolled over on his stomach and levered his body away from the thrusting surface of the—the *floor*, downsiders called the direction from which the vector of gravitational force came—and crept to the nearest window, pulling himself alongside it. The light that poured through it was taking on a strange diffuse quality, diminishing. "It's all white—Claire, I think we must be entering a cloud!"

Claire had watched clouds from orbit above for hours, as they slowly billowed in the convection of Rodeo's atmosphere. They had always seemed massive as moons. She longed to go look.

Andy was clutching her blue T-shirt. She rolled over, as Tony had, palms to the surface, and pushed up. Andy, turning his head toward his father, reached out with his upper hands and tried to shove off from Claire with his lowers. The floor leaped up and smacked him.

For a moment he was too stunned to howl. Then his little mouth went from round to square and poured out the vibrating scream of true pain. The sound knifed through every nerve in Claire's body.

Tony too jerked at the noise, and scrambled down from the window and back toward them. "Why did you drop him? What do you think you're doing? Oh, make him be quiet, quick!"

Claire rolled onto her back again, pulling Andy onto the elastic softness of her abdomen, and patted and kissed him frantically. The timbre of his screams began to change from the frightening high-pitched cry of pain to the less piercing bellows of indignation, but the volume was just as loud.

"They'll hear him all the way up in the pilot's compartment!" Tony hissed in anguish. "*Do* something!"

"I'm *trying*," Claire hissed back. Her hands shook. She tried to push Andy's head toward her breast, standard comfort, but he turned his head away and screamed louder. Fortunately, the sound of the atmosphere rushing over the shuttle's skin had risen to a deafening thunder. By the time the noise peaked and faded, Andy's cries had become whimpering hiccups. He rubbed his face, slimy with tears and mucous, mournfully against Claire's T-shirt. His weight on Claire's stomach and diaphragm half stopped her breath, but she dared not lay him down.

Another set of clunks reverberated through the shuttle. The engines' vibrations changed their pitch, and Claire was plucked this way and that by changing acceleration vectors, none as strong as the one emanating from the floor. She spared two hands from comforting Andy to brace herself against the plastic crates.

Tony lay beside them, biting his lips in helpless

anxiety. "We must be coming down to land on the surface."

Claire nodded. "At one of the shuttleports. There'll be people there—downsiders—maybe we can tell them we got trapped aboard this shuttle by accident. Maybe," she added hopefully, "they'll send us right back up home."

Tony's right upper hand clenched. "No! We can't give up now! We'd never get another chance!"

"But what else can we do?"

"We'll sneak off this ship and hide, until we can get on another one, one that's going to the Transfer Station." His voice turned earnest with urgent pleading as a puff of dismay escaped Claire's parted lips. "We did it once, we can do it again."

She shook her head doubtfully. Further argument was interrupted by a startling series of thumps that shook the whole ship and then blended into a low continuous rumble. The light falling through the window shifted its beam around the cargo bay as the shuttle landed, taxied, and turned. Then it winked out, the cargo bay dimmed, and the engines whined to an equally startling silence.

Claire cautiously unbraced herself. Of all the acceleration vectors, only one remained. Isolated, it became overwhelming.

Gravity. Silent, implacable, it pressed against her back—she struggled with a nasty illusion that it might suddenly cease, and the thrust it imparted slam her into the ceiling above, smashing Andy between. In an accompanying optical illusion, the whole cargo bay seemed to be chugging in a slow circle around her. She closed her eyes in self-defense.

Tony's hand tightened warningly on her left lower wrist. She looked up and froze as the outside cargo bay door at the forward end of the compartment slid open.

A pair of downsiders wearing company maintenance coveralls entered. The access door in the center of the shuttle's fuselage dilated, and Ti the shuttle co-pilot stuck his head through.

"Hi, guys. What's the big rush-rush?"

"We're supposed to have this bird turned around and reloaded in an hour, that's what," replied the maintenance man. "*You* have just time to pee and eat lunch."

"What's the cargo? I haven't seen this much hopping around since the last medical emergency."

"Equipment and supplies for some sort of show they're supposed to be putting on up at your Habitat for the Vice President of Operations."

"That's not till next week."

The maintenance man snickered. "That's what everybody thought. The VP just flew in a week early on her private courier, with a whole commando squad of accountants. Seems she likes surprise inspections. Management, naturally, is overjoyed."

"Don't laugh too soon," Ti warned. "Management has ways of sharing their joy with the rest of us."

"Don't I know it," the maintenance man groaned. "C'mon, c'mon, you're blocking the door . . ." The three of them clattered forward.

"*Now*," whispered Tony, with a nod at the open cargo bay door.

Claire rolled to her side and laid Andy gently on the deck. His face crumpled, working up to a cry. Claire quickly rolled onto her palms, tested her balance. Her right lower arm seemed to be the one she could most easily spare. She scooped Andy back up one-handed and held him under her torso.

Plastered against the planet-ward side of the cargo

bay by the dreadful gravity, she began a three-handed crawl toward the door. Andy's weight pulled at her arm as though a strong spring were drawing him to the floor, and his head bobbed backwards at an alarming angle. Claire inched her palm up under his head to support it, painfully awkward for her arm.

Beside her, Tony too achieved a three-handed stance. With his free hand he jerked the cord to their pack of supplies. The pack, stuck to the downside surface as if by suction, didn't budge.

"Shit," Tony swore under his breath. He swarmed over the pack, gripped and lifted it, but it was too bulky to carry under his belly. "*Double*-shit."

"Can we give up yet?" Claire asked in a tiny voice, knowing the answer.

"*No!*" He grabbed the pack backwards over both shoulders with his upper hands and rocked forward violently. It came up and balanced precariously on his back. He kept his left upper hand on it to steady it and hopped forward on his right, his lower palms shuffling along under his hips. "I got it, go, go!"

The shuttle was parked in a cavernous hangar, a vast dim gulf of space roofed by girders. The girders behind the overhead lights would have been an excellent hiding place, if only one could swoop up there. But everything not rigidly fastened was doomed to fly to the one side of the room only, and stick there until forcibly removed. There was a lopsided fascination to it. . . .

"Oh . . ." Claire hesitated. Leading from the hatch to the hangar floor was a kind of corrugated ramp. Clearly, it was designed to break down the dangerous fight with the omnipresent gravity into little manageable increments. "*Stairs*." Claire paused, head down. Her blood seemed to pool dizzyingly in her face. She gulped.

"Don't *stop*," Tony gasped pleadingly behind her, then gulped himself.

"Uh . . . uh . . ." In a moment of inspiration, Claire turned around and began to back down, her free lower palm slapping the metal treads with each hop. It was still uncomfortable, but at least possible. Tony followed.

"Where now?" Claire panted when they reached the bottom.

Tony pointed with his chin. "Hide in that jumble of equipment over there, for now. We daren't get too far from the shuttles."

They scuttled along over the downside surface of the hangar. Claire's hands quickly became smudged with oil and dirt, a psychological irritation as fierce as an unscratchable itch; she felt she might gladly risk death for a chance to wash them. Claire remembered watching beads of condensed humidity creeping by capillarity across surfaces in the Habitat, until she'd smeared them to oblivion with her dry-rag, just as she and Tony crept now.

As they reached the area where some pieces of heavy equipment were parked, a loader rolled into the hangar and a dozen coveralled men and women jumped off it and began swarming over the shuttle, organized confusion. Claire was glad for their noise, for Andy was still emitting an occasional whimper. Fearfully, she watched the maintenance crew through the metal arms of the machinery. How late was too late to surrender?

Leo, half suited-up in the equipment locker, glanced up anxiously as Pramod swooped across the room to fetch up gracefully beside him.

"Did you find Tony?" Leo asked. "As gang foreman, he's supposed to be leading this parade. I'm only supposed to be watching."

Pramod shook his head. "He's not in any of the usual places, sir."

Leo hissed under his breath, not quite swearing. "He should've answered his page by now . . ." He drifted to the plexiport.

Outside in the vacuum, a small pusher was just depositing the last of the sections for the shell of the new hydroponics bay in their carefully arranged constellation. It was to be built before the Operations Vice President's eyes by the quaddies. So much for Leo's faint hope that screw-ups and delays in other departments might cover those in his own. It was time for his welding crew to make its debut.

"All right, Pramod, get suited up. You'll take over Tony's position, and Bobbi from Gang B will take yours." Leo hurried on before the startlement in Pramod's eyes could turn to stage fright. "It's nothing you haven't practiced a dozen times. And if you have the least doubts about the quality or safety of any procedure, I'll be right there. Reality first—you people are going to be living in the structure you build today long after Vice President Apmad and her travelling circus are gone. I guarantee she'll have more respect for a job done right, however slowly, than for a piece of slap-dash fakery."

For God's sake make it look smooth, Van Atta had instructed Leo urgently, earlier. *Keep to the schedule, no matter what—we'll fix the problems later, after she's gone. We're supposed to be making these chimps seem cost-effective.*

"You don't have to try and seem to be anything but what you are," Leo told Pramod. "You *are* efficient—and you are good. Instructing you all has been one of the great unexpected pleasures of my career. Be off, now, I'll catch up with you shortly."

Pramod sped away to find Bobbi. Leo frowned briefly to himself, and floated up the length of the locker room to the comconsole terminal at the end.

He keyed in his ID. "Page," he instructed it. "Dr. Sondra Yei." At the same moment a message square in the corner of the vid began to blink with his own name, and a number. "Cancel that instruction."

He punched up the number and raised his brows in surprise as Dr. Yei's face appeared on his vid. "Sondra! I was just about to call you. Do you know where Claire is?"

"How odd. I was calling to ask you if you knew where I could reach Tony."

"Oh?" said Leo, in a voice suddenly drained to neutrality. "Why?"

"Because I can't find her anywhere, and I thought Tony might know where she is. She's supposed to be giving a demonstration of child care techniques in free fall to Vice President Apmad after lunch."

"Is, um," Leo swallowed, "Andy at the creche, or with Claire, do you know?"

"With Claire, of course."

"Ah."

"Leo . . ." Dr. Yei's attention sharpened, her lips pursed. "Do you know something I don't?"

"Ah . . ." he eyed her. "I know Tony has been unusually inattentive at work for the last week. I might even say—depressed, except that's supposed to be your department, eh? Not his usual cheerful self, anyway." A knot of unease, tightening in Leo's stomach, gave his tongue an unaccustomed edge. "You, ah, got any concerns that you may have forgotten to share with me, lady?"

Her lips thinned, but she ignored the bait. "Sched-

ules have been moved up in all departments, you
know. Claire received her new reproduction assignment. It didn't include Tony."

"Reproduction assignment? You mean, having a
baby?" Leo could feel his face flushing. Somewhere
within him, a long-controlled steam pressure began
to build. "Do you hide what you're really doing from
yourselves with those weasel-words, too? And here I
thought the propaganda was just for us peons." Yei
started to speak, but Leo overrode her, bursting out,
"Good God! Were you born inhuman, or did you
grow so by degrees—M.S., M.D., Ph.D. . . ."

Yei's face darkened, her accent grew clipped. "An
engineer with romance in his soul? Now I've seen
everything. Don't get carried away with your scenario, Mr. Graf. Tony and Claire were assigned to
each other in the first place by the exact same system, and if *certain people* had been willing to abide
by my original timetable, this problem could have
been avoided. I fail to see the point of paying for an
expert and then blithely ignoring her advice, really I
do. Engineers . . . !"

Ah, hell, she's suffering from as bad a case of Van
Atta as I am, Leo realized. The insight blunted his
momentum, without bleeding off internal pressure.

"—I didn't invent the Cay Project, and if I were
running it I'd do it differently, but I have to play the
hand I'm dealt, Mr. Graf. Blast—" she controlled
herself, almost visibly wrenching the conversation
back on its original track. "I've got to find her soon,
or I'll have no choice but to let Van Atta start the
show ass-backwards. Leo, it's absolutely essential that
Vice President Apmad get the creche tour first, before she has time to start forming any—do you have
any idea at all where those kids may be?"

Leo shook his head; an inspiration turned the truthful gesture to a lie even before he'd finished it. "But will you give me a call if you find them before I do?" he pleaded, his humble tone offering truce.

Yei's stiffness wilted a bit. "Yes, certainly." She shrugged wryly, a silent apology, and broke off.

Leo swung back to his locker, peeled out of his work suit, donned coveralls, and hastened off to track down his inspiration before Dr. Yei duplicated it independently. He was certain she would, and shortly, too.

Silver checked the work schedule on her vid display. Bell peppers. She floated across the hydroponics bay to the seed locker, found the correct labeled drawer, and withdrew a pre-counted paper packet. She gave the packet an absent shake, and the dried seeds made a pleasing rattle.

She collected a plastic germination box, tore open the packet, and coaxed the little pale seeds into the container, where they bounced about cheerfully. To the hydration spigot next. She thrust the water tube through the rubber doughnut seal on the side of the germination box and administered a measured squirt, and gave the box an extra shake to break up the shimmering globule of liquid that formed. Shoving the germination box into its slot in the incubation rack, she set it for the optimum temperature for peppers, bell, hybrid phototropic non-gravitational axial differentiating clone 297-X-P, and sighed.

The light from the filtered windows plucked insistently at her attention, and she paused for the fourth or fifth time this shift to weave among the grow tubes and stare out at the portion of Rodeo this bay's angle of view allowed her to see. Somewhere down there, at the bottom of that well of air, Claire and Tony were crawling now—if they had not already surrendered—or managed to make it to another shuttle—or met some horrible catastrophe. . . . Silver's imagination, unbidden, supplied her with a string of sample catastrophes.

She tried to crowd them out with a firm mental picture of Tony and Claire and Andy successfully sneaking onto a shuttle bound for the Transfer Station, but the picture wavered into a scenario of Claire, attempting to jump some gap to the shuttle's hatchway (what gap? from where, for pity's sake?) forgetting that all such tangents were bent to parabolas by the gravitational force, and missing the target. Silver thought of the peculiar ways things moved in dense gravitational fields. The scream, chopped off by the splat on the concrete below—no, surely Claire would be holding Andy—the *double* splat on the concrete below. . . . Silver kneaded her forehead with the heels of her upper hands, as if she might physically press the grisly vision back out of her brain. Claire had seen the same vids of life downside, surely she'd remember.

The hiss of the airseal doors twitched Silver back to present reality. Better look busy—what was she supposed to be doing next? Oh, yes, cleaning used grow tubes, in preparation for their placement day after tomorrow in the new bay they were building to show off everybody's skills to the Ops VP. Damn the Ops VP. But for her, there'd be a chance Tony and Claire might go un-missed for two shifts, even three. Now . . .

Her heart shrank, as she saw who had entered the hydroponics bay. Now, indeed.

Ordinarily, Silver would have been glad to see Leo. He seemed a big, clean man—no, not large, but solid somehow, full of a prosaic calmness that spilled over in the very scent of him, reminiscent of

downsider things Silver had chanced to handle, wood
and leather and certain dried herbs. In the light of
his slow smile, ghastly scenarios thinned to mist. She
might yet be glad to talk to Leo. . . .

He was not smiling now. "Silver . . . ? You in
here?"

For a wild moment Silver considered trying to
hide among the grow tubes, but the foliage rustled as
she turned, giving away her position. She peeked
over the leaves. "Uh . . . hi, Leo."

"Have you seen Tony or Claire lately?" Trust Leo
to be direct. *Call me Leo*, he'd told her the first time
she'd "Mr. Graf'd" him. *It's shorter*. He drifted over
to the grow tubes; they regarded each other across a
barrier of bush beans.

"I haven't seen anybody but my supervisor all
shift," said Silver, momentarily relieved to be able to
give a perfectly honest answer.

"When did you last see either one of them?"

"Oh—last shift, I guess." Silver tossed her head
airily.

"Where?"

"Uh . . . around." She giggled vacuously. Mr. Van
Atta might have flung up his hands in disgust at this
point, and abandoned any attempt to wring sense
from so empty a head as hers.

Leo frowned at her thoughtfully. "You know, one
of the charms of you kids is the literal precision with
which you answer any question."

The comment hung in air expectantly, as Leo did.
The picture of Tony, Claire, and Andy scooting across
the shuttle loading bay flashed in Silver's mind with
hallucinatory clarity. She groped in memory for their
prior meeting, where the final plans had been laid,
to offer up as a half-truth. "We had the mid-shift
meal together last shift at Nutrition Station Seven."

Leo's lips quirked. "I see." He tilted his head, studying her as if she were some puzzle, such as two metallurgically incompatible surfaces he had to figure out how to join.

"You know, I just heard about Claire's new, ah, reproduction assignment. I'd wondered what was bothering Tony the last few weeks. He was pretty broken up about it, eh? Pretty . . . distraught."

"They'd had plans," Silver began, caught herself, shrugged casually. "I don't know. *I'd* be glad to get any reproduction assignment. There's no pleasing some people."

Leo's face grew stern. "Silver—just how distraught were they? Kids often mistake a temporary problem for the end of the world, they have no sense of the fullness of time. Makes 'em excitable. Think they might have been upset enough to do something . . . desperate?"

"Desperate?" Silver smiled rather desperately herself.

"Like a suicide pact or something?"

"Oh, no!" said Silver, shocked. "Oh, they'd never do anything like that."

Did relief flash for a moment in Leo's brown eyes? No, his face puckered in intensified concern.

"That's just what I'm afraid they might have done. Tony didn't show up for his work shift, and that's unheard of; Andy's gone too. They can't be found. If they felt so desperate—trapped—what could be easier than slipping out an airlock? A flash of cold, a moment's pain, and then—escape forever." His single pair of hands clasped earnestly. "And it's all my fault. I should have been more perceptive—said something . . ." He paused, looking at her hopefully.

"Oh, no, it was nothing like that!" Silver, horrified, hastened to dissuade him. "How awful for you to think that. Look . . ." She glanced around the hydroponics bay, lowered her voice. "Look, I shouldn't tell you this, but I can't let you go around thinking— thinking those fearful things." She had his entire attention, grave and intent. How much dare she tell him? Some suitably edited reassurance . . . "Tony and Claire—"

"Silver!" Dr. Yei's voice rang out as the airseal doors slid open. Echoed by Van Atta's bellow, "Silver, what do you know about all this?"

"Aw, shit," Leo snarled under his breath. His piously clasped hands clenched to fists of frustration.

Silver drew back in understanding and indignation. "You—!" And yet she almost laughed; Leo, so subtle and tricksy? She'd underestimated him. Did they both wear masks before the world, then? If so, what unknown territories did his bland face conceal?

"Please, Silver, before they get here—I can't help you if . . ."

It was too late. Van Atta and Yei tumbled into the room.

"Silver, do you know where Tony and Claire have gone?" Dr. Yei demanded breathlessly. Leo drew back into reserved silence, appearing to take an interest in the fine structure of the white bean blossoms.

"Of course she knows," Van Atta snapped, before Silver could reply. "Those girls are in each others' pockets, I tell you—"

"Oh, I *know*," Yei muttered.

Van Atta turned sternly to Silver. "Cough it up, Silver, if you know what's good for you."

Silver's lips closed, firmed into a line; her chin lifted.

Dr. Yei rolled her eyes at her superior's back. "Now, Silver," she began placatingly, "this isn't a good time for games. If, as we suspect, Tony and Claire have tried to leave the Habitat, they could be in very serious trouble by now, even physical danger. I'm pleased that you feel you should be loyal to your friends, but I beg you, make it a responsible loyalty—friends don't let friends get hurt."

Silver's eyes puddled in doubt; her lips parted, inhaling for speech.

"Damn it," cried Van Atta, "I don't have time to stand around sweet-talking this little cunt. That snake-eyed bitch that runs Ops is waiting up there *right now* for the show to go on. She's starting to ask questions, and if she doesn't get the answers pronto she'll come looking for 'em herself. That one plays hardball. Of all the times to pick for this outbreak of idiocy, this has gotta be the worst possible. It's got to be deliberate. Nothing this fouled up could be by chance."

His red-faced rage was having its usual effect on Silver; her belly trembled, her vision blurred with unshed tears. She had once felt she would give him anything, do anything at all, if only he would calm down and smile and joke again.

But not this time. Her initial awed infatuation with him had been emptied out of her, bit by bit, and it startled her to realize how little was left. A hollowed shell could be rigid and strong. . . . "You," she whispered, "can't *make* me say anything."

"Just as I thought," snarled Van Atta. "Where's your *total socialization* now, Dr. Yei?"

"If you would," said Dr. Yei through her teeth, "kindly refrain from teaching my subjects anti-social behavior, you wouldn't have to deal with its consequences."

"I don't know what you're whining about. I'm an

executive. It's my job to be hard-assed. That's why
GalacTech put me in charge of this orbiting money-
sink. Behavior control is your department's responsibility, Yei, or so you claimed. So do your job."

"Behavior *shaping*," Dr. Yei corrected frostily.

"What the hell's the use of that if it breaks down
the minute the going gets tough? I want something
that works all the time. If you were an engineer
you'd never get past the reliability specs. Isn't that
right, Leo?"

Leo snapped off a bean leaf stem, smiled blandly.
His eyes glittered. He must have been chewing on
his reply; at any rate, he swallowed *something*.

Silver grasped at a simple plan. So simple, surely
she could carry it out. All she had to do was nothing.
Do nothing, say nothing; eventually, the crisis must
pass. They could not physically damage her, after all,
she was valuable GalacTech property. The rest was
only noise. She shrank into the safety of thing-ness,
and stony silence.

The silence grew thick as cold oil. She nearly
choked on it.

"So," hissed Van Atta to her, "that's the way you
want to play it. Very well. Your choice." He turned
to Yei. "You got something in the Infirmary like
fast-penta, Doctor?"

Yei's lips rippled. "Fast-penta is only legal for
police departments, Mr. Van Atta."

"Don't they need a court order to use it, too?"
inquired Leo, not looking up from the bean leaf he
twirled between his fingers.

"On citizens, Leo. That," Van Atta pointed at Silver, "is not a citizen. What about it, Doctor?"

"To answer your question, *Mr.* Van Atta, no, our
Infirmary does *not* stock illegal drugs!"

"I didn't say fast-penta, I said something *like* it,"

said Van Atta irritably. "Some sort of anesthetic or something, to do in a pinch."

"Are we in a pinch?" asked Leo in a mild tone, still twirling his leaf; it was getting frayed. "Pramod is substituting for Tony, surely one of the other girls with babies can take over for Claire. Why should the Ops VP know the difference?"

"If we end up having to scrape two of our workers off the pavement downside—"

Silver winced at this echo of her own ghastly scenario.

"—or find them floating freeze-dried outside somewhere up here, it'll be damned hard to conceal from her. You haven't met the woman, Leo. She has a nose for trouble like a weasel's."

"Mm," said Leo.

Van Atta turned back to Yei. "What about it, Doctor? Or would you rather wait until someone calls us up asking what to do with the bodies?"

"IV Thalizine-5 is a bit like fast-penta," muttered Dr. Yei reluctantly, "in certain doses. It will make her sick for a day, though."

"That's her choice." He wheeled on Silver. "Your last chance, Silver. I've had it. I despise disloyalty. Where did they go? Tell me, or it's the needle for you, right now."

She was driven from thing-ness at last to a more painful, active human courage. "If you do that to me," Silver whispered in desperate dignity, "we're through."

Van Atta recoiled in sputtering outrage. "Through? You and your little friends conspire to sabotage my career in front of the company brass and you tell *me* we're through? You're damn right we're through!"

"Company Security, Shuttleport Three, Captain

Bannerji speaking," George Bannerji recited into his comconsole. "May I help you?"

"You in charge here?" the well-dressed man in his vid began abruptly. He was clearly laboring under strong emotion, breathing rapidly. A muscle jumped in his clamped jaw.

Bannerji took his feet off his desk and leaned forward. "Yes, sir?"

"I'm Bruce Van Atta, Head of Project at the Habitat. Check my voiceprint, or whatever it is you do."

Bannerji sat up straight, tapped out the checkcode; the word "cleared" flashed for a moment across Van Atta's face. Bannerji sat up straighter still. "Yes, sir, go ahead."

Van Atta paused as if groping for words, speaking slowly despite the jostling urgency of thought apparent in his tense face. "We have a little problem here, Captain."

Red lights and sirens went off in Bannerji's head. He could recognize an ass-covering understatement when he heard one. "Oh?"

"Three of our—experimental subjects have escaped the Habitat. We interrogated their co-conspirator, and we believe they stowed away on shuttle flight B119, and are now loose somewhere in Shuttleport Three. It is of the utmost urgency that they be captured and returned to us as quickly as possible."

Bannerji's eyes widened. Information about the Habitat was under a tight company security lid, but no one could work on Rodeo for long without learning that some kind of genetic experiments on humans were taking place up there, in careful isolation. It usually took a little longer for new employees to figure out that the more exotic monster stories told by the old hands were a form of hazing, practiced upon their credulity. Bannerji had transferred in to Rodeo about a month ago.

The project chief's words rang through Bannerji's head. *Escaped. Captured.* Criminals escaped. Dangerous zoo animals escaped, when their keepers screwed up, then some poor shmuck of a cop got the job of capturing them. Occasionally, horrifying biological weapons escaped. What the hell was he dealing with?

"How will we recognize them, sir? Do they," Bannerji swallowed, "look like human beings?"

"No." Van Atta evidently read the dismay in Bannerji's face, for he snorted ironically. "You'll have no trouble recognizing them, I assure you, Captain. And when you do find them, call me at once on my private code. I don't want this going out over broadcast channels. For God's sake keep it quiet, understand?"

Bannerji envisioned public panic. "Yes, sir. I understand completely."

His own panic was a private matter. He wouldn't be collecting the fat salary he did if Security was expected to be all extended coffee breaks and pleasant evening strolls around perfectly deserted property. He'd always known the day would come when he'd have to earn his pay.

Van Atta broke off with a grim nod. Bannerji put in a call on the comconsole for his subordinate, and placed pages for both his off-duty men as well. Something that had the executive hierarchy pouring sweat was nothing for a newly-promoted Security grunt to take chances with.

He unlocked the weapons cabinet and signed out stunners and holsters for himself and his team. He weighed a stunner thoughtfully in his palm. It was such a light little diddly thing, almost a toy; GalacTech risked no lawsuits over stray shots from weapons like these.

Bannerji stood a moment, then turned to his own desk and keyed open the drawer with his personal palm-lock. The unregistered pistol nestled in its own locked box, its shoulder holster coiled around it like a sleeping snake. By the time Bannerji had buckled it on and shrugged his uniform jacket back over it, he was feeling much better. He turned decisively to greet his patrolmen reporting for duty.

Chapter 5

Leo paused outside the airseal doors to the Habitat's infirmary to gather his nerve. He had been
secretly relieved when a frantic call from Pramod
had pulled him, shaking inside, away from the excruciating interrogation of Silver; as secretly ashamed of
his relief. Pramod's problem—fluctuating power levels in his beam welder, traced at last to poisoning of
the electron-emitting cathode by gas contamination—
had occupied Leo for a time, but with the welding
show over, shame had driven him back here.

*So what are you going to do for her at this late
hour?* his conscience mocked him. *Assure her of
your continued moral support, as long as it doesn't
involve you in anything inconvenient or unpleasant?
What a comfort.* He shook his head, tapped the door
control.

Leo drifted silently past the medtech's station without signing in. Silver was in a private cubicle, a
quarter-wedge of the infirmary's circumference at
the very end of the module. The distance had helped
muffle the yelling and crying.

Leo peered through the observation window. Silver was alone, floating limply in the locked sleep
restraints against the wall. In the light from the

fluoros her face was greenish, pale and damp. Her eyes seemed drained of their sparkling blue color, blurred leaden smudges. A yet-unused spacesick sack was clutched, hot and wrinkled, in an upper hand.

Sickened himself, Leo glanced up the corridor to be sure he was still unobserved, swallowed the clot of impotent rage growing in his throat, and slipped inside.

"Uh . . . hi, Silver," Leo began with a weak smile. "How you doing?" He cursed himself silently for the inanity of his own words.

Her smeary eyes found and focused on him uncomprehendingly. Then, "Oh. Leo. I think I was asleep for . . . for a while. Funny dreams . . . I still feel sick."

The drug must be wearing off. Her voice had lost the slurred, dreamy quality it had had during the interrogation earlier; now it was small and tight and self-aware. She added with a quaver of indignation, "That stuff made me throw up. And I've never thrown up before, not ever. It *made* me."

There were, Leo had learned, the most intense social inhibitions against vomiting in free fall, in Silver's little world. She would probably have been far less embarrassed at being stripped naked in public.

"It wasn't your fault," he hastened to reassure her.

She shook her head, her hair waving in lank strands unlike its usual bright aureole, her mouth pinched. "I should have—I thought I could . . . the Red Ninja never told *his* enemies his secrets, and they drugged and tortured him both!"

"Who?" asked Leo, startled.

"Oh . . . !" Silver's voice flattened to a wail. "They found out about our books, too! This time they'll find them all. . . ." Her lashes clotted with tears that could not fall, but only accumulate until blotted away.

When her eyes widened to stare at Leo in a horrified realization, two or three droplets flew off in shimmering tangents. "And now Mr. Van Atta thinks Ti must have known Tony and Claire were on his shuttle—collusion—he says he's going to get Ti fired! And he'll find Tony and Claire down there—I don't know what he'll do to them. I've never seen Mr. Van Atta so angry."

Leo's set jaw had ground his smile to a grimace. Still he tried to speak reasonably. "But you told them—under drugs—that Ti didn't know, surely."

"He didn't believe it. Said I was lying."

"But that would be logically inconsistent—" Leo began, cut himself short. "No, you're right, that wouldn't faze him. God, what an asshole."

Silver's mouth opened in shock. "You mean—Mr. Van Atta?"

"I mean Brucie-baby. You can't tell me you've been around the man for what, eleven months, and not figured that out."

"I thought it was me—something wrong with me . . ." Silver's voice was still small and teary, but her eyes began to brighten with a sort of pre-dawn light. She overcame her inner miseries enough to regard Leo with increased attention. ". . . Brucie-baby?"

"Huh." The memory of one of Dr. Yei's lectures about *maintaining unified and consistent authority* gave Leo pause. It had seemed to make great sense at the time. . . . "Never mind. But there's nothing wrong with you, Silver."

Her regard was sharpening to something almost scientific. "You're not afraid of him." Her tone of wonder suggested she found this an unexpected and remarkable discovery.

"Me? Afraid? Of Bruce Van Atta?" Leo snorted. "Not likely."

"When he first came, and took over Dr. Cay's position, I thought—thought he would be like Dr. Cay."

"Look, ah . . . there is a very ancient rule of thumb that states, people tend to get promoted to the level of their incompetence. So far I think I've managed to avoid that unenviable plateau. So, I gather, did your Dr. Cay." *Screw Yei's scruples*, Leo thought, and added bluntly, "Van Atta hasn't."

"Tony and Claire would never have tried to run away if Dr. Cay were still here." A straggling species of hope began in her eyes. "Are you saying you think this mess could be Mr. Van Atta's fault?"

Leo stirred uneasily, pronged by secret convictions he had not yet voiced even to himself. "Your s—, s—," *slavery* "situation seems intrinsically, intrinsically," *wrong* his mind supplied, while his mouth fishtailed, "susceptible to abuse, mishandling of all sorts. Because Dr. Cay was so passionately dedicated to your welfare—"

"Like a father to us," Silver confirmed sadly.

"—this, er, susceptibility remained latent. But sooner or later it's inevitable that someone begin to exploit it, and you. If not Van Atta, someone else down the line. Someone . . ." *worse?* Leo had read enough history. Yes. "Much worse."

Silver looked as if she were struggling to imagine something worse than Van Atta, and failing. She shook her head dolefully. She raised her face to Leo; eyes like morning glories, targeting the sun. The target, struck, jerked out an involuntary smile.

"What's going to happen now, to Tony and Claire? I tried not to give them away, but that stuff made me so woozy—it was dangerous for them before, and now it's worse. . . ."

Leo attempted a tone of bluff and hearty reassurance. "Nothing's going to happen to them, Silver. Don't let Bruce's snit spook you. There's not really much he can do to them, they're much too valuable to GalacTech. He'll yell at them, no doubt, and you can't blame him for that; I'm ready to yell at them myself. Security will pick them up downside—they can't have gone far—they'll get the lecture of their young lives, and in a few weeks it'll all blow over. Lessons learned," Leo faltered. Just what lessons would they learn from this fiasco? "—all around."

"You act like—like getting yelled at—was nothing."

"It comes with age," he offered. "Someday you'll feel that way too." Or was it power that this particular immunity came with? Leo was suddenly unsure. But he had no power to speak of, except the ability to build things. Knowledge as power. Yet who had power over him? The line of logic trailed off in confusion; he turned his thoughts impatiently from it. Mental wheel-spinning, as unproductive as philosophy class in college.

"I don't feel that way now," said Silver practically.

"Look, uh . . . tell you what. If it'll make you feel better, I'll go along downside when they locate those kids. Maybe I can kind of keep things under control."

"Oh, would you? Could you?" Silver asked with relief. "Like you were trying to help me?"

Leo felt like biting his tongue off. "Uh, yeah. Something like that."

"You're not afraid of Mr. Van Atta. You can stand up to him." Her eyebrows quirked self-deprecatingly, and she waved her lower arms. "As you can see, I'm not equipped to stand up to anybody. Thank you, Leo." There was even a little color in her face now.

"Uh, right. I better hustle along now, if I'm to catch the shuttle going down to 'Port Three. We'll have 'em back safe and sound by breakfast. Think of it this way; at least GalacTech can't dock their pay for the extra shuttle trip." This even won a brief smile from her.

"Leo . . ." her voice sobered, and he paused on his way out the door. "What are we going to do if . . . if there's ever anyone worse than Mr. Van Atta?"

Cross that bridge when you come to it, he wanted to say, evading the question. But one more platitude and he'd gag. He smiled and shook his head, and fled.

The warehouse made Claire think of a crystal lattice. It was all right angles, stretching away at ninety degrees in each dimension, huge slotted shelves reaching to the ceilings, endless rows, cross corridors. Blocking vision, blocking flight.

But there was no flight here. She felt like a stray molecule caught in the interstices of a doped crystal wafer, out of place but trapped. In retrospect the cozy curves of the Habitat seemed like enclosing arms.

They huddled now in one empty cell of a shelf stack, one of the few they had not found occupied by supplies, measuring some two meters on a side. Tony had insisted on climbing to the third tier, to be above the eye level of any chance downsider walking along the corridor upright on his long legs. The ladders set at intervals along the shelves had actually proved easier to manage then creeping along the floor, but getting the pack up had been a dreadful struggle, as its cord was too short to climb up and draw it up after themselves.

Claire was secretly unnerved. Andy was already finding an ability to push and grunt and wriggle against the gravity, still only a few centimeters at a time, but she had a nasty vision of him falling over the edge. Claire was developing a distaste for edges.

A robotic forklift whirred past. Claire froze, cowering in the back of their recess, clutching Andy to her, grabbing one of Tony's hands. The whirring trailed off into the distance. She breathed again.

"Relax," Tony squeaked. "Relax . . ." He breathed deeply in an apparent effort to follow his own advice.

Claire peered doubtfully out of the cubicle at the forklift, which had stopped farther down the corridor and was engaged in retrieving a plastic carton from its coded cell.

"Can we eat now?" She had been nursing Andy on and off for the last three hours in an effort to keep him quiet, and was drained in every sense. Her stomach growled, and her throat was dry.

"I guess," said Tony, and dug a couple of ration bars out of their hoard in the pack. "And then we'd better try and work our way back to the hangar."

"Can't we rest here a little longer?"

Tony shook his head. "The longer we wait, the more chance they'll be looking for us. If we don't get on a shuttle for the Transfer Station soon, they may start searching the outbound Jump ships, and there goes our chance of stowing away undiscovered until after they boost past the point of no return."

Andy squeaked and gurgled; a familiar aroma wafted from his vicinity.

"Oh, dear. Would you please get out a diaper?" Claire asked Tony.

"Again? That's the fourth time since we left the Habitat."

"I don't think I brought near enough diapers," Claire worried, smoothing out the laminated paper and plastic form Tony handed her.

"Half our pack is filled with diapers. Can't you— make it last a little longer?"

"I'm afraid he may be getting diarrhea. If you

leave that stuff on his bottom too long, it eats right through his skin—gets all red—even bleeds—gets infected—and then he screams and cries every time you touch it to try and clean it. Real loud," she emphasized.

The fingers of Tony's lower right hand drummed on the shelf floor, and he sighed, biting back frustration. Claire wrapped the used diaper tightly in itself and prepared to stash it back in their pack.

"Do we have to cart those along?" Tony asked suddenly. "Everything in the pack is going to reek after a while. Besides, it's heavy enough already."

"I haven't seen a disposal unit anywhere," said Claire. "What else can we do with them?"

Tony's face screwed up with inner struggle. "Just leave it," he blurted. "On the floor. It's not like it's going to float off down the corridor and get into the air recirculation, here. Leave them all."

Claire gasped at this horrific, revolutionary idea. Tony, following up his own suggestion before his nerve failed, collected the four little wads and stuffed them into the far corner of the storage cubicle. He smiled shakily, in mixed guilt and elation. Claire eyed him in worry. Yes, the situation was extraordinary, but what if Tony was developing a habit of criminal behavior? Would he return to normal when they got—wherever they were going?

If they got wherever they were going. Claire pictured their pursuers following the dirty diapers, like a trail of flower petals dropped by that heroine in one of Silver's books, across half the galaxy. . . .

"If you've got him back together," said Tony with a nod at his son, "maybe we better start back toward the hangar. That mob of downsiders may be cleared out by now."

"How are we going to pick a shuttle this time?"

asked Claire. "How will we know that it's not just going right back up to the Habitat—or taking up a cargo to be unloaded in the vacuum? If they vent the cargo bay into space while we're in it . . ."

Tony shook his head, lips tight. "I don't know. But Leo says—to solve a big problem, or complete a big project, the secret is to break it down into little parts and tackle them one at a time, in order. Let's—just get back to the hangar, first. And see if there's any shuttles there at all."

Claire nodded, paused. Andy was not the only one of them plagued by biology, she reflected grimly. "Tony, do you think we can find a toilet on the way back? I need to go."

"Yeah, me too," Tony admitted. "Did you see any on the way here?"

"No." Locating the facilities had not been uppermost on her mind then, on that nightmare journey, creeping over the floors, dodging hurrying downsiders, squeezing Andy tightly to her for fear that he might cry out. Claire wasn't even sure she could reconstruct the route they'd taken, when they'd been driven out of their first hiding place by the busy work crew descending upon their machines and powering them up.

"There's got to be something," Tony reasoned optimistically, "people work here."

"Not in this section," Claire noted, gazing out at the wall of storage cells across the aisle. "It's all robots."

"Back toward the hangar, then. Say . . ." his voice faltered, "uh . . . do you happen to know what a gravity-field toilet chamber looks like? How do they manage? Air suction couldn't possibly fight the gee forces."

One of Silver's smuggled historical vid dramas had

involved a scene with an outhouse, but Claire was certain that was obsolete technology. "I think they use water, somehow."

Tony wrinkled his nose, shrugged away his bafflement. "We'll figure it out." His eye fell rather wistfully on the little wad of diapers in the corner. "It's too bad . . ."

"No!" said Claire, repelled. "Or at least—at least let's *try* to find a toilet first."

"All right. . . ."

A distant rhythmic tapping was growing louder. Tony, about to swing out on the ladder, muttered "Oops," and recoiled back into the cubicle. He held a finger to his lips, panic in his face, and they all scuttled to the back of the cell.

"Aaah?" said Andy. Claire snatched him up and stuffed the tip on one breast into his mouth. Full and bored, he declined to nurse, turning his head away. Claire let her T-shirt fall back down and tried to distract him by silently counting all his busy fingers. He too had become smudged with dirt, as she had; no big surprise, planets were *made* of dirt. Dirt looked better from a distance. Say, a couple of hundred kilometers. . . .

The tapping grew louder, passed under their cell, faded.

"Company Security man," Tony whispered in Claire's ear.

She nodded, hardly daring to breathe. The tapping was from those hard downsider footcoverings striking the cement floor. A few minutes passed, and the tapping did not return. Andy made only small cooing noises.

Tony stuck his head cautiously out the chamber, looked right and left, up and down. "All right. Get ready to help me lower the pack as soon as this next forklift goes by. It'll have to fall the last meter, but maybe the sound of the forklift will cover that some."

Together they shoved the pack toward the edge of the cell, and waited. The whirring robolift was approaching down the corridor, an enormous plastic storage crate almost as large as a cubicle positioned on its lift.

The forklift stopped below them, beeped to itself, and turned ninety degrees. With a whine, its lift began to rise.

At this point, Claire recalled that theirs was the only empty cell in this stack.

"It's coming *here*! We're going to get squashed!"

"Get out! Get out on the ladder!" Tony yelped.

Instead she scuttled back to grab Andy, whom she'd laid at the rear of the chamber as far as possible from the frightening edge while she'd helped Tony shove the pack forward. The chamber darkened as the rising crate eclipsed the opening. Tony barely squeezed past it onto the ladder as it began to grind inward.

"Claire!" Tony screamed. He pounded uselessly on the side of the huge plastic crate. "Claire! No, no! Stupid robot! Stop, stop!"

But the forklift, clearly, was not voice-activated. It kept coming, bulldozing their pack before it. There were only a few centimeters' clearance on the sides and top of the crate. Claire retreated, so terrified her screams clotted in her throat like cotton, and she emitted only a smeary squeak. Back, back; the cold metal wall behind froze her. She flattened against it as best she could, standing on her lower hands, holding Andy with her uppers. He was howling now, infected by her terror, earsplitting shrieks.

"Claire!" Tony cried from the ladder, a horrified bellow laced with tears. "ANDY!"

The pack, beside them, compressed. Little crunching noises came from it. At the last moment, Claire transferred Andy to her lower arms, below her torso, bracing against the crate, against gravity, with her uppers. Perhaps her crushed body would hold the crate off just far enough to save him—the robolift's servos skreeled with overload. . . .

And began to withdraw. Claire sent a silent apology to their oversized pack for all the curses she and Tony had heaped upon it in the past hours. Nothing in it would ever be the same, but it had saved them.

The robolift hiccoughed, gears grinding bewilderedly. The crate shifted on its pallet, out of sync now. As the lift withdrew, the crate skidded with it, dragged by friction and gravity, skewing farther and farther from true.

Claire watched open-mouthed as it tilted and fell from the opening. She rushed forward. The crash shook the warehouse as the crate hit the concrete, followed by a booming shattered echo, the loudest sound Claire had ever heard. The crate took the forklift with it, its wheels whirring helplessly in air as it banged onto its side.

The power of gravity was stunning. The crate split, its contents spilling. Hundreds of round metal wheelcovers of some kind burst forth, ringing like a stampede of cymbals. A dozen or so rolled down the aisle in either direction as if bent on escape, wobbling into the corridor walls and falling onto their sides, still spinning, in ever-diminishing whanging pulses of sound. The echoes rang on in Claire's ears for a moment in the stupendous silence that followed.

"Oh, Claire!" Tony swarmed back into the cell and wrapped all his arms around her, Andy between them, as if he might never let go again. "Oh, Claire . . ." His voice cracked as he rubbed his face against her soft short hair.

Claire looked over his shoulder at the carnage they had created below. The overturned robolift was beeping again, like an animal in pain. "Tony, I think we better get out of here," she suggested in a small voice.

"I thought you were coming behind me, onto the ladder. Right behind me."

"I had to get Andy."

"Of course. You saved him, while I—saved myself. Oh, Claire! I didn't mean to leave you in there . . ."

"I didn't think you did."

"But I jumped—"

"It would have been plain stupid not to. Look, can we talk about it *later*? I *really* think we ought to get out of here."

"Yes, oh yes. Uh, the pack . . . ?" Tony peered into the dimness of the recess.

Claire didn't think they were going to have time for the pack, either—yet how far could they get without it? She helped Tony drag it back to the edge with frantic haste.

"If you brace yourself back there, while I hang onto the ladder, we can lower it—" Tony began.

Claire pushed it ruthlessly over the edge. It landed on the mess below, tumbled to the concrete. "I don't think there's any more point in worrying about the breakables now. Let's *go*," she urged.

Tony gulped, nodded, moved quickly onto the ladder, sparing one upper arm to help support Andy, whom Claire held in her lowers, her upper hands slapping down the rungs. Then they were back to the floor and their slow, frustrating, crabwise locomotion along it. Claire was beginning to hate the cold, dusty smell of concrete.

They were only a few meters down the corridor when Claire heard the pounding of downsider footcoverings again, moving fast, with uncertain pauses as if for direction. A row or two over; the steps must shortly thread the lattice to them. Then an echo of the steps—no, another set.

What happened next seemed all in a moment, suspended between one breath and the next. Ahead of them, a grey-uniformed downsider leaped from a cross-corridor into their own with an unintelligible shout. His legs were braced apart to support his half-crouch, and he clutched a strange piece of equipment in both hands, held up half a meter in front of his face. His face was as white with terror as Claire's own.

Ahead of her, Tony dropped the pack and reared up on his lower arms, his upper hands flung wide, crying, "No!"

The downsider recoiled spasmodically, his eyes wide, mouth gaping in shock. Two or three bright flashes burst from his piece of equipment, accompanied by sharp cracking bangs that echoed, splintered, all through the great warehouse. Then the downsider's hands jerked up, the object flung away. Had it malfunctioned or short-circuited, burning or shocking him? His face drained further, from white to green.

Then Tony was screaming, flopping on the floor, all his arms curling in on himself in a tight ball of agony.

"Tony? Tony!" Claire scrambled toward him, Andy clamped tightly to her torso and crying and screaming in fear, his racket mingling with Tony's in a terrifying cacophony. "Tony, what's wrong?" She didn't see the blood on his red T-shirt until some drops spattered on the concrete. The bicep of his left lower arm, as he rolled toward her, was a scrambled, pulsing, scarlet and purple mess. "Tony!"

The company security guard had rushed forward.
His face was harrowed with horror, his hands empty
now and fumbling with a portable comm link hooked
to his belt. It took him three tries to detach it.
"Nelson! Nelson!" he called into it. "Nelson, for God's
sake call the medical squad, quick! It's just *kids*! I
just shot a *kid!*" His voice shook. "It's just some
crippled *kids!*"

Leo's stomach sank at the sight of the yellow pulses
of light reflecting off the warehouse wall. Company
medical squad; yes, there was their electric truck,
blinkers flashing, parked in the wide central aisle.
The breathless words of the clerk who'd met their
shuttle tumbled through his brain—. . . *found in
the warehouse . . . there's been an accident . . .
injury* . . . Leo's steps quickened.

"Slow down, Leo, I'm getting dizzy," Van Atta,
behind him, complained irritably. "Not everybody
can bounce back and forth between null-gee and
one-gee like you do with no effects, you know."

"They said one of the kids was hurt. . . ."

"So what are you going to do that the medics
can't? I, personally, am going to crucify that idiot
Security team for this. . . ."

"I'll meet you there," Leo snarled over his shoulder, and ran.

Aisle 29 looked like a war zone. Smashed equipment, stuff scattered everywhere—Leo half tripped
over a couple of round metal cover plates, kicked
them impatiently out of his way. A pair of medics
and a Security guard were huddled over a stretcher
on the floor, an IV bag hoisted on a pole like a flag
above them.

Red shirt; Tony, it was Tony who'd been hurt.
Claire was crouched on the floor a little farther down

the aisle, clutching Andy, tears streaming silently down her ragged white mask of a face. On the stretcher, Tony writhed and cried out with a hoarse sob.

"Can't you at least give him something for pain?" the security guard urged the medtech.

"I don't *know*." The medtech was clearly flustered. "I don't know what all they've done to their metabolisms. Shock is shock, I'm safe with the IV and the warmers and the synergine, but as for the rest of it—"

"Patch in an emergency comm link to Dr. Warren Minchenko." Leo advised, kneeling beside them. "He's chief medical officer for the Cay Habitat, and he's on his month's downside leave right now. Ask him to meet you at your infirmary; he'll take over the case there."

The Security guard eagerly unhooked his comm link and began punching in codes.

"Oh, thank God," said the medtech, turning to Leo. "At last, somebody who knows what the hell they're doing. Do you know what I can give him for pain, sir?"

"Uh . . ." Leo did a quick mental review of his first aid. "Syntha-morph should be all right, until you get in touch with Dr. Minchenko. But adjust the dose—these kids weigh less than they look like they ought to—I think Tony masses about, um, 42 kilos."

The peculiar nature of Tony's injuries dawned on Leo at last. He had been picturing a fall, broken bones, maybe spinal cord or cranial damage. . . . "What *happened* here?"

"Gunshot wound," reported the medtech shortly. "Left lower abdomen and . . . and, um, not femur— left lower limb. That's just a flesh wound, but the abdominal one is serious."

"Gunshot!" Leo stared aghast at the guard, who reddened. "Did you—I thought you guys carried stunners—why in the name of God—"

"When that damned hysteric called down from the Habitat, yammering about his escaped monsters, I thought—I thought—I don't know what I thought." The guard glowered at his boots.

"Didn't you look before you fired?"

"I *damn* near shot the girl with the baby." The guard shuddered. "I hit this kid by accident, jerking my aim away."

Van Atta panted up. "Holy shit, what a mess!" His eye fell on the security guard. "I thought I told you to keep this quiet, Bannerji. What did you do, set off a bomb?"

"He shot Tony," said Leo through his teeth.

"You idiot, I told you to capture them, not murder them! How the hell am I supposed to sweep *this*—" he waved his arm down Aisle 29, "under the rug? And what the hell were you doing with a pistol anyway?"

"You said—I thought—" the guard began.

"I swear I'll have you canned for this. Of all the ass-backwards—did you think this was some kind of feelie-dream drama? I don't know whose judgment is worse, yours or the jerk's who hired you—"

The guard's face had gone from red to white. "Why you stupid son-of-a-bitch, you set me up for this—"

Somebody had better keep a level head, Leo thought wretchedly. Bannerji had retrieved and holstered his unauthorized weapon, a fact Van Atta seemed to be unconscious of—the temptation to shoot the project chief shouldn't be allowed to get too overwhelming— Leo intervened. "Gentlemen, may I suggest that charges and defenses would be better saved for a formal investigation, where everyone will be cooler and, er, more reasoned. Meantime we have some hurt and frightened kids to take care of."

Bannerji fell silent, simmering with injustice. Van Atta growled assent, contenting himself with a black look toward Bannerji that boded ill for the guard's future career. The two medtechs snapped down the wheels of Tony's stretcher and began rolling him down the aisle toward their waiting truck. One of Claire's hands reached out after him, fell back hopelessly.

The gesture caught Van Atta's attention. Full of suppressed rage, he discovered he had an object on which to vent it after all. "You—!" he turned on Claire.

She flinched into a tighter huddle.

"Do you have any idea what this escapade of yours is going to cost the Cay Project, first to last? Of all the irresponsible—did you con Tony into this?"

She shook her head, eyes widening.

"Of course you did, isn't it always the way. The male sticks his neck out, the female gets it chopped off for him. . . ."

"Oh, no. . . ."

"And the timing—were you deliberately trying to smear me? How did you find out about the Ops VP—did you figure I'd cover up for you just because she was here? Clever, clever—but not clever enough. . . ."

Leo's head, eyes, ears throbbed with the beating of his blood. "Lay off, Bruce. She's had enough for one day."

"The little bitch nearly gets your best student killed, and you want to stand up for her? Get serious, Leo."

"She's already scared out of her wits. Lay off."

"She damn well better be. When I get her back to the Habitat . . ." Van Atta strode past Leo, grabbed Claire by an upper arm, yanked her cruelly and painfully up. She cried out, nearly dropping Andy; Van Atta overrode her. "You wanted to come downside, you can bloody well just *try* walking—back to the shuttle, then."

Leo could not, afterwards, recall running forward or swinging Van Atta around to face him, but only Van Atta's surprised, open-mouthed expression. "Bruce," he sang through a red haze, "you smarmy creep—lay *off.*"

The uppercut to Van Attta's jaw that punctuated this command was surprisingly effective, considering it was the first time Leo had struck a man in anger in his life. Van Atta sprawled backwards on the concrete.

Leo surged forward in a kind of dizzy joy. He would rearrange Van Atta's anatomy in ways that even Dr. Cay had never dreamed of—

"Uh, Mr. Graf," the security guard began, touching him hesitantly on the shoulder.

"It's all right, I've been waiting to do this for weeks," Leo assured him, going for a grip on Van Atta's collar.

"It's not that, sir . . ."

A cold new voice cut in. "Fascinating executive technique. I must take notes."

Vice President Apmad, flanked by her flying wedge of accountants and assistants, stood behind Leo in Aisle 29.

Chapter 6

"Well, it wasn't *my* fault," snapped Shuttleport Administrator Chalopin. "I wasn't even told this was going on." She glowered pointedly at Van Atta. "How am I supposed to control my jursidiction when *other* administrators hopscotch my properly established channels of command, blithely hand out orders to my people without even informing me, violate protocol . . ."

"The situation was extraordinary. Time was of the essence," muttered Van Atta truculently.

Leo secretly sympathized with Chalopin's testiness. Her smooth routine disrupted, her office abruptly appropriated for the Ops VP's inquest— Apmad did not believe in wasting time. The official company investigation of the incident had commenced, by her fiat, a bare hour ago in Aisle 29; he'd be surprised if it took her more than another hour to finish sifting the case.

The windows of Shuttleport Three's adminstrative offices, sealed against the internal pressure of the building, framed a panorama of the complex—the runways, loading zones, warehouses, offices, hangars, workers' dormitories, the monorail running off to the refinery glittering on the horizon and the eerily rugged mountains beyond. And the vital power plant; Rodeo's atmosphere had oxygen, nitrogen, and carbon dioxide, but in the wrong proportions and at too low a pressure to suit human metabolism. The air conditioning labored constantly to adjust the gas mix and filter out the contaminants. A human might live for fifteen minutes outside without a breath mask; Leo was uncertain whether to think of it as a safety margin or just a slow death. Definitely not a garden spot.

Bannerji had sidled around behind the shuttleport administrator. Hiding behind her, Leo thought. It might be the best strategy for the security guard at that. From her smart shoes through her trim Galac-Tech uniform to her swept-back coiffure, not a hair out of place, and her set, clean jawline, Chalopin radiated both the will and the ability to defend her turf.

Apmad, refereeing the scrimmage, was another type altogether. Dumpy, on the high end of middle age, frizzy grey hair cut short, she might have been somebody's grandmother, but for her eyes. She made no attempt to dress for success. As if she already possessed so much power, she was beyond that game. So far from regulating tempers, her laconic comments had served to stir the pot, as if she was curious what might float to the top. Definitely not a grandmother's eyes . . .

Leo was still close to a boil himself. "The project is twenty-five years old. Time can't be that much of the essence."

"God almighty," cried Van Atta, "am I the only man here conscious of what the bottom line means?"

"Bottom line?" said Leo. "GalacTech is closer to its payoff from the Cay Project than ever before. To screw things up now with an impatient, premature attempt to wring profits is practically criminal. You're on the verge of the first real results."

"Not really," observed Apmad coolly. "Your first group of fifty workers is merely a token. It will take another ten years to bring the whole thousand on-line." Cool, yes; but Leo read a fierce concealed tension in her the source of which he could not yet identify.

"So, call it a tax loss. You can't tell me this," Leo waved a hand toward the window, indicating Rodeo, "can't use a tax loss or two."

Apmad rolled her eyes at the man who stood silently at her shoulder. "Tell this young man the facts of life, Gavin."

Gavin was a big rumpled goon with a broken nose whom Leo had taken at first for some kind of bodyguard. He was in fact the Ops VP's chief accountant, and when he spoke it was with startlingly precise and elegant elocution, in impressive rounded paragraphs.

"GalacTech had been offsetting the Cay Project's very considerable losses with Rodeo's paper profits since its inception. I'd better recapitulate a little history for you, Mr. Graf." Gavin scratched his nose thoughtfully.

"GalacTech holds Rodeo on a ninety-nine-year lease with the government of Orient IV. The original terms of the lease were extremely favorable to us, since Rodeo's unique mineral and petrochemical resources were at that time still undiscovered. And so they remained for the first thirty years of the lease.

"The next thirty years saw an enormous investment of materials and labor on the part of GalacTech to develop Rodeo's resources. Of course," he prodded the air with a didactic finger, "as soon as Orient IV began to see our profit passing through their wormhole nexus, they began to regret the terms of the lease, and to seek a larger cut of the action. Rodeo was chosen as the site for the Cay Project in the first place in part, besides certain unique legal advantages, precisely so that its projected expenses could be charged against Rodeo's profits generally, and reduce the, er, unhealthy excitement said profits were generating on Orient IV.

"GalacTech's lease of Rodeo now has some fourteen years left to run, and the government of Orient IV is getting, ah, how shall I put this, infected with anticipatory greed. They've just changed their tax laws, and from the end of this fiscal year they propose to tax the company's Rodeo operation upon gross not net profit. We lobbied against it, but we failed. Damn provincials," he added reflectively.

"So. After the end of this fiscal year, the Cay Project losses can no longer be offset against Orient IV tax savings; they will be real, and passed through to us. The terms of the new lease at the end of the next fourteen years are not expected to be favorable. In fact, we project Orient IV is preparing to drive GalacTech out and take over its Rodeo operations at a fraction of their real worth. Expropriation by any other name doth smell the same. The economic blockade is already beginning. The time to start limiting further investment and maximizing profit is now."

"In other words," said Apmad, a hard angry glitter in her eyes, "let them take over a hollow shell."

Could be hard on the last guys out, Leo thought, chilled. Didn't those jerks on Orient IV realize that cooperation and compromise would increase everybody's profit, in the end? The GalacTech negotiators were probably not without fault, either, he reflected grimly. He'd seen other versions of the hostile takeover scenario before. He glanced out the window at the large, lively, *working* facilities laid out below, hard-won results of two generations of sincere labor, and groaned inwardly at the thought of the waste to come. From the horrified look on Chalopin's face, she had a similar vision, and Leo's heart went out to her. How much of her blood had gone into the building-up of this place? How many people's sweat and dedication, cancelled at the stroke of a pen?

"That was always your problem, Leo," said Van Atta rather venomously. "You always get your head balled up in the little details, and miss the big picture."

Leo shook his head to clear it, grasped for the lost thread of his original argument. "Nevertheless, the Cay Project's viability—" he paused abruptly, seized by a breathtaking inspiration as delicate as a soap bubble. The stroke of a pen. Could freedom be won with the stroke of a pen? As simply as that? He gazed at Apmad with a new intensity, two orders of magnitude more at least. "Tell me, ma'am," he said carefully, "what happens if the Cay Project's viability is *dis*proved?"

"We shut it down," she said simply.

Oh, the tales out of school he might tell—and sink Brucie-baby forever as an added bonus— Leo's nerves thrilled. He opened his mouth to pour out destruction—

And closed it, sucked on his tongue, regarded his fingernails, and asked instead casually, "And what happens to the quaddies then?"

The Ops VP frowned as if she'd bitten into something nasty: that hidden tension again, the most expression Leo had yet seen upon her face. "That presents the most difficult problem of all."

"Difficult? Why difficult? Just let them go. In fact," Leo strove to conceal his rising excitement behind a bland face, "if GalacTech would let them go immediately, before the end of this fiscal year, it could still take whatever it chooses to calculate as its investment in them as a tax loss against Rodeo's profits. One last fling, as it were, one last bite out of Orient IV." Leo smiled attractively.

"Let them go where? You seem to forget, Mr. Graf, that the bulk of them are still mere children."

Leo faltered. "The older ones could help take care of the younger ones, they already do, some. . . . Perhaps they could be moved for a few years to some other sector that could absorb the loss from their upkeep—it couldn't cost GalacTech *that* much more than a like number of workers on pensions, and only for a few years. . . ."

"The company retirement pension fund is self-supporting," Gavin the accountant observed elliptically. "Roll-over."

"A moral obligation," Leo offered desperately. "Surely GalacTech must admit some moral obligation to them—we created them, after all." The ground was shifting under his feet, he could see it in her unsympathetic face, but he could not yet discern in what direction the tilt was going.

"Moral obligation indeed," agreed Apmad, her hands clenching. "And have you overlooked the fact that Dr. Cay created these creatures fertile? They are a new species, you know; he dubbed them *Homo quadrimanus*, not *Homo sapiens* race *quadrimanus*. He was the geneticist, we may presume he knew what he was talking about. What about GalacTech's moral obligation to society at large? How do you imagine it will react to having these creatures and all their problems just dumped into its systems? If you think they overreact to chemical pollution, just imagine the flap over genetic pollution!"

"Genetic pollution?" Leo muttered, trying to attach some rational meaning to the term. It *sounded* impressive.

"No. If the Cay Project is proved to be GalacTech's most expensive mistake, we will containerize it properly. The Cay workers will be sterilized and placed in some suitable institution, there to live out their lives otherwise unmolested. Not an ideal solution, but the best available compromise."

"St—st . . ." Leo stuttered. "What crime have they committed, to be sentenced to life in prison? And where, if Rodeo is to be closed down, will you find or build another suitable orbital habitat? If you're worried about expense, lady, *that'll* be expensive."

"They will be placed planetside, of course, at a fraction of the cost."

A vision of Silver creeping uncomfortably across the floor like a bird with both wings broken burst in Leo's brain. "That's *obscene*! They'll be no better than cripples."

"The obscenity," snapped Apmad, "was in creating them in the first place. Until Dr. Cay's death brought his department under mine, I had no idea that his 'R&D—Biologicals' was concealing such enormously invasive manipulations of human genes. My home world embraced the most painfully draconian measures to ensure our gene pool not be overrun with accidental mutations—to go out and deliberately introduce mutations seems the most vile . . ." she caught her breath, contained her emotions again, except what escaped her nervously drumming fingers. "The *right* thing to do is euthanasia. Terrible as it seems at first glance, it might actually be less cruel in the long run."

Gavin the accountant, squirming, twitched an uncertain smile at his boss. His eyebrows had gone up in surprise, down in dismay, and at last settled on up again—not taking her seriously, perhaps. Leo didn't think she'd been joking, but Gavin added in a facetiously detached professional tone, "It *would* be more cost effective. If it were done before the end of this fiscal year, we could indeed take them as a loss—total—against Orient taxes."

Leo felt suspended in glass. "You can't do that!" he whispered. "They're people—children—it would be murder—"

"No, it would not," denied Apmad. "Repugnant, certainly, but not murder. That was the other half of the reason for locating the Cay Project in orbit around Rodeo. Besides physical isolation, Rodeo exists in legal isolation. It's in the ninety-nine-year lease. The only legal writ in Rodeo local space is GalacTech regulation. I fear this has less to do with foresight than with Dr. Cay's successful blocking of any interference with his schemes. But if GalacTech chooses not to define the Cay workers as human beings, company regulations regarding crimes do not apply."

"Oh, really?" Bannerji brightened slightly.

"How *does* GalacTech define them?" asked Leo, glassily curious. "Legally."

"Post-fetal experimental tissue cultures," said Apmad.

"And what do you call murdering them? Retroactive abortion?"

Apmad's nostrils grew pinched. "Simple disposal."

"Or," Gavin glanced sardonically at Bannerji, "vandalism, perhaps. Our one legal requirement is that experimental tissue be cremated upon disposal. IGS Standard Biolab rules."

"Launch them into the sun," Leo suggested tightly. "That'd be cheap."

Van Atta stroked his chin gently and regarded Leo uneasily. "Calm down, Leo. We're just talking contingency scenarios here. Military staffs do it all the time."

"Quite," agreed the Ops VP. She paused to frown at Gavin, whose flippancy apparently did not please her. "There are some hard decisions to be made here, which I am not anxious to face, but it seems they have been dealt to me. Better me than someone blind to the long-term consequences to society at large like Dr. Cay. But perhaps, Mr. Graf, you will wish to join Mr. Van Atta in showing how Dr. Cay's original vision might still be carried out at a profit, so we can *all* avoid having to make the hardest choices."

Van Atta smiled at Leo, smarmily triumphant. Vindicated, vindictive, calculating . . . "To return to the matter at hand," Van Atta said, "I've already requested that Captain Bannerji be summarily terminated for his poor judgment and," he glanced at Gavin, "and vandalism. I might also suggest that the cost of TY-776-424-X-G's hospitalization be charged to his department." Bannerji wilted, Administrator Chalopin stiffened.

"But it's increasingly apparent to me," Van Atta went on, fixing his most unpleasant smile on Leo, "that there's another matter to be pursued here. . . ."

Ah shit, thought Leo, he's going to get me on an assault charge—an eighteen-year career up in smoke—and I did it to myself—and I didn't even get to *finish* the job. . . .

"Subversion."

"Huh?" said Leo.

"The quaddies have been growing increasingly restive in the past few months. Coincidentally with *your* arrival, Leo." Van Atta's gaze narrowed. "After today's events I wonder if it was a coincidence. I rather think not. Isn't it so that," he wheeled and pointed dramatically at Leo, "*you* put Tony and Claire up to this escapade?"

"Me!" Leo sputtered in outrage, paused. "True, Tony did come to me once with some very odd questions, but I thought he was just curious about his upcoming work assignment. I wish now I'd . . ."

"You admit it!" Van Atta crowed. "You have encouraged defiant attitudes toward company authority among the hydroponics workers, and among your own students entrusted to you—ignored the psych department's carefully developed guidelines for speech and behavior while aboard the Habitat—infected the workers with your own bad attitudes—"

Leo realized suddenly that Van Atta was not going to let him get a word of defense in edgewise if he could possibly help it. Van Atta was onto something infinitely more valuable than mere vengeance for a punch in the jaw—a scapegoat. A perfect scapegoat, upon whom he could pin every glitch in the Project for the past two months—or longer, depending on his ingenuity—and sacrifice qualmlessly to the company gods, himself emerging squeaky-clean and sinless.

"No, by God!" Leo roared. "If I were running a revolution, I'd do a damn sight better job of it than *that*—" he waved in the general direction of the warehouse. His muscles bunched to launch himself at Van Atta again. If he was to be fired anyway, he'd at least get some satisfaction out of it—

"Gentlemen." Apmad's voice sluiced down like a bucket of ice water. "Mr. Van Atta, may I remind you that terminations from outlying facilities like Rodeo are discouraged. Not only is GalacTech contractually obligated to provide transportation home to the terminees, but there is also the expense and large time delay of importing their replacements. No, we shall finish it this way. Captain Bannerji shall be suspended for two weeks without pay, and an official reprimand added to his permanent record for carrying an unauthorized weapon on official company duty. The weapon shall be confiscated. Mr. Graf shall be officially reprimanded also, but return immediately to his duties, as there is no one to replace him in them."

"But I was screwed," complained Bannerji.

"But I'm totally innocent!" cried Leo. "It's a fabrication—a paranoid fantasy—"

"You can't send Graf back to the Habitat now," yelped Van Atta. "Next thing you know he'll be trying to unionize 'em—"

"Considering the consequences of the Cay Project's failure," said the Ops VP coldly, "I think not. Eh, Mr. Graf?"

Leo shivered. "Eh."

She sighed without satisfaction. "Thank you. This investigation is now complete. Further complaints or appeals by any party may be addressed to GalacTech headquarters on Earth." *If you dare*, her quirked eyebrow added. Even Van Atta had the sense to keep his mouth shut.

The mood in the shuttle for the return trip to the Habitat was, to say the least, constrained. Claire, accompanied by one of the Habitat's infirmary nurses pulled off her downside leave three days early for the duty, huddled in the back clutching Andy. Leo and Van Atta sat as far from each other as the limited space allowed.

Van Atta spoke once to Leo. "I told you so."

"You were right," Leo replied woodenly. Van Atta

nearly purred at the stroke, smug. Leo would rather have stroked him with a pipe wrench.

Could Van Atta be all right, as well? Was his disruptive pressure for instant results a sign of concern for the quaddies' welfare, even survival? No, Leo decided with a sigh. The only welfare that truly concerned Bruce was his own.

Leo let his head rest on the padded support and stared out his window as the acceleration of takeoff thrust him back in his seat. A shuttle ride was still a bit of a thrill to something deep in him, even after the countless trips he'd made. There were people—billions, the vast majority—who never set foot off their home planets in their lives. He was one of the lucky few.

Lucky to have his job. Lucky in the results he'd achieved, over the years. The vast Morita Deep Space Transfer Station had probably been the crown of his career, the largest project he was ever likely to work on. He'd first viewed the site when it was empty, icy vacuum, as nothing as nothing could possibly be. He'd passed through it again just last year, making a changeover from a ship from Ylla to a ship for Earth. Morita had looked good, really good; alive, even undergoing expansion of its facilities, several years sooner than anyone had expected. Smooth expansion; plans for it had been incorporated into the original designs. Over-ambitious they'd called it then. Far-sighted, they called it now.

And there had been other projects too. Every day, from one end of the wormhole nexus to the other, countless accidents of structural failure did *not* occur because he, and people he'd trained, had done their jobs well. The work of a harried week, the early detection of the propagating micro-cracks in the reactor coolant lines at the great Beni Ra orbital factory alone had saved, perhaps, three thousand lives. How many surgeons could claim to save three thousand lives in ten years of their careers? On that memorable inspection tour, he'd done it once a month for a year. Invisibly, unsung; disasters that never happen don't normally make headlines. But he knew, and the men and women who worked alongside him knew, and that was enough.

He regretted slugging Bruce. The moment's red joy had certainly not been worth risking his job for. The eighteen years of accumulating pension benefits, the stock options, the seniority, yes, maybe; with no family to support, they were all Leo's, to piss into the wind if he chose. But who would take care of the next Beni Ra?

When they returned to the Habitat, he would cooperate. Apologize handsomely to Bruce. Redouble his training efforts, increase his care. Bite his tongue, speak only when spoken to. Be polite to Dr. Yei. Hell, even do what she told him.

Anything else was impossibly risky. There were a thousand kids up there. So many, so varied—so *young*. A hundred five-year-olds, a hundred and twenty six-year-olds alone, cramming the creche modules, playing games in their free-fall gym. No one individual could possibly take responsibility for risking all those lives on something chancy. It would be endless, all-consuming. Impossible. Criminal. Insane. Revolt—where could it lead? No one could possibly forsee all the consequences. Leo couldn't even see around the next corner. No one could. No one.

They docked at the Habitat. Van Atta shooed Claire and Andy and the nurse ahead of him through the hatchway, as Leo slowly unfastened his seat harness.

"Oh, no," Leo heard Van Atta say. "The nurse will take Andy to the creche. You will return to your old dormitory. Taking that baby downside was criminally irresponsible. It's clear you are totally unfit to have charge of him. I can guarantee, you'll be struck from the reproduction roster, too."

Claire's weeping was so muffled as to be nearly inaudible.

Leo closed his eyes in pain. "God," he asked, "why me?"

Releasing his last restraint, he fell blindly into his future.

Chapter 7

"Leo!" Silver anchored one hand and pounded softly and frantically with the other three on the door to the engineer's sleeping quarters. "Leo, quick! Wake up, help!" She laid her cheek against the cold plastic, muffling her bursting howl to a small, sliding "Leo?" She dared not cry louder, lest she attract more than Leo's ear.

His door slid open at last. He wore red T-shirt and shorts, barefoot. His sleep sack against the far wall hung open like an empty cocoon, and his thinning sandy hair stuck out in odd directions. "What the hell . . . Silver?" His face was rumpled with sleep, eyes dark-ringed but focusing fast.

"Come quick, come quick!" Silver hissed, grabbing his hand. "It's Claire. She tried to go out an airlock. I jammed the controls. She can't get the outer door open, but I can't get the inner door open either, and she's trapped in there. Our supervisor will be back soon, and then I don't know *what* they'll do to us. . . ."

"Son-of-a . . ." he allowed her to draw him into the corridor, then lurched back into his cabin to grab a tool belt. "All right, go, go, lead on."

They sped through the maze of the Habitat, offer-

119

ing strained bland smiles to those quaddies and downsiders they flew past in the corridors. At last, the familiar door to "Hydroponics D" closed behind them.

"What happened? How did this happen?" Leo asked her as they brushed through the grow-tubes to the far end of the module.

"They wouldn't let me go see Claire day before yesterday, when you brought her back on the shuttle, even though we were both in the Infirmary. Yesterday we were on different work teams. I think it was on purpose. Today I made Teddie trade with me." Silver's voice smeared with her distress. "Claire said they won't even let her into the creche to see Andy on her off-shift. I went to get fertilizer from Stores to charge the grow-tubes we were working on, and when I came back, the lock was just starting to cycle. . . ." If only she hadn't left Claire alone—if only she had not let the shuttle take them downside in the first place—if only she had not betrayed them to Dr. Yei's drugs—if only they'd been born down-siders—or not been born at all. . . .

The airlock at the end of the hydroponics module was almost never used, merely waiting to become the airseal door to the next module that future growth might demand. Silver pressed her face to the observation window. To her immense relief, Claire was still within.

But she was ramming herself back and forth between door and door, her face smeared with tears and blood, fingers reddened. Whether she gulped for air or only screamed Silver could not tell, for all sound was silenced by the barrier door, like a turned-down holovid. Silver's own chest seemed so tight she could scarcely breathe.

Leo glanced in. His lips drew back in a fierce

scowl in his whitened face, and he turned to hiss at
the lock mechanism, scrabbling at his tool belt. "You
fixed it but good, Silver . . ."

"I had to do something quick. Shorting it that way
blocked the alarm from going off in Central Systems."

"Oh . . ." Leo's hands hesitated briefly. "Not so
random a stab as it looks, then."

"Random? In an airlock control box?" She stared at
him in surprise, and some indignation. "I'm not a
five-year-old!"

"Indeed not." A crooked grin lightened his tense
face for a moment. "Any quaddie of six would know
better. My apologies, Silver. So the problem then, is
not how to open the door, but how to do so without
tripping the alarm."

"Yes, right." She hovered anxiously.

He looked the mechanism over, glanced up rather
more hesitantly at the airlock door, which vibrated to
the thumping from within. "You sure Claire doesn't
need—more help anyway?"

"She may need help," snapped Silver, "but what
she'll get is Dr. Yei."

"Ah . . . right." His grin thinned out altogether.
He clipped a couple of tiny wires and rerouted them.
With one last doubtful look at the lock door, he
tapped a pressure plate within the mechanism.

The inner door slid open and Claire tumbled out,
gasping rawly, ". . . let me *go*, let me *go*, oh, why
didn't you let me go—I can't stand this . . ." She
curled up in a huddled ball in midair, face hidden.

Silver darted to her, wrapped her arms around
her. "Oh, Claire! Don't *do* things like that. Think—
think how Tony would feel, stuck in that hospital
downship, when they told him . . ."

"What does it matter?" demanded Claire, muffled
against Silver's blue T-shirt. "They'll never let me

see him again. I might as well be dead. They'll never let me see Andy . . ."

"Yes," Leo chimed in, "think of Andy. Who will protect him, if you're not around? Not just today, but next week, next year . . ."

Claire unwound, and fairly screamed at him. "They won't even let me see him! They threw me out of the creche . . ."

Leo seized her upper hands. "Who? Who threw you out?"

"Mr. Van Atta . . ."

"Right, I might have known. Claire, listen to me. The proper response to Bruce isn't suicide, it's murder."

"Really?" said Silver, her interest sparking. Even Claire was drawn out of her tight wad of misery enough to meet Leo's eyes directly for the first time.

"Well . . . perhaps not literally. But you can't let the bastard grind you down. Look, we're all smart here, right? You kids are smart—I've been known to knock down a problem or two, in my time—we've got to be able to think our way out of this mess, if we try. You're not alone, Claire. We'll help. I'll help."

"But you're a company man—a downsider—why should you . . . ?"

"GalacTech's not God, Claire. You shouldn't have to sacrifice your firstborn to it. GalacTech—any company—is just a way, one way, for people to organize themselves to do a job that's too big for one person to do alone. It's not God, it's not even a being, for pity's sake. It doesn't have a free will to answer for. It's just a collection of people, working. Bruce is only Bruce, there's got to be some way to get around him."

"You mean go over his head?" asked Silver thoughtfully. "Maybe to that vice president who was here last week?"

Leo paused. "Well . . . maybe not to Apmad. But I've been thinking—for three days, I've been thinking of nothing else but how to blow up this whole rotten set-up. But you've got to hang on, for me to have time to work—Claire, can you hang on? Can you?" His hands tightened on hers urgently.

She shook her head doubtfully. "It hurts so much . . ."

"You have to. Look, listen. There's nothing I can do here at Rodeo, it's in this peculiar legal bubble. If it were a regular planetary government, I swear I'd go into debt to my eyebrows and buy each and every one of you a ticket out of here, but then, if it were a regular planet, I wouldn't need to. Anyway GalacTech has a monopoly on Jump ship seats here, you travel on a company ship or not at all. So we have to wait, and bide our time.

"But in a little time—just a few months—the first quaddies will leave Rodeo on the first real work assignments. Working in and passing through real planetary jurisdictions. Governments too big and powerful even for GalacTech to mess with. I'm sure— pretty sure, if I pick the right venue—not Apmad's planet, of course, but say, Earth—Earth's by far the best bet, I'm a citizen there—I can bring a class-action suit declaring you legal persons. I'll probably lose my job, and the costs will eat me, but it can be done. Not exactly the life's work I had in mind . . . but eventually, you can be cracked loose from GalacTech."

"So long a time," sighed Claire.

"No, no, delay is our friend. The little ones grow older every day. By the time the legal case goes through, you'll all be ready. Go as a group—hire out—find work—even GalacTech wouldn't be so bad as an employer, if you were citizens and regular employees, with all the legal protections. Maybe even the Spacer's Union would take you in, though that might constrain—well, I'm not sure. If they don't perceive you as a threat . . . anyway, something can be worked out. But you've got to hang on! Promise me?"

Silver breathed again when Claire nodded slowly. She drew Claire away to the first aid kit on the wall, to apply antisepts and plastic bandages to her torn fingernails, and wipe the blood from her bruised face. "There. There. Better . . ."

Leo meanwhile restored the airlock control to its original working order, then drifted over to them. "All right now?" He turned his face to Silver. "Is she going to be all right?"

Silver could not help glowering. "As all right as any of us . . . it's not fair!" she burst out. "This is my home, but it's beginning to feel like an overpressurized oxy bottle. Everybody's upset, all the quaddies, about Tony and Claire. There hasn't been anything like this since Jamie was killed in that awful pusher accident. But this—this was *on purpose*. If they'd do that to Tony, who was so good, what about—about me? Any of us? What's going to happen next?"

"I don't know." Leo shook his head grimly. "But I'm pretty sure the idyll is over. This is only the beginning."

"But what will we do? What can we do?"

"Well—don't panic. And don't despair. Especially don't despair—"

The airseal doors at the end of the module slid open, and the downsider hydroponics supervisor's voice lilted in. "Girls? We got the seed delivery on the shuttle after all—is that grow-tube ready yet?"

Leo twitched, but turned back one last time before hastening away, to grasp a hand of each quaddie with determined pressure. "It's just an old saying, but I know it's true from personal experience. Chance favors the prepared mind. So stay strong—I'll get back to you . . ." he escaped past the hydroponics supervisor with an elaborately casual yawn, as if he'd merely stopped in to kibbitz a moment upon the work in progress.

Silver's stomach churned as she watched Claire fearfully. Claire sniffled, and turned hurriedly away to busy herself with the grow tube, hiding her face from their supervisor. Silver shivered with relief. All right for now.

The churning in Silver's stomach was slowly replaced by something hot and unfamiliar, filling it, crowding out the fear. *How dare they do this to her—to me—to us? They have no right, no right, no right. . . .*

Rage made her head pound, but it was better than the knotting fear. There was almost an exultation in it. The expression Silver bent her head to conceal from the supervisor was a small, fierce frown.

The nutrition assistant, a quaddie girl of perhaps thirteen, handed Leo's lunch tray to him through the serving window without her usual bright smile. When Leo smiled and said "Thank you," the responding upward twitch of her mouth was mechanical, and fell away instantly. Leo wondered in what scrambled form the story of Claire's and Tony's downside disaster of the previous week had reached her ears. Not that the correct facts weren't distressing enough. The whole Habitat seemed plunged into an atmosphere of wary dismay.

Leo felt a flash of horrible weariness of the quaddies and their everlasting troubles. He shied away from a collection of his students eating their lunches near

the serving window, though they waved to him with
assorted hands, and instead floated down the module
until he saw a vacant space to velcro his tray next to
somebody with legs. By the time Leo realized the
legged person was the supply shuttle captain, Durrance, it was too late to retreat.

But Durrance's greeting grunt was without animosity. Evidently he did not, unlike some others
Leo could name, hold the engineer obscurely responsible for his student Tony's spectacular fiasco.
Leo hooked his feet into the straps to free his hands
to attack his meal, returned the grunt, and sucked
hot coffee from his squeeze bulb. There wasn't enough
coffee in the universe to dissolve his dilemmas.

Durrance, it appeared, was even in the mood for
polite conversation. "You going to be taking your
downside leave soon?"

"Soon . . ." In about a week, Leo realized with a
start. Time was getting away from him, like everything else around here. "What's Rodeo like?"

"Dull." Durrance spooned some sort of vegetable
pudding into his mouth.

"Ah." Leo glanced around. "Is Ti with you?"

Durrance snorted. "Not likely. He's downside, on
ice. He's appealing." A twisted grimace and raised
eyebrows pointed up the double meaning. "Not, you
understand, from my point of view. I got a reprimand on my record because of that damn tadpole. If
it had been his first screw-up, he might have been
able to duck getting fired, but now I don't think he
has a chance. Your Van Atta wants his pelt riveted to
the airlock doors."

"He's not *my* Van Atta," Leo denied strenuously.
"If he was, I'd trade him for a dog—"

"—and shoot the dog," finished Durrance. A grin
twitched his mouth. "Van Atta. That's all right. If the

rumor I heard is true, he may not have so long to strut either."

"Ah?" Leo's ears pricked hopefully.

"I was talking yesterday to the Jump pilot from the weekly personnel ship from Orient IV—he'd just finished his month's gravity leave there—listen up to *this* one. He swears the Betan embassy there is demonstrating an artificial gravity device."

"What! How—?"

"Piping it in from wormhole space for all I know. You bet Beta Colony is sitting on the math of it, till they make their initial killing in the marketplace and recoup their R&D costs. It's apparently been kept under wraps by their military for a couple of years already, till they got their head start, damn 'em. GalacTech and everybody else will be on the scramble to catch up. Every other R&D project in the company is going to have to kiss their budget good-bye for a couple of years, you watch."

"My God." Leo glanced up the length of the cafeteria module, crowded with quaddies. *My God . . .*

Durrance scratched his chin reflectively. "If it's true, do you have any idea what it's going to do to the space transport industry? The Jump pilot claims the Betans got the damned thing there in two months—from Beta Colony!—boosting at fifteen gees and insulating the crew from the acceleration using it. There'll be no limit to acceleration now but fuel costs. It probably won't affect bulk cargos much for that very reason, but the passenger trade'll be revolutionized. The speed news travels, which'll affect the rate of exchange between planetary currencies— military transport, where they don't care what they spend on fuel—and you can bet *that'll* affect inter-planetary politics—it's a whole new game all around."

Durrance finished scraping the last globs of food

out of the pockets of his lunch tray. "Damn the colonials. Good old conservative Earth-based Galac-Tech left in the lurch again. You know, I'm really tempted to emigrate out to the farther end of the wormhole nexus sometimes. The wife's got family on Earth, though, so I don't suppose we ever will . . ."

Leo hung stunned in his straps as Durrance droned on. After a moment he swallowed the bite of squash still in his mouth, there being no more practical way to dispose of it. "Do you realize," he choked, "what this will do to the quaddies?"

Durrance blinked. "Not much, surely. There's still going to be plenty of jobs to do in free fall."

"It will destroy their edge in profitability versus ordinary workers, that's what. It was the downside medical leaves that were boosting the personnel costs. Eliminate them, and there's nothing to choose between—can this thing provide artificial gravity on a space station?"

"If they could mount it on a ship, they can put it on a station," opined Durrance. "It's not some kind of perpetual motion, though," he cautioned. "It sucks power like crazy, the Jump pilot said. That'll cost something."

"Not as much—and surely they'll find more design efficiencies as they go along—oh, God."

This chance wasn't going to favor the quaddies. This chance favored no one. Damn, damn, damn the timing! Ten years from now, even one year from now, it could have been their salvation. Here, now, might it be—a death sentence? Leo flipped his feet out of the straps and coiled to launch himself toward the module doors.

"You just leaving this tray here?" asked Durrance. "Can I have your dessert . . . ?"

Leo waved a hand in impatient assent as he sprang away.

*   *   *

One look at Bruce Van Atta's glum and hostile face, as Leo swung into his Habitat office, confirmed Durrance's story. "Have you heard this artificial gravity rumor?" Leo demanded anyway, one last lurch of hope—let Van Atta deny it, name it fraud. . . .

Van Atta glared at him in profound irritation. "How the hell did you find out about it?"

"It's none of your business where I found out about it. Is it true?"

"Oh, yes it is my business. I want to keep this under wraps for as long as possible."

It was true, then. Leo's heart shrank. "Why? How long have you known about it?"

Van Atta's hand flipped the edges of a pile of plastic flimsies, computer printouts and communiques, magnetized to his desk. "Three days."

"It's official, then."

"Oh, quite official." Van Atta's mouth twisted in disgust. "I got the word from GalacTech district headquarters on Orient IV. Apmad apparently met the news on her way home, and made one of her famous field decisions."

He rattled the flimsies again, and frowned. "There's no way around it. Do you know what came in yesterday on the heels of this thing? Kline Station has cancelled its construction contract with GalacTech, the first one we were going to send the quaddies out on. Paid the penalty without a murmur. Kline Station's out toward Beta Colony, they must have found out about this weeks ago—months. They've switched to a Betan contractor who, we may presume, is undercutting us. The Cay Project is cooked. Nothing left to do but wrap it up and get the hell out of here, the sooner the better. Damn! So now I'm associated with a loser project. I'll come out reeking with odor of loss."

"Wrap, wrap how? What do you mean, wrap?"

"That bitch Apmad's most favored scenario. I'll bet she was purring when she cut these orders—the quaddies gave her nervous palpitations, y'know. They're to be sterilized and stashed downside. Any pregnancies in progress to be aborted—shit, and we just started fifteen of 'em! What a fiasco. A year of my career down the tubes."

"My God, Bruce, you're not going to carry out those orders, are you?"

"Oh no? Just watch me." Van Atta stared at him, chewing his lip. Leo could feel himself tensing, pale with his suppressed fury. Van Atta sniffed. "What d'you want, Leo? Apmad could have ordered them exterminated. They're getting off lightly. It could have been worse."

"And if it had been—if she had ordered the quaddies killed—would you have carried it out?" inquired Leo, deceptively calm.

"She didn't. C'mon, Leo. I'm not inhuman. Sure, I'm sorry for the little suckers. I was doing my damndest to make 'em profitable. But there's no way I can fight this. All I can do is make the wrap as quick and clean and painless as possible, and cut the losses as much as I can. Maybe *somebody* in the company hierarchy will appreciate it."

"Painless to whom?"

"To everybody." Van Atta grew more intent, and leaned toward Leo with a scowl. "That means I don't need a lot of panic and wild rumors floating around, you hear? I want business as usual right up to the last minute. You and all the other instructors will go on teaching your classes just as if the quaddies really were going out on a work project, until the downside facility is ready and we can start shuttling 'em. Maybe take the little ones first—the salvageable parts of the

Habitat are supposed to be moved around the orbit to the Transfer Station, we might cut some costs by using quaddies for that last job."

"To imprison them downside—"

"Oh, come off the dramatics. They're being placed in a perfectly ordinary drilling workers' dormitory, only abandoned six months ago when the field ran dry." Van Atta brightened slightly in self-congratulation. "I found it myself, looking over the possible sites to place 'em. It'll cost next to nothing to refurbish it, compared to building new."

Leo could just picture it. He shuddered. "And what happens in fourteen years, when and if Orient IV expropriates Rodeo?"

Van Atta ruffled his hair with both hands in exasperation. "How the hell should I know? At that point, it becomes Orient IV's problem. There's only so much one human being can do, Leo."

Leo smiled slowly, in grim numbness. "I'm not sure . . . what one human being can do. I've never pushed myself to the limit. I thought I had, but I realize now I hadn't. My self-tests were always carefully non-destructive."

This test was a higher order of magnitude altogether. This Tester, perhaps, scorned the merely humanly possible. Leo tried to remember how long it had been since he'd prayed, or even believed. Never, he decided, like this. He'd never *needed* like this before. . . .

Van Atta frowned at him suspiciously. "You're weird, Leo." He straightened his spine, as if seeking a posture of command. "Just in case you missed my message, let me repeat it loud and clear. You are to mention this artificial gravity business to no one, that means especially no quaddies. Likewise, keep their downside destination secret. I'll let Yei figure out how to make them swallow it without kicking, it's time she earned her overinflated salary. No rumors, no panics, no goddamn workers' riots—and if there are, I'll know just whose hide to nail to the wall. Got it?"

Leo's smile was canine, concealing—everything. "Got it." He withdrew without turning his back, or speaking another word.

Dr. Yei was not usually easy to track down, it being her habit to circulate often among the quaddies, observing behavior, taking notes, making suggestions. But this time Leo found her at once, in her office, with plastic flimsies stuck to every available surface and her desk console lit like a Christmas tree. Did they have Christmas at the Cay Habitat? Leo wondered. Somehow, he thought not.

"Did you hear—"

Her glum slouch answered his question, even as his white face and rapid breathing finished asking it.

"Yes, I've heard," she said wearily, glancing up at him. "Bruce just dumped the whole Habitat's personnel evacuation logistics on my desk to organize. He, he tells me, being an engineer, will be doing facility dismantling and equipment salvage flow charts. Just as soon as I get the bodies out of his way. Excuse me, the damned bodies."

Leo shook his head helplessly. "Are you going to do it?"

She shrugged, her lips compressed. "How can I not do it? Quit in high dudgeon? It wouldn't change a thing. This affair would not be rendered one iota less brutal for my walking out, and it could get a lot worse."

"I don't see how," Leo ground out.

"You don't?" she frowned. "No, I don't suppose

you do. You never appreciated what a dangerous legal edge the quaddies are balanced on here. But I did. One wrong move and—oh, damn it all. I knew Apmad needed careful handling. Everything got away from me. Although I suppose this artificial gravity thing would have killed the project whoever was in charge, we are very, very lucky that she didn't order the quaddies exterminated. You have to understand, she had something like four or five pregnancies terminated for genetic defects, back on her home world when she was a young woman. It was the law. She eventually gave up, got divorced, took an off-planet job with GalacTech—came up through the ranks. She has a deep emotional vested interest in her prejudices against genetic tampering, and I knew it. And blew it . . . She still could order the quaddies killed—do you understand that? Any report of trouble, unrest, magnified by her genetic paranoias, and . . ." she squeezed her eyes shut, massaged her forehead with her fingertips.

"She could order it—who says you've got to carry it out? You said you cared about the quaddies. We've got to *do* something!" said Leo.

"What?" Yei's hands clenched, spread wide. "What, what, what? One or two—even if I could adopt one or two, take them away with me—smuggle them out somehow, who knows?—what then? To live on a planet with me, socially isolated as cripples, freaks, mutants—and sooner or later they would grow to adulthood, and then what? And what about the others? A *thousand*, Leo!"

"And if Apmad did order them exterminated, what excuse would you find then for doing nothing?"

"Oh, go *away*," she groaned. "You have no appreciation for the complexities of the situation, none. What do you think one person can do? I used to have a life of my own, once, before this job swallowed it. I've given six years—which is five and three-quarters more than *you* have—I've given all I can. I'm burned out. When I get away from this hole, I never want to hear of quaddies again. They're not my children. *I* haven't had *time* to have children."

She rubbed her eyes angrily, and sniffed, inhaling—tears?—or just bile. Leo didn't know. Leo didn't care.

"They're not anybody's children," Leo growled. "That's the trouble. They're some kind of . . . genetic orphans or something."

"If you're not going to say anything useful, please go *away*," she repeated. A wave of her hand encompassed the mass of flimsies. "I have work to do."

Leo had not struck a female since he was five years old. He removed himself, shaking.

He drifted slowly through the corridors, back toward his own quarters, cooling. And whatever had he hoped to get from Yei anyway? Relief from responsibility? Was he to dump his conscience on her desk, a la Bruce, and say, "Take care of it . . ."

And yet, and yet, and yet . . . there was a solution in here somewhere. He could feel it, a palpable dim shape, like a tightness in the gut, a mounting, screaming frustration. The problem that refused to fall into the right pieces, the elusive solution—he'd solved engineering problems that presented themselves at first as such solid, unscalable walls. He did not know where the leaps beyond logic that ultimately topped them came from, except that it was not a conscious process, however elegantly he might diagram it post facto. He could not solve it and he could not leave it alone, but picked uselessly at it, counterproductive like picking a scab, in a rising compulsive frenzy. The wheels spun, imparting no motion.

"It's in here," he whispered, touching his head. "I can feel it. I just . . . can't . . . *see* it . . ."

They had to get out of Rodeo local space somehow, that much was certain. All the quaddies. There was no future here. It was the damn peculiar legal set-up. What was he to do—hijack a Jump ship? But the personnel Jump ships carried no more than three hundred passengers. He could, just barely, picture himself holding a—a what? what weapon? he had no gun, his pocket knife featured mainly screwdrivers—right, hold a screwdriver to the pilot's head and cry, "Jump us to Orient IV!"—where he would promptly be arrested and jailed for the next twenty years for piracy, leaving the quaddies to do . . . what? In any case, he could not possibly hijack three ships at the same time, and that was the minimum number needed.

Leo shook his head. "Chance favors," he muttered, "chance favors, chance favors . . ."

Orient IV would not want the quaddies. Nobody was going to want the quaddies. What, indeed, could their future be even if freed from GalacTech? Gypsy orphans, alternately ignored, exploited, or abused, in their dependency on the narrow environment of humanity's chain of space facilities. Talk about technology traps. He pictured Silver—he had little doubt just what sort of exploitation would be her lot, with that elegant face and body of hers. No place for her out there . . .

No! Leo denied silently. The universe was so damned *big*. There had to be a place. A place of their own, far, far from the trappings and traps of human so-called civilization. The histories of previous utopian social experiments in isolation were not encouraging, but the quaddies were exceptional in every way.

Between one breath, and the next, the vision took him. It came not as a chain of reason, more words words words, but as a blinding image, all complete in its first moment, inherent, holistic, gestalt, inspired. Every hour of his life from now on would be but the linear exploration of its fullness.

A stellar system with an M or G or K star, gentle, steady, pouring out power for the catching. Circling it, a Jovian gas giant with a methane- and water-ice ring, for water, oxygen, nitrogen, hydrogen. Most important of all, an asteroid belt.

And some equally important absences; no Earth-like planet orbiting there also to attract competition; not on a wormhole Jump route of strategic importance to any potential conquistadors. Humanity had passed over hundreds of such systems, in its obsessive quest for new Earths. The charts were glutted with them.

A quaddie culture spreading out along the belt from their initial base, a society of the quaddies, by the quaddies, for the quaddies. Burrowing into the rocks for protection against radiation, and to seal in their precious air, expanding, leapfrogging from rock to rock, to drill and build new homes. Minerals all around, more than they could ever use. Whole hydroponics farms for Silver. A new world to build. A space world to make Morita Station look like a toy.

"Why," Leo's eyes widened with delight, "it's an *engineering* problem after all!"

He hung limply in air, entranced; fortunately, the corridor was empty of passers-by at the moment, or they would surely have thought him mad or drugged.

The solution had been lying around him in pieces all this time, invisible until *he'd* changed. He grinned dementedly, possessed. He yielded himself up to it without reservation. All. All. There was no limit to what one man might do, if he gave all, and held back nothing.

Didn't hold back, didn't look back—for there would be no going back. Literally, medically, that was the heart of it. Men adapted to free fall, it was the going *back* that crippled them.

"*I* am a quaddie," Leo whispered in wonder. He regarded his hands, clenched and spread his fingers. "Just a quaddie with legs." He wasn't going back.

As for that initial base—he was floating in it right now. It merely required relocating. His cascading thought clicked over the connections too rapidly to analyze. He didn't need to hijack a spaceship; he was in one. All it needed was a bit of power.

And the power lay ready-to-hand in Rodeo orbit, being gratuitously wasted even at this moment to shove mere bulk petrochemicals out of orbit. What might a petrochemical pod-bundle mass, compared to a chunk of the Cay Habitat? Leo didn't know, but he knew he could find out. The numbers would be on his side, anyway, whatever their precise magnitudes.

The cargo thrusters could handle the Habitat, if it were properly reconfigured, and anything the thrusters could handle, one of the monster cargo Super-jumpers could manage too. It was all there, all—for the taking.

For the taking . . .

Chapter 8

It took an hour of stalking before Leo was able to catch Silver alone, in a monitor blind spot in a corridor leading from the free fall gym.

"Is there someplace we can talk in private?" he asked her. "I mean really private."

Her wary glance around confirmed that she understood him perfectly. Still she hesitated. "Is it important?"

"Vital. Life or death for every quaddie. That important."

"Well . . . wait a minute or two, then follow me."

He trailed her slowly and casually through the Habitat, a flash of shimmering hair and blue jersey at this or that cross-branching. Then, down one corridor, he suddenly lost her. "Silver . . . ?"

"Sh!" she hissed at his ear. A wall panel hinged silently inward, and one of her strong lower hands reached out to yank him in like a fish on a line.

It was dark and narrow behind the wall for only a moment, then airseal doors parted with a whisper to reveal an odd-shaped chamber perhaps three meters across. They slipped within.

"What's this?" asked Leo, stunned.

"The Clubhouse. Anyway, we call it that. We built

139

it in this little blind pocket. You wouldn't notice it from Outside unless you were looking for it at just the right angle. Tony and Pramod did the outside walls. Siggy ran the ductwork in, others did the wiring . . . the airseals we built from spare parts."

"Weren't they missed?"

Her smile was not in the least innocent. "Quaddies do the computer records entry, too. The parts just sort of ceased to exist in inventory. A bunch of us worked together on it—we just finished it about two months ago. I was sure Dr. Yei and Mr. Van Atta would find out about it, when they were questioning me," her smile faded to a frown in memory, "but they never asked just the right question. Now the only vids we have left are the ones that happened to be stored in here, and Darla doesn't have the vid system up yet."

Leo followed her glance to a dead holovid set, obviously in process of repair, fixed to the wall. There were other comforts: lighting, handy straps, a wall cabinet that proved to be stuffed with little bags of dried snacks abstracted from Nutrition, raisins, peanuts and the like. Leo orbited the room slowly, nervously examining the workmanship. It was tight. "Was this place your idea?"

"Sort of. I couldn't have done it alone, though. You understand, it's strictly against our rules for me to bring you in here," Silver added somewhat truculently. "So this better be good, Leo."

"Silver," said Leo, "it's your uniquely pragmatic approach to rules that makes you the most valuable quaddie in the Habitat right now. I need you—your daring, and all the other qualities that Dr. Yei would doubtless call anti-social. I've got a job to do that I can't do alone either." He took a deep breath. "How would you quaddies like to have your own asteroid belt?"

"What?" her eyes widened.

"Brucie-baby is trying to keep it under wraps, but the Cay Project has just been scheduled for termination—and I mean that in the most sinister sense of the word."

He detailed the anti-gravity rumor to her, all that he had yet heard, and Van Atta's secret plans for the quaddies' disposal. With rising passion, he described his vision of escape. He didn't have to explain anything twice.

"How much time do we have left?" she asked whitely, when he had finished.

"Not much. A few weeks at most. I have only six days until I'm forced downside by my gravity leave. I've got to figure out some way to duck that, I'm afraid I might not be able to get back here. We— you quaddies—have to choose *now*. And I can't do it for you. I can only help with some of the parts. If you cannot rescue yourselves, you will be lost, guaranteed."

She blew out her breath in a silent whistle, looking troubled indeed. "I thought—watching Tony and Claire—they were doing it the wrong way. Tony talked about finding work, but do you know, he didn't think to take a work-suit with him? I didn't want to make the same mistakes. We aren't made to travel alone, Leo. Maybe it's something that was built into us."

"But can you bring in the others?" Leo asked anxiously. "In secret? Let me tell you, the quickest end-scenario for this little revolution I can imagine would be for some quaddie to panic and tell, trying to be good. This is a real conspiracy, all rules off. I sacrifice my job, risk legal prosecution, but you risk much more."

"There are some who, um, should be told last," said Silver thoughtfully. "But I can bring the important ones in. We've got some ways of keeping things private from the downsiders."

Leo glanced around the chamber, subtly reassured.

"Leo . . ." her blue eyes targeted him searchingly, "*how* are we going to get rid of the downsiders?"

"Well, we won't be able to shuttle them down to Rodeo, that's for certain. From the moment this thing comes out in the open, you can count on the Habitat being cut off from re-supply." *Besieged*, was the word Leo's mind suggested, and carefully edited. "The way I thought of was to collect them all in one module, throw in some emergency oxygen, cut it off the Habitat, and use one of the cargo pushers to move it around orbit to the Transfer Station. At that point they become GalacTech's problem, not ours. Hopefully it'd ball things up a bit at the Transfer Station, too, and give us a little more time."

"How do you plan to—to make them all get into the module?"

Leo stirred uncomfortably. "Well, that's the point of no return, Silver. There are weapons all around us here, we just don't recognize them because we call them 'tools'. A laser-solderer with the safety removed is as good as a gun. There's a couple of dozen of them in the workshops. Point it at the downsiders and say 'Move!'—and they'll move."

"What if they don't?"

"Then you must fire it. Or choose not to, and be taken downside to a slow and sterile death. And you choose for everybody, when you make that choice, not just for yourself."

Silver was shaking her head. "I don't think that's

such a good idea, Leo. What if somebody panicked and actually fired one? The downsider would be horribly burned!"

"Well . . . yes, that's the idea."

Her face crumpled with dismay. "If I have to shoot Mama Nilla, I'd rather go downside and die!"

Mama Nilla was one of the quaddies' most popular creche mothers, Leo recalled vaguely, a big elderly woman—he'd barely met her, as his classes didn't involve the younger quaddies. "I was thinking more in terms of shooting Bruce," Leo confessed.

"I'm not sure I could even do that to Mr. Van Atta," said Silver slowly. "Have you ever seen a bad burn, Leo?"

"Yes."

"So have I."

A brief silence fell.

"We can't bluff our teachers," said Silver finally. "All Mama Nilla would have to do is say 'Give that over now, Siggy!' in that *voice* of hers, and he would. It's not—it's not a *smart* scenario, Leo."

Leo's hands clenched in exasperation. "But we must get the downsiders off the Habitat, or nothing else can be done! If we can't, they'll just re-take it, and you'll be worse off than when you started."

"All right, all right! We've got to get rid of them. But that's not the way." She paused, looking at him more doubtfully. "Could you shoot Mama Nilla? Do you really think—say—Pramod, could shoot you?"

Leo sighed. "Probably not. Not in cold blood. Even soldiers in battle have to be brought to a special state of mental excitement to shoot total strangers."

Silver looked relieved. "All right, so what else would have to be done? Saying we could take over the Habitat."

"Re-configuring the Habitat can be done with tools and supplies already aboard, though everything will have to be carefully rationed. The Habitat will have to be defended from any attempt by GalacTech to recapture it while this is going on. The high-energy-density beam welders could be quite effective discouragements to shuttles attempting to board us—if anybody could be induced to fire one," he added with a dry edge. "Company inventory doesn't include armored attack ships, fortunately. A real military force would make short work of this little revolution, you realize." His imagination supplied the details, and his stomach bunched queasily. "Our only real defense is to get gone before GalaTech can produce one. That will require a Jump pilot."

He studied her anew. "That's where you come in, Silver. I know a pilot who's going to be passing through the Transfer Station very soon who might be, um, easier to kidnap than most. Especially if *you* came along to lend your personal persuasion."

"Ti."

"Ti," he confirmed.

She looked dubious. "Maybe."

Leo fought down another and stronger wave of queasiness. Ti and Silver had a relationship predating his arrival. He wasn't really playing pimp. Logic dictated this. He realized suddenly that what he really wanted was to remove her as far from the Jump pilot as possible. *And do what? Keep her for yourself? Get serious. You're too old for her.* Ti was what—twenty-five, maybe? Perhaps violently jealous, for all Leo knew. She must prefer him. Leo tried virtuously to feel old. It wasn't hard; most of the quaddies made him feel about eighty anyway. He wrenched his mind back to business.

"The third thing that has to be done first," Leo

thought over the wording of that, and concluded
unhappily that it was all too accurate, "is nail down a
cargo Jumper. If we wait until we boost the Habitat
all the way out to the wormhole, GalacTech will have
time to figure out how to defend them. Such as
Jumping them all to the Orient IV side and thumb-
ing their noses at us until we are forced to surrender.
That means," he contemplated the next logical step
with some dismay, "we've got to send a force out to
the wormhole to hijack one. And I can't go with it,
and be here to defend and reconfigure the Habitat
both . . . it'll have to be a force of quaddies. I don't
know . . ." Leo ran down, "maybe this isn't such a
great idea after all."

"Send Ti with them," suggested Silver reasonably.
"He knows more about the cargo Jumpers than any
of us."

"Mm," said Leo, drawn back to optimism. If he
was going to pay attention to the odds against this
escapade succeeding, he might as well give up now
and avoid the rush. Screw the odds. He would believe in Ti. If necessary, he would believe in elves,
angels, and the tooth fairy.

"That makes, um, suborning Ti step one in the
flow chart," Leo reasoned aloud. "From the moment
he's missed we're out in the open, racing the clock.
That means all the advance planning for moving the
Habitat had better be done—in advance. And—oh.
Oh, my." Leo's eyes lit.

"What?"

"I just had a *brilliant* idea to buy us a head
start . . ."

Leo timed his entrance carefully, waiting until Van
Atta had been holed up in his Habitat office nearly
the first two hours of the shift. The project chief

would be starting to think about his coffee break by
now, and reaching the degree of frustration that
always attended the first attack on a new problem, in
this case dismantling the Habitat. Leo could picture
the entangled stage of his planning precisely; he'd
gone through it himself about eight hours previously,
locked in his own quarters, brainstorming on his
computer console after a brief pause to render his
programs inaccessible to snoops. The leftover military security clearance from the Argus cruiser project
worked wonders. Leo was quite sure no one in the
Habitat, not Van Atta and certainly not Yei, possessed a higher key.

Van Atta frowned at him from the clutter of printouts, his computer vid scintillating multi-screened
and colorful with assorted Habitat schematics. "Now
what, Leo? I'm busy. Those who can, do; those who
can't, teach."

And those who can't teach, Leo finished silently,
go into administration. He maintained his usual bland
smile, not letting the edged thought show by any
careless gleam or reflection. "I've been thinking,
Bruce," Leo purred. "I'd like to volunteer for the job
of dismantling the Habitat."

"You would?" Van Atta's brows rose in astonishment, lowered in suspicion. "Why?"

Van Atta would hardly believe it was out of the
goodness of his heart. Leo was prepared. "Because
as much as I hate to admit it, you were right again.
I've been thinking about what I'm going to bring
away from this assignment. Counting travel time,
I've shot four months of my life—more, before this is
done—and I've got nothing to show for it but some
black marks on my record."

"You did it to yourself." Van Atta, reminded, rubbed

his chin upon which the bruise was fading to a green shadow, and glowered.

"I lost my perspective for a little while, it's true," Leo admitted. "I've got it back."

"A bit late," sneered Van Atta.

"But I could do a good job," argued Leo, wondering how one could achieve the effect of a hangdog shuffle in free fall. Better not overdo it. "I really need a commendation, something to counterweight those reprimands. I've had some ideas that could result in an unusually high salvage ratio, cut the losses. It would take all the scut work off your hands and leave you free to administer."

"Hm," said Van Atta, clearly enticed by a vision of his office returning to its former pristine serenity. He studied Leo, his eyes slitting. "Very well—take it. There's my notes, they're all yours. Ah, just send the plans and reports through my office, I'll send 'em on. That's my real job, after all, administration."

"Certainly." Leo swept up the clutter. *Yes, send 'em through you—so you can replace my name with your own.* Leo could almost see the wheels turn, in the smug light of Van Atta's eyes. Let Leo do the work, and Van Atta siphon off the credit. *Oh, you'll get the credit for how this project ends all right, Brucie-baby—all of it.*

"I'll need a few other things," Leo requested humbly. "I want all the quaddie pusher crews that can be spared from their regular duties, in addition to my own classes. These useless children are going to learn to work like they never worked before. Supplies, equipment, authorization to sign out pushers and fuel—gotta start some on-site surveying—and I need to be able to commandeer other quaddie spot labor as needed. All right?"

"Oh, are you volunteering for the hands-on part

too?" A fleeting vindictive greediness crossed Van Atta's face, followed by doubt. "What about keeping this under wraps till the last minute?"

"I can present the pre-planning as a theoretical class exercise, at first. Buy a week or two. They'll have to be told eventually, you know."

"Not too soon. I'll hold you responsible for keeping the chimps under control, you copy?"

"I copy. Do I have my authorization? Oh—and I'll need to get an extension against my downside gravity leave."

"HQ docsn't like that. Liability."

"It's either me or you, Bruce."

"True . . ." Van Atta waved a hand, already sinking back gratefully from harried to languid mode. "All right. You got it."

A blank check. Leo tamped a wolfish grin into a fawning smile. "You'll remember this, won't you Bruce—later?"

Van Atta's lips too drew back. "I guarantee, Leo, I'll remember *everything*."

Leo bowed himself out, mumbling gratitude.

Silver poked her head through the door to the creche mother's private sleep cubicle. "Mama Nilla?"

"Sh!" Mama Nilla held her finger to her lips and nodded toward Andy, asleep in a sack on the wall with his face peeping out. She whispered, "For heaven's sake don't wake the baby. He's been so fussy—I think the formula disagrees with him. I wish Dr. Minchenko were back. Here, I'll come out in the corridor."

The airseal doors swished shut behind her. In preparation for sleep Mama Nilla had exchanged her pink working coveralls for a set of flowered pajamas cinched in around her ample waist. Silver suppressed an urge to clamp herself to that soft torso as she had in desperate moments when she was little—she was much too grown-up to be cuddled anymore, she told herself sternly. "How's Andy doing?" she asked instead, with a nod toward the closed doors.

"Hm. All right," said Mama Nilla. "Though I hope I can get this formula problem straightened out soon. And . . . well . . . I'm not sure you could call it depression, exactly, but his attention span seems shorter, and he fusses—don't tell Claire that, though, poor dear, she has enough troubles. Tell her he's all right."

Silver nodded. "I understand."

Mama Nilla frowned introspectively. "I wrote up a protest, but my supervisor blocked it. Ill-timed, she said. Ha. More like Mr. Van Atta has her spooked. I could just . . . ahem. Anyway, I've been turning in overtime chits like crazy, and I requested an extra assistant be assigned to my creche unit. Maybe when they realize that this foolishness is costing them money, they'll give in. You can tell Claire that, I think."

"Yes," said Silver, "she could use a little hope."

Mama Nilla sighed. "I feel so badly about this. Whatever possessed those children to try and run off, anyway? I could just shake Tony. And as for that stupid Security guard, I could just . . . well . . ." she shook her head.

"Have you heard any more about Tony, that I could pass on to Claire?"

"Ah. Yes." Mama Nilla glanced up and down the corridor, to assure herself of their privacy. "Dr. Minchenko called me last night on the personal channel. He assures me Tony's out of danger now, they got that infection under control. But he's still very weak. Dr. Minchenko means to bring him back up to the Habitat when he finishes his own gravity leave. He thinks Tony will complete his recovery faster up here. So that's a bit of good news you can pass on to Claire."

Silver calculated, her lower fingers tapping out the days unobtrusively below Mama Nilla's line of sight, and breathed relief. That was one massive problem she could report to Leo as solved. Tony would be back before their revolt broke into the open. His safe return might even become the signal for it. A smile lit her face. "Thanks, Mama Nilla. That is good news."

Revolution 101 for the Bewildered, Leo decided grimly, should be his course title. Or worse; *050: Remedial Revolution* . . .

The shell of floating quaddies hovering expectantly around him in the lecture module had been officially augmented by both the off-duty pusher crews, and loaded with all the off-shift older quaddies Silver had been able to contact covertly. Sixty or seventy altogether. The lecture module was jammed, causing Leo to jump ahead mentally and think about oxygen consumption and regeneration plans for the reconfigured Habitat. There was tension, as well as carbon dioxide, in the air. Rumors were afloat already, Leo realized, God knew in what mutant forms. It was time to replace rumors with facts.

Silver waved all clear from the airseal doors, turning all four thumbs up and grinning at Leo, as one last T-shirted quaddie scurried within. The airseal doors slid shut, eclipsing her as she turned to take up guard duty in the corridor.

Leo took up his lecture station in the center. The center, the hub of the wheel, where stresses are most concentrated. After some initial whispering, poking, and prodding, they hushed for him, to an almost frightening attentiveness. He could hear them breathing. *We would need you even if you weren't an engineer, Leo*, Silver had remarked. *We're all too used to taking orders from people with legs.*

Are you saying you need a front man? he'd asked, amused.

Is that what it's called? Her gaze upon him had been coolly pragmatic.

He was getting too old, his brain was short-circuiting to some distant rock beat, slipping back to the noisier rhythms of his adolescence. *Let me be your front man, baby. Call me Leo. Call me anytime, day or night. Let me help.* He eyed the closed airseal doors. Was the man waving the baton at the front of the parade pulling it after him—or being pushed along ahead of it? He had a queasy premonition he was going to learn the answer. He woofed a breath, and returned his attention to the lecture chamber.

"As some of you have already heard," Leo began, words like pebbles in the pool of silence, "a new gravity technology has arrived from the outlying planets. It's apparently based on a variation of the Necklin field tensor equations, the same mathematics that underlie the technology we use to punch through those wrinkles in space-time we call wormholes. I haven't been able to get hold of the tech specs yet myself, but it seems it's already been developed to the marketable stage. The theoretical possibility was not, strictly speaking, new, but I for one never expected to see its practical capture in my lifetime. Evidently, neither did the people who created you quaddies.

"There is a kind of strange symmetry to it. The spurt forward in genetic bioengineering that made you possible was based on the perfection of a new technology, the uterine replicator, from Beta Colony. Now, barely a generation later, the new technology that renders you obsolete has arrived from the same source. Because that's what you have become, before you even got on-line—technologically obsolete. At least from GalacTech's point of view." Leo drew breath, watching for their reactions.

"Now, when a machine becomes obsolete, we scrap it. When a man's training becomes obsolete, we send him back to school. But your obsolescence was bred in your bones. It's either a cruel mistake, or, or, *or*," he paused for emphasis, "the greatest opportunity you will ever have to become a free people.

"Don't . . . don't take notes," Leo choked, as heads bent automatically over their scribble boards, illuminating his key words with their light pens as the autotranscription marched across their displays. "This isn't a class. This is real life." He had to stop a moment to regain his equilibrium. He was positive some child at the back was still highlighting "no notes—real life", in reflexive virtue.

Pramod, floating near, looked up, his dark eyes agitated. "Leo? There was a rumor going around that the company was going to take us all downside and shoot us. Like Tony."

Leo smiled sourly. "That's actually the least likely scenario. You are to be taken downside, yes, to a sort of prison camp. But this is how guilt-free genocide is handled. One administrator passes you on to the next, and him to the next, and him to the next. You become a routine expense on the inventory. Expenses rise, as they always do. In response, your downsider support employees are gradually withdrawn, as the company names you 'self-sufficient.' Life support equipment deteriorates with age. Breakdowns happen more and more often, maintenance and resupply become more and more erratic.

"Then one night—without anybody ever giving an order or pulling a trigger—some critical breakdown occurs. You send a call for help. Nobody knows who you are. Nobody knows what to do. Those who placed you there are all long gone. No hero takes initiative, initiative having been drained by administrative bitching and black hints. The investigating inspector, after counting the bodies, discovers with relief that you were merely inventory. The books are quietly closed on the Cay Project. Finis. Wrap. It might take twenty years, maybe only five or ten. You are simply forgotten to death."

Pramod's hand touched his throat, as if he already felt the rasp of Rodeo's toxic atmosphere. "I think I'd rather be shot," he muttered.

"*Or,*" Leo raised his voice, "you can take your lives into your own hands. Come with me and put all your risks up front. The big gamble for the big payoff. Let me tell you," he gulped for courage, mustered megalomania—for surely only a maniac could drive this through to success—"let me tell you about the Promised Land. . . ."

Chapter 9

Leo stretched for a look out the viewport of the cargo pusher at the rapidly-enlarging Transfer Station. Damn. The weekly passenger ship from Orient IV was already docked at the hub of the wheel. Newly arrived, it was doubtless still in the off-loading phase, but nothing seemed more likely to Leo than for a pilot—or ex-pilot—like Ti to invite himself aboard early, to kibbitz.

The Jump ship was blocked from view as they spiraled around the station to their own assigned shuttle hatch. The quaddie piloting the pusher, a dark-haired, copper-skinned girl named Zara in the purple T-shirt and shorts of the pusher crews, brought her ship smartly into alignment and clicked it delicately into the clamps on the landing spoke. Leo was encouraged toward belief in her top rating among the pusher pilots after all, despite his qualms about her age, barely fifteen.

The mild acceleration vector of the Station's spin at this radius tugged at Leo, and his padded chair swung in its gimbals to the newly-defined "upright" position. Zara grinned over her shoulder at Leo, clearly exhilarated by the sensation. Silver, in the quaddie-formfit acceleration couch beside Zara, looked more dubious.

Zara completed the formal litany of cross-checks with Transfer Station traffic control, and shut down her systems. Leo sighed illogical relief that traffic control hadn't questioned the vaguely-worded purpose of their filed flight plan—"Pick up material for the Cay Habitat." There was no reason they should have. Leo wasn't even close to exceeding his powers of authorization. Yet.

"Watch, Silver," said Zara, and let a light-pen fall from her fingers. It fell slowly to the padded strip on the wall-now-floor, and bounced in a graceful arc. Zara's lower hand scooped it back out of the air.

Leo waited resignedly while Silver tried it once too, then said, "Come on. We've got to catch Ti."

"Right." Silver pulled herself up by her upper hands on her headrest, swung her lowers free, and hesitated. Leo shook out his pair of grey sweat pants he'd brought for the purpose, and gingerly helped her pull them over her lower arms and up to her waist. She waved her hands and the ends of the pant legs flopped and flapped over them. She grimaced at the unaccustomed constraint of the bundled cloth upon her dexterity.

"All right, Silver," said Leo, "now the shoes you borrowed from that girl running Hydroponics."

"I gave them to Zara to stow."

"Oh," said Zara. One of her upper hands flew to her lips.

"What?"

"I left them in the docking bay."

"Zara!"

"Sorry . . ."

Silver blew out her breath against Leo's neck. "Maybe your shoes, Leo," she suggested.

"I don't know . . ." Leo kicked out of his shoes, and Zara helped Silver slip her lower hands into them.

"How do they look?" said Silver anxiously.

Zara wrinkled her nose. "They look kinda big."

Leo sidled around to catch their reflection in the darkened port. They looked absurd. Leo regarded his feet as though he'd never seen them before. Did they look that absurd on him? His socks seemed suddenly like enormous white worms. Feet were insane appendages. "Forget the shoes. Give 'em back. Just let the pant legs cover your hands."

"What if someone asks what happened to my feet?" Silver worried aloud.

"Amputated," suggested Leo, "due to a terrible case of frostbite suffered on your vacation to the Antarctic Continent."

"Isn't that on Earth? What if they start asking questions about Earth?"

"Then I'll—I'll quash them for rudeness. But most people are pretty inhibited about asking questions like that. We can still use the original story about your wheelchair being Lost Luggage, and we're on our way to try and get it back. They'll believe that. Come on." Leo backed up to her. "All aboard." Her upper arms twined around his neck, and her lowers clamped around his waist with slightly paranoid pressure, as she cautiously entrusted her newfound weight to him. Her breath was warm, and tickled his ear.

They ducked through the flex tube and into the Transfer Station proper. Leo headed for the elevator stack that ran up—or down—the length of the spoke to the rim where the transient rest cubicles were to be found.

Leo waited for an empty elevator. But it stopped again, and others boarded. Leo had a brief spasm of terror that Silver might try to strike up a friendly conversation—he should have told her explicitly not to talk to strangers—but she maintained a shy reserve. Transfer Station personnel gave them a few uncomfortable covert stares, but Leo gazed coldly at the wall and no one attempted to broach the silence.

Leo staggered, exiting the elevator at the outer rim where the gee forces were maximized. Little though he wished to admit it, three months of null-gee deconditioning had had its inevitable effect. But at half-gee, Silver's weight didn't even bring their combined total up to his Earthside norm, Leo told himself sternly. He shuffled off as rapidly as possible away from the populated foyer.

Leo knocked on the numbered cubicle door. It slid open. A male voice, "Yeah, what?" They had cornered the Jump pilot. Leo plastered an inviting smile on his face, and they entered.

Ti was propped up on the bed, dressed in dark trousers, T-shirt, and socks, idly scanning a hand-viewer. He glanced up in mild irritation at Leo, unfamiliar to him, then his eyes widened as he saw Silver. Leo dumped Silver as unceremoniously as a cat on the foot of the bed, and plopped into the cubicle's sole chair to catch his breath. "Ti Gulik. Gotta talk to you."

Ti had recoiled to the head of the bed, knees drawn up, hand viewer rolled aside and forgotten. "Silver! What the hell are you doing here? Who's this guy?" He jerked a thumb at Leo.

"Tony's welding teacher. Leo Graf," answered Silver smearily. Experimentally, she rolled over and pushed her torso upright with her upper hands. "This feels weird." She raised her upper hands, balancing, Leo thought, for all the world like a seal on a tripod formed by her lower arms. "Huh." She returned her upper hands to the bed, to lend support, achieving a dog-like posture, fine hair flattened, all her grace stolen by gravity. No doubt about it, quaddies belonged in null-gee.

"We need your help, Lieutenant Gulik," Leo began as soon as he could. "Desperately."

"Who's *we*?" asked Ti suspiciously.

"The quaddies."

"Hah," said Ti darkly. "Well, the first thing I would like to point out is that I am not Lieutenant Gulik any more. I'm plain Ti Gulik, unemployed, and quite possibly unemployable. Thanks to the quaddies. Or at any rate, one quaddie." He frowned at Silver.

"I told them it wasn't your fault," said Silver. "They wouldn't listen to me."

"You might at least have covered for me," said Ti petulantly. "You owed me that much."

He might as well have hit her, from the look on her face. "Back off, Gulik," Leo growled. "Silver was drugged and tortured to extract that confession. Seems to me any owing in here goes in the other direction."

Ti flushed. Leo bit back his annoyance. They couldn't afford to piss the Jump pilot off, they needed him too much. Besides, this wasn't the conversation Leo had rehearsed. Ti should be leaping through hoops for those morning-glory eyes of Silver's, the psychology of reward and all that—surely he must respond to a plea for her good. If the young lout didn't appreciate her, he didn't deserve to have her— Leo forced his thoughts back to the matter at hand.

"Have you heard about this new artificial gravity field technology yet?" Leo began again.

"Something," admitted Ti warily.

"Well, it's killed the Cay Project. GalacTech's dropping out of the quaddie business."

"Huh. Yeah, well, that makes sense."

Leo waited a beat for the next logical question,

which didn't come. Ti wasn't an idiot, he was therefore being deliberately dense. Leo pushed on relentlessly. "They plan to ship the quaddies downside to Rodeo, to an abandoned workers' barracks—" he repeated the forgotten-to-death scenario he had described to Pramod a week earlier, and looked up to gauge its effect.

The pilot's face was closed and neutral. "Well, I'm very sorry for them," Ti did not look at Silver, "but I totally fail to see what I'm supposed to do about it. I'm leaving Rodeo in six hours, never to return— which is just fine with me, by the way. This place is a pit."

"And Silver and the quaddies are being dropped into that pit and the lid clamped over them. And the only crime they've committed is to become technologically obsolete. Doesn't that mean anything to you?" cried Leo heatedly.

Ti bolted upright indignantly. "You want to talk about technological obsolescence? I'll show you technological obsolescence. This!" His hand touched the implant plugs at midforehead and temples, the cannula at the nape of his neck. "This! I trained for two years and waited in line for a year for the surgery to implant my Jump set. It's a tensor bit-code version, because that's the Jump system GalacTech uses, and they underwrote part of the cost of it. Trans-Stellar Transport and a few independents also use it. Everybody else in the universe is gearing up to Necklin color-drive. You know what my chances of being hired by TST are, after being fired by GalacTech? Zilch. Zero. Nada. If I want a Jump pilot's job, I need this surgically removed and a new implant. Without a job, I can't afford an implant. Without an implant, I can't get a job. Screw you, Ti Gulik!" He sat, panting.

Leo leaned forward. "I'll give you a pilot's berth, Gulik," he said clearly. "On the biggest Jump ship ever to fly." Rapidly, before the pilot could interrupt, he detailed his vision of the Habitat converted to colony ship. "It's all here. All we need is a pilot. A pilot who can plug into the GalacTech drive system. All we need—is you."

Ti looked perfectly appalled. "You're not just talking grand lunacy—you're talking grand larceny! Do you realize what the cash value of the total configuration would *be*? They wouldn't let you out of jail till the next millennium!"

"I'm not going to jail. I'm going to the stars with the quaddies."

"*Your* cell will be padded."

"This isn't crime. This is—war, or something. Crime is turning your back and walking away."

"Not by any legal code I know of."

"All right then; sin."

"Oh, brother." Ti rolled his eyes. "Now it comes out. You're on a mission from God, right? Let me off at the next stop, please."

God's not here. Somebody's got to fill in. Leo backed off hastily from that line of thought. Padded cells, indeed. "I thought you were in love with Silver. How can you abandon her to a slow death?"

"Ti's not in love with me," interrupted Silver in surprise. "Whatever gave you that idea, Leo?"

Ti gave her an unsettled look. "No, of course not," he agreed faintly. "You, ah—you always knew, right? We just had a mutually beneficial little arrangement, is all."

"That's right," confirmed Silver. "I got books and vids, Ti got relief from physiological stress. Downsider males need sex to stay healthy, you know, they can't cope with stress. It makes them disruptive. Wild genes, I suppose."

"Where did *that* line of bullshit come from—?" Leo began, and broke off. "Never mind." He could guess. He closed his eyes, pressed them with his fingertips, and groped for his lost argument. "Right. So to you, Silver is just . . . disposable. Like a tissue. Sneeze in her and toss her away."

Ti looked stung. "Give it up, Graf. I'm no worse than anyone else."

"But I'm giving you the chance to be better, don't you see—"

"Leo," Silver interrupted again. She was now sprawled on her stomach on the bed, her chin propped awkwardly on one upper hand. "After we get to our asteroid belt—wherever it turns out to be—what are we going to do with the Superjumper?"

"The Superjumper?"

"We'll be detaching the Habitat and opening it out again, surely—building on to it—the Jumper unit would just be sitting there in parking orbit. Can't we give it to Ti?"

"What?" said Leo and Ti together.

"As payment. He jumps us to our destination, he gets to keep the Jump ship. Then he can go off and be a pilot-owner, set up his own transport business, whatever he likes."

"In a stolen ship?" yipped Ti.

"If we're far enough away that GalacTech can't catch up with us, we're far enough away that GalacTech can't catch up with you," said Silver logically. "Then you'll have a ship that fits your neural implant, and nobody will be able to fire you again, because you'll be working for yourself."

Leo bit his tongue. He'd brought Silver along expressly to help persuade Ti—so what if it wasn't the blandishment he'd envisioned? From the blitzed look on the pilot's face, they'd gotten through to his launch-button at last. Leo lidded his eyes and smiled encouragement at her.

"Besides," she went on, her eyelashes fluttering in return, "if we do succeed in Jumping out of here, Habitat and all, Mr. Van Atta's going to be left looking an awful fool." She let her head flop back on the bed and smiled sideways at Ti.

"Oh," said Ti in a tone of enlightenment. "Ah . . ."

"Are your bags all packed?" asked Leo helpfully.

"Over there," Ti nodded to a pile of luggage in the corner. "But . . . but . . . dammit, if this thing crashes, they'll crucify me!"

"Ah," said Leo. "Here, see . . ." he opened his red coveralls at the neck and drew out the laser-solderer concealed in an inner pocket. "I jimmied the safety on this thing; it'll fire an extremely intense beam for quite a distance now, until the atmosphere dissipates it—farther than the distance across this room, certainly." He waved it negligently; Ti ducked, eyes widening. "If we end up under arrest, you can truthfully testify that you were kidnapped at gunpoint by a crazed engineer and his mad mutant assistant and made to cooperate under duress. You may be a hero one way—or another."

The mad mutant assistant smiled blindingly at Ti, her eyes like stars.

"You, ah—wouldn't really fire that thing, would you?" choked Ti cautiously.

"Of course not," Leo said jovially, baring his teeth. He put the solderer away.

"Ah." Ti's mouth twitched briefly in response. But his eye returned often thereafter to the lump in Leo's coveralls.

When they made it back to the shuttle hatch where the pusher was docked, Zara was gone.

"Oh, God," moaned Leo. Had she wandered off? Gotten lost? Been forcibly removed? A frantic inventory found no message left on the comm, no note pinned anywhere.

"Pilot, she's a pilot," Leo reasoned aloud. "Is there anything she could have needed to do? We've plenty of fuel—communicating with traffic control is done right from here . . ." He realized, with a cold chill, that he hadn't actually forbidden her to leave the pusher. It had been so self-evident that she was to stay out of sight, and on guard. Self-evident to himself, Leo realized. Who could say what was self-evident to a quaddie?

"I could fly this thing, if necessary," said Ti in a most unpressing tone, looking over the control deck. "It's all manual."

"That's not the point," said Leo. "We can't leave without her. The quaddies aren't supposed to be over here at all. If she gets picked up by the Station authorities and they start asking questions—always assuming she hasn't been picked up by something worse . . ."

"What worse?"

"I don't *know* what worse, that's the trouble."

Silver meanwhile had rolled off the acceleration couch to the deck strip. After a moment of thoughtful experimentation, she achieved a four-handed forward shuffle, and marched off past Leo's knees, pant legs trailing.

"Where are you going?"

"After Zara."

"Silver, stay with the ship. We don't need two of you lost, for God's sake," Leo ordered sternly. "Ti and I can move much faster, we'll find her."

"I don't think so," murmured Silver distantly. She reached the flex tube, stared up and down the corridor which curved away to right and left, ringing the spoke. "You see, I don't think she's gone far."

"If she got on the elevator, she could be practically anywhere on the Station by now," said Ti.

Silver reared up on her tripoded lower arms, raised her uppers over her head, and narrowed her eyes for a look around the elevator foyer to her left. "The controls would be hard for a quaddie to reach. Besides, she'd know she was more likely to run into downsiders there. I think she went this way." She raised her chin and shuffled determinedly off to her right on all fours. After a moment she picked up speed by changing her gait to a series of gazelle-like bounds in the low-gee of the spoke. Leo and Ti, of necessity, bounded after her. Leo felt absurdly like a man chasing a runaway pet. It was an optical illusion of the quadrimanual locomotion—quaddies even *looked* more human in free fall.

A strange rumbling noise approached around the curve of the corridor. Silver hooted, and skidded to one side against the outer wall.

"Oh, sorry!" cried Zara, whizzing past torso-down and chin up on a low roller-pallet, all four hands going like paddle wheels to propel her along the deck. Braking proved more difficult than acceleration, and Zara fetched up beside Silver with a crash.

Leo, horrified, bounded over to them, but Zara was already disentangling herself and sitting up cheerfully. Even the roller pallet was undamaged.

"Look Silver," Zara said, flipping the pallet over, "wheels! I wonder how they're beating the friction, inside those casings? Feel, they're not hot at all."

"Zara," cried Leo, "why did you leave the ship?"

"I wanted to see what a downsider toilet chamber looked like," said Zara, "but there wasn't one on this level. All I found was a closet full of cleaning supplies, and this," she patted the roller pallet. "Can I take the wheels apart and see what's inside?"

"No!" roared Leo.

She looked quite put-out. "But I want to know!"

"Bring it along," Silver suggested, "and take it apart later." Her eyes flicked up and down the corridor; Leo was slightly consoled that at least one quaddie shared his sense of urgency.

"Yes, later," Leo agreed, for the sake of expediency. "Let's *go* now." He tucked the roller pallet firmly under his arm, to thwart further experimentation. The quaddies, he reflected, didn't seem to have a very clear idea of private property. Probably came from a lifetime spent in a communal space habitat, with its tight ecology. Planets were communal in the same way, really, except that their enormous size put so much slack in their systems, it was disguised.

Habits of thought, indeed. Here he was worried over the theft of a roller pallet, while planning the greatest space heist in human history. Ti almost bolted when he found out what the rest of the assignment they had planned for him was to be. Leo, prudently, didn't fill in these details until the pusher was safely launched from the Transfer Station and halfway back to the Habitat.

"You want *me* to hijack the Superjumper!" yelped Ti.

"No, no," Leo soothed him. "You're only going along as an advisor. The quaddies will take the ship."

"But *my* ass will depend on whether or not *they* can—"

"Then I suggest you advise well."

"Ye gods."

"The trouble with you, Ti," lectured Leo kindly, "is that you lack teaching experience. If you had, you'd have faith that the most unlikely people can learn the most amazing things. After all, you weren't born knowing how to pilot a Jump—yet lives depended on your doing it right the first time, and every time thereafter. Now you'll know how your instructors felt, that's all."

"How do instructors feel?"

Leo lowered his voice and grinned. "Terrified. Absolutely terrified."

A second pusher, packed with fuel and supplies for its long-range excursion, was waiting in the slot next to theirs as they docked at the Habitat. Leo resisted a strong urge to take Ti aside and fill his ear with advice and suggestions for his mission. Alas, their experience in criminal theft was all too comparable—zero equalled zero no matter how unequal the years each was multiplied by.

They floated through the hatch into the docking module to find several anxious quaddies waiting for them.

"I've modified more solderers, Leo," Pramod began unnecessarily—three of his four hands clutched the improvised arsenal to his torso. "One each for five people."

Claire, hovering at his shoulder, eyed the weapons with dread fascination.

"Good. Give them to Silver, she'll have charge of them until the pusher gets to the wormhole," said Leo.

They made their way down the hand grips to the next hatch. Zara swung within to begin her pre-flight checks.

Ti craned his neck after her nervously. "Are we leaving right now?"

"Time is critical," said Leo. "We don't have more than four hours till you're missed at the Transfer Station."

"Shouldn't there be a—a briefing, or something?"

Ti too, Leo appreciated, was having trouble committing himself to falling free. Well, *jumped* or *was pushed*, after the initial impulse it would make no practical difference.

"You'll have almost twenty-four hours, boosting at one gee to midpoint and then flipping and braking the rest of the way, to work out your plan of attack. Silver will be depending on your knowledge of the Superjumpers. We've already discussed various methods of achieving surprise. She'll fill you in."

"Oh, is Silver going?"

"Silver," Leo enlightened him gently, "is in command."

Ti's face flickered through an array of expressions, settled on dismay. "Screw this. There's still time for me to go back and catch my ship—"

"And *that*," Leo overrode him, "is precisely why Silver is in charge. Your capture of a cargo Jumper is the signal for a quaddie uprising here on the Habitat. And that uprising is their death warrant. When GalacTech discovers it cannot control the quaddies, it will almost certainly be frightened into an attempt to violently exterminate them. Escape must be assured before we tip our hand. The ship you must catch is out that way." Leo pointed. "I can depend on Silver to remember that. You," Leo smiled thinly, "are no worse than anyone else."

Ti subsided at that, although not happily.

Silver, Zara, Siggy, a particularly husky quaddie from the pusher crews named Jon, and Ti. Five, crammed into a ship meant for a crew of two and not designed for overnight use in any case. Leo sighed. The Superjumpers carried a pilot and an engineer. Five-to-two wasn't altogether bad odds, but Leo wished he could have loaded them even more overwhelmingly in the quaddies' favor.

They filed through the flex tube into the pusher. Silver, at the end, paused to embrace Pramod and Claire, who had lingered to see them off.

"We're going to get Andy back," Silver murmured to Claire. "You'll see."

Claire nodded, and hugged her hard.

Silver turned last to Leo, who was gazing doubtfully at the flex tube through which the crew he'd drafted had gone.

"I thought the quaddies were going to be the weak link in this hijacking operation," jittered Leo, "now I'm not so sure. Don't let Ti cave on you, eh, Silver? Don't let him bring you down. You have to succeed."

"I know. I'll try. Leo . . . why did you think Ti was in love with me?"

"I don't know. . . . You were intimate—the power of suggestion, maybe. All those romances."

"Ti doesn't read romances, he reads *Ninja of the Twin Stars*."

"Weren't you in love with him? At first, anyway?"

She frowned. "It was exciting, to be beating the rules with him. But Ti is . . . well, is Ti. Love like in the books—I always knew it wasn't really real. When I got to looking around, at our own downsiders, nobody was like that. I guess I was stupid, to like those stories so much."

"I suppose they're not realistic—I haven't read them either, to tell you the truth. But it's not stupid to want something more, Silver."

"More than what?"

More than to be worked over by a lot of self-centered legged louts, that's what. We're not all like that . . . are we? Why, after all, was he being moved *now* to lay a load of his own on her, when she needed all her concentration for the task ahead? Leo shook his head. "Anyway, don't let Ti get confused between his Ninja-whatsit and what you're trying to do, either."

"I don't think even Ti could mistake a company Jumpship crew for the Black League of Eridani," said Silver.

Leo could have wished for more certainty in her tone. "Well . . ." he cleared his throat, inexplicably blocked, "take care. Don't get hurt."

"You be careful too." She did not hug him, as she had Pramod and Claire.

"Right."

And don't ever believe, his mind cried after her as she vanished into the flex tube, *that nobody could love you, Silver . . .* But it was too late to call the words aloud. The airseal doors shut with a sigh like regret.

Chapter 10

The freight shuttle docking bay was chilly, and
Claire rubbed all her hands together to warm them.
Only her hands seemed cold, her heart beat hot with
anticipation and dread. She looked sideways at Leo,
floating as seeming-stolid as ever by the airseal doors
with her.

"Thanks, for pulling me off my work shift for this,"
Claire said. "Are you sure you won't get into trouble,
when Mr. Van Atta finds out?"

"Who's to tell him?" said Leo. "Besides, I think
Bruce is losing interest in tormenting you. Everything's so obviously futile. All the better for us.
Anyway, I want to talk to Tony too, and I figure I'll
have a better chance of getting his undivided attention after you've got the reunion-bit over with." He
smiled reassuringly.

"I wonder what condition he'll be in?"

"You may be sure he's much better, or Dr.
Minchenko wouldn't be subjecting him to the stresses
of travel, even to keep him close under his eye."

A thump, and the whir and grind of machinery,
told Claire that the shuttle had arrived in its clamps.
Her hands reached out, drew in self-consciously.
The quaddie manning the control booth waved to

two others in the bay, and they locked the flex tubes into position and sealed them. The personnel tube opened first, and the shuttle's engineer stuck his head through to double check everything, then whipped back out of sight. Claire's heart lurched in her chest, and her throat constricted dryly.

Dr. Minchenko emerged at last and hovered a moment, one hand anchored to a grip by the hatch. A leathery-faced, vigorous man, his hair was as white as the GalacTech medical service coveralls he wore. He had been a big man, now shrunken to his frame like a withered apricot, but, like a withered apricot, still sound. Claire had the impression he only needed to be re-hydrated and he'd pop back to like-new condition.

Dr. Minchenko shoved off from the hatchway and crossed the bay toward them, landing accurately by the grips around the airseal doors. "Why, hullo, Claire," he said in a surprised voice. "And, ah—Graf," he added less cordially. "You're the one. Let me tell you, I don't appreciate being leaned on to authorize violation of sound medical protocol. You are to spend double time in the gym for the duration of your extension, you hear?"

"Yes, Dr. Minchenko, thank you," said Leo promptly, who was not, as far as Claire knew, spending any time in the gym at all these days. "Where's Tony? Can we help you get him to the infirmary?"

"Ah," he looked more closely at Claire. "I see. Tony's not with me, dear, he's still in hospital downside."

Claire stifled a gasp. "Oh, no—is he worse?"

"Not at all. I had fully intended to bring him with me. In my opinion, he needs free fall to complete his recovery. The problem is, um, administrative, not medical. And I'm on my way right now to resolve it."

"Did Bruce order him kept downside?" asked Leo.

"That's right." He frowned at Leo. "And I'm not pleased to have my medical responsibilities interfered with, either. He'd better have a mighty convincing explanation. Daryl Cay wouldn't have permitted a screw-up like this."

"You, um . . . haven't heard the new orders yet, then?" said Leo carefully, with a warning glance at Claire—*hush*. . . .

"What new orders? I'm on my way to see the little schmuck—that is, the man right now. Get to the bottom of this . . ." He turned to Claire, switching firmly to a kinder tone. "It's all right, we'll get it straightened out. All Tony's internal bleeding is stopped, and there's no further sign of infection. You quaddies are tough. You hold your health much better in gravity than we downsiders do in free fall. Well, we explicitly designed you not to undergo deconditioning. I could only wish the confirming experiment hadn't happened under such distressing conditions. Of course," he sighed, "youth has something to do with it. . . . Speaking of youth, how's little Andy? Sleeping better for you now?"

Claire almost burst into tears. "I don't know," she squeaked, and swallowed hard.

"What?"

"They won't let me see him."

"*What?*"

Leo, studying his fingernails distantly, put in, "Andy was removed from Claire's care. On charges of childendangering, or some such thing. Didn't Bruce tell you that either?"

Dr. Minchenko's face was darkening to a brick-red hue. "Removed? From a breast-feeding mother—obscene!" His eyes swept back over Claire.

"They gave me some medicine to dry me up," explained Claire.

"Well, that's something . . ." his mollification was slight. "Who did?"

"Dr. Curry."

"He didn't report it to me."

"You were on leave."

" 'On leave' doesn't mean 'incommunicado.' You, Graf! Spit it out. What the hell's going on around here? Has that pocket-martinet lost his mind?"

"You really haven't heard. Well, you'd better ask Bruce. I'm under direct orders not to discuss it."

Minchenko gave Leo a stabbing glare. "I shall." He pushed off and entered the corridor through the airseal doors, muttering under his breath.

Claire and Leo were left looking at each other in dismay.

"How are we going to get Tony back now?" cried Claire. "It's less than twenty-four hours till Silver's signal!"

"I don't know—but don't cave now! Remember Andy. He's going to need you."

"I'm not going to cave," Claire denied. She took a steadying gulp of air. "Not ever again. What can we do?"

"Well, I'll see what strings I can pull, to try and have Tony brought up—bullshit Bruce, tell him I have to have Tony to supervise his welding gang or something—I'm not sure. Maybe Minchenko and I together can work something, though I don't want to risk rousing Minchenko's suspicions. If I can't," Leo inhaled carefully, "we'll have to work out something else."

"Don't lie to me, Leo," said Claire dangerously.

"Don't leap to conclusions. Yes, I know—you know—the possibility exists that we won't be able to retrieve him, all right, I said it, right out loud. But please note any, er, alternative scenarios depend on Ti to pilot a shuttle for us, and must wait until we re-connect with the hijack crew. At which point we will have captured a Jumpship, and I will begin to believe that anything is possible." His brows quirked, stressed. "And if it's possible, we'll try it. Promise."

There was a growing coldness in her. She firmed her lips against their tremble. "You can't risk everybody for the sake of just one. That's not right."

"Well . . . there are a thousand things that can go wrong between now and some—point of no return for Tony. It may turn out to be quite academic. I do know, dividing our energies among a thousand what-ifs instead of concentrating them for the one sure next-step is a kind of self-sabotage. It's not what we do next week, it's what we do next, that counts most. What must you do next?"

Claire swallowed, and tried to pull her wits back together. "Go back to work . . . pretend like nothing's going on. Continue the secret inventory of all possible seed stocks. Uh, finish the plan of how we're going to hook up the grow-lights to keep the plants going while the Habitat is moved away from the sun. And as soon as the Habitat is ours, start the new cuttings and bring the reserve tubes on-line, to start building up extra food stocks against emergencies. And, uh, arrange cryo-storage of samples of every genetic variety we have on board, to re-stock in case of disaster—"

"That's enough!" Leo smiled encouragement. "The next step only! And you *know* you can do that."

She nodded.

"We need you, Claire," he added. "All of us, not just Andy. Food production is one of the fundamentals of our survival. We'll need every pair, er, every set of expert hands. And you'll have to start training youngsters, passing on that how-to knowledge that the library, no matter how technically complete, can't duplicate."

"I am not going to cave," Claire reiterated through her teeth, answering the undercurrent, not the surface, of his speech.

"You scared me, that time in the airlock," he apologized, embarrassed.

"I scared myself," she admitted.

"You had a right to be angry. Just remember, your true target isn't in here—" he touched her collarbone, above her heart, fleetingly. "It's out there."

So, he had recognized it was rage, rage blocked and turned inward, and not despair, that had brought her to the airlock that day. In a way, it was a relief to put the right name to her emotion. In a way it was not.

"Leo . . . that scares me too."

He smiled quizzically. "Welcome to the human club."

"The next step," she muttered. "Right. The next *reach*." She gave Leo a wave, and swung into the corridor.

Leo turned back to the freight bay with a sigh. The next-step speech was all very well, except when people and changing conditions kept switching your route around in front of you while your foot was in the air. His gaze lingered a moment on the quaddie docking crew, who had connected the flex tube to the shuttle's large freight hatch and were unloading the cargo into the bay with their power handlers. The cargo consisted of man-high grey cylinders, that Leo did not at first recognize.

But the cargo wasn't supposed to be unrecognizable.

The cargo was supposed to be a massive stock of spare cargo-pusher fuel rods. "For dismantling the Habitat," Leo had sung dulcetly to Van Atta, when jamming the requisition through. "So I won't have to stop and reorder. So what if we have leftovers, they can go to the Transfer Station with the pushers when they're relocated. Credit them to the salvage."

Disturbed, Leo drifted over to the cargo workers. "What's this, kids?"

"Oh, Mr. Graf, hello. Well, I'm not quite sure," said the quaddie boy in the canary-yellow T-shirt and shorts of Airsystems Maintenance, of which Docks & Locks was a subdivision. "I don't think I've ever seen it before. It's massive, anyway." He paused to unhook a report panel from his power-handler and gave it to Leo. "There's the freight manifest."

"It was supposed to be cargo-pusher fuel rods. . . ." The cylinders *were* about the right size. They surely couldn't have redesigned them. Leo tapped the manifest keypad—item, a string of code numbers, quantity, astronomical.

"They gurgle," the yellow-shirted quaddie added helpfully.

"Gurgle?" Leo looked at the code number on the report panel more closely, glanced at the grey cylinders—they matched. Yet he recognized the code for the pusher rods—or did he? He entered 'Fuel Rods, Orbital Cargo Pusher Type II, cross ref, inventory code.' The report panel blinked and a number popped up. Yes, it was the same—no, by God! G77618PD, versus the G77681PD emblazoned on the cylinders. Quickly he tapped in 'G77681PD.' There was a long pause, not for the report panel but for Leo's brain to register.

"Gasoline?" Leo croaked in disbelief. "*Gasoline?*

Those idiots actually shipped a hundred tons of gasoline to a space station . . . ?"

"What is it?" asked the quaddie.

"Gasoline. It's a hydrocarbon fuel used downside, to power their land rovers. A freebie by-product from the petrochemical cracking. Atmospheric oxygen provides the oxidant. It's a bulky, toxic, volatile, flammable—explosive!—liquid at room temperature. For God's sake don't let any of those barrels get open."

"Yes, *sir*," promised the quaddie, clearly impressed with Leo's list of hazards.

The legged supervisor of the orbital pusher crews arrived at that moment in the bay, trailed by a gang of quaddies from his department.

"Oh, hello, Graf. Look, I think it was a mistake letting you talk me into ordering this load—we're going to have a storage problem—"

"Did you order this?" Leo demanded.

"What?" the supervisor blinked, then took in the scene before him. "What the—where are my fuel rods? They told me they were here."

"I mean did you, personally, place the order. With your own little fingers."

"Yes. You asked me to, remember?"

"Well," Leo took a breath, and handed him the report panel, "you made a typo."

The super glanced at the report panel, and paled. "Oh, God."

"And they did it," Leo gibbered, running his hands through what was left of his hair, "they filled it—I can't believe they filled it. Loaded all this stuff onto the shuttle without once questioning it, sent a hundred tons of gasoline to a space station without *once* noticing that it was utterly absurd. . . ."

"I can believe it," sighed the super. "Oh, God. Oh, well. We'll just have to send it back, and reorder. It'll probably take about a week. It's not like our fuel rod stocks are really low, in spite of the rate you've been using them up for that 'special project' you're so hushy-hush about."

I don't have a week, thought Leo frantically. *I have twenty-four hours, maybe*.

"I don't have a week," Leo found himself raging. "I want them *now*. Put it on a rush order." He lowered his voice, realizing he was becoming conspicuous.

The super was offended enough to overcome his guilt. "There's no need to throw a fit, Graf. It was my mistake and I'll probably have to pay for it, but it's plain stupid to charge my department for a rush shuttle trip on top of this one when we can perfectly well wait. This is going to be bad enough as it is." He waved at the gasoline. "Hey, kids," he added, "stop unloading! This load's a mistake, it's all gotta go back downside."

The shuttle pilot was just exiting the personnel hatch in time to hear this. "What?" He floated over to them, and Leo gave him a brief explanation in very short words of the error.

"Well, you can't send it back this trip," said the shuttle pilot firmly. "I'm not fueled up to take a full load. It'll have to wait." He shoved off, to take his mandatory safety break in the cafeteria.

The quaddie cargo handlers looked quite reproachful, as the direction of their work was reversed for the second time. But they limited their implied criticism to a plaintive, "Are you sure now, sir?"

"Yes," sighed Leo. "But find some place to store this stuff in a detached module, you can't leave it in here."

"Yes, sir."

Leo turned again to the pusher crew supervisor. "I've still got to have those fuel rods."

"Well, you'll just have to wait. I won't do it. Van Atta's going to have enough of my blood for this already."

"You can charge it to my special project. I'll sign for it."

The super raised his eyebrows, slightly consoled. "Well . . . I'll try, all right, I'll try. But what about your blood?"

Already sold, thought Leo. "That's my look-out, isn't it?"

The super shrugged. "I guess." He exited, muttering. One of the pusher crew quaddies, trailing him, gave Leo a significant look; Leo returned a severe shake of his head, emphasized by a throat-cutting gesture with his index finger, indicating, Silence!

He turned and nearly rammed Pramod, waiting patiently at his shoulder. "Don't sneak up on me like that!" he yelped, then got better control of his fraying nerves. "Sorry, you startled me. What is it?"

"We've run into a problem, Leo."

"But of course. Who ever tracks me down to impart good news? Never mind. What is it?"

"Clamps."

"Clamps?"

"There's a lot of clamped connections Outside. We were going over the flow chart for the Habitat disassembly, for, um, tomorrow, you know—"

"I know, don't say it."

"We thought a little practice might speed things up."

"Yes, good . . ."

"Hardly any of the clamps will unclamp. Even with power tools."

"Uh . . ." Leo paused, taken aback, then realized what the problem was. "Metal clamps?"

"Mostly."

"Worse on the sun side?"

"Much worse. We couldn't get any of those to come at all. Some of them are visibly fused. Some idiot must have welded them."

"Welded, yes. But not by some idiot. By the sun."

"Leo, it doesn't get *that* hot—"

"Not directly. What you're seeing is spontaneous vacuum diffusion welding. Metal molecules are evaporating off the surfaces of the pieces in the vacuum. Slowly, to be sure, but it's a measurable phenomenon. On the clamped areas they migrate into their neighboring surfaces and eventually achieve quite a nice bond. A little faster for the hot pieces on the sun side, a little slower for the cold pieces in the shade—but I'll bet some of those clamps have been in place for twenty years."

"Oh. But what do we do about them?"

"They'll have to be cut."

Pramod's lips pursed in worry. "That will slow things down."

"Yeah. And we'll have to have a way set up to re-clamp each connection in the new configuration, too . . . gonna need more clamps, or something that can be made to work as clamps. . . . Go round up all your off-shift work gang. We're going to have to have a little emergency scrounging session."

Leo stopped wondering if he was going to survive the Great Takeover, and started wondering if he was going to survive *until* the Great Takeover. He prayed devoutly that Silver was having an easier time of it than himself.

*   *   *

Silver hoped earnestly that Leo was having an easier time of it than herself.

She hitched herself around in the acceleration couch, increasingly uncomfortable after their first eight hours of flight, and rested her chin on the padding to regard her crew, crammed in the pusher's cabin. The other quaddies were drooped and draped as she was; only Ti seemed comfortable, feet propped up and leaning back in his seat in the steady gee-forces.

"I saw this great holovid," Siggy waved some hands enthusiastically, "that had a boarding battle. The marines used magnetic mines to blow holes like bubble cheese in the side of the mothership and just poured through." He added a weird ululating cry for sound effects. "The aliens were running every which way, stuff flying everywhere as the air blew out—"

"I saw that one," said Ti. "*Nest of Doom*, right?"

"You got it for us," reminded Silver.

"Did you know it had a sequel?" said Ti aside to Siggy. "*The Nest's Revenge*."

"No, really? Do you suppose—"

"First of all," said Silver, "nobody has found any intelligent aliens yet, hostile or not, secondly, we don't have any magnetic mines," *thanks be*, "and thirdly, I don't think Ti wants a lot of unsightly holes blown in the side of his ship."

"Well, no," conceded Ti.

"We will go in through the airlock," said Silver firmly, "which was designed for just that purpose. I think the jumpship crew will be surprised enough when we put them in their escape pod and launch it, without, um, frightening them into doing who-knows-what with a lot of premature whooping. Even if Colonel Wayne in *Nest of Doom* led his troops into battle with his rebel yell over their comm links, I don't think real marines would do that. It would be bound to interfere with their communications." She frowned Siggy into submission.

"We'll just do it Leo's way," Silver went on, "and point the laser-solderers at them. They don't know us, they wouldn't know whether we'd fire or not." How, after all, could strangers know what she didn't know herself? "Speaking of which, how do we know which Superjumper to," she groped for terminology, "cut out of the herd? It ought to be easier to get permission to come aboard if the crew's someone Ti knows well. On the other hand, it might be harder to . . ." she trailed off, disliking the thought. "Especially if they tried to fight back."

"Jon could wrestle them into submission," offered Ti. "That's what he's here for, after all."

Husky Jon gave him a woeful look. "I thought I was here as the pusher back-up pilot. You wrestle them if you want, they're your friends. I'll hold a solderer."

Ti cleared his throat. "Anyway, I'd like to get D771, if it's there. We aren't going to have much choice, though. There's only likely to be a couple of Superjumpers working this side of the wormhole at any one time anyway. Basically, we go for whatever ship that's just jumped over from Orient IV and dumped its empty pod bundles, and hasn't started to load on new ones yet. That'll give us the quickest getaway. There's not that much to plan, we just go *do* it."

"The real trouble will start," said Silver, "when they've figured out what we're really up to and start trying to take the ship back."

A glum silence fell. For the moment, even Siggy had no suggestions.

Leo found Van Atta in the downsiders' gym, tramping determinedly on the treadmill. The treadmill was a medical torture device like a rack in reverse. Spring-loaded straps pulled the walker toward the tread surface, against which his or her feet pushed, for an hour or more a day by prescription, an exercise designed to slow, if not stop, the lower body decon-ditioning and long bone demineralization of free fall dwellers.

By the expression on Van Atta's face he was stamp-ing out the measured treads today with considerable personal animosity. Cultivated irritation was indeed one way to muster the energy to tackle the boring but necessary task. After a moment's thoughtful study Leo decided upon a casual and oblique approach. He slipped out of his coveralls and velcroed them to the wall-strip, retaining his red T-shirt and shorts, and floated over and hooked himself into the belt and straps of the unoccupied machine next to Van Atta's.

"Have they been lubricating these things with glue?" he puffed, grasping the hand holds and straining to start the treads moving against his feet.

Van Atta turned his head and grinned sardonically. "What's the matter, Leo? Did Minchenko the medi-cal mini-dictator order a little physiological revenge on you?"

"Yeah, something like that . . ." he got it started at last, his legs flexing in an even rhythm. He *had* skipped too many sessions lately. "Have you talked to him since he came up?"

"Yeah." Van Atta's legs drove against his machine, and angry whirring spurted from its gears.

"Have you told him what's going to be happening to the Project yet?"

"Unfortunately, I had to. I'd hoped to put him off to the last, with the rest. Minchenko is probably the most arrogant of Cay's Old Guard—he's never made

it a secret that he thought he should have succeeded
Cay as Head of Project, instead of bringing in an
outsider, namely me. If he hadn't been slated for
retirement in a year, I'd damn well have taken steps
to get rid of him before this."

"Did he, ah—voice objections?"

"You mean, did he yowl like a stuck pig? You bet
he did. Carried on like *I* was personally responsible
for inventing the damned artificial gravity. I don't
need this shit." Van Atta's treadmill moaned in coun-
terpoint to his words.

"If he's been with the Project from the beginning,
I guess the quaddies are practically his life's work,"
allowed Leo reasonably.

"Mm." Van Atta marched. "It doesn't give him the
right to go on strike in a snit, though. Even you had
more sense, in the end. If he doesn't show signs of a
more cooperative attitude when he's had a chance to
calm down and think through how useless it is, it
may be easier to extend Curry's rotation and just
send Minchenko back downside."

"Ah." Leo cleared his throat. This didn't exactly
smell like the good opening he'd been hoping for.
But there was so little time. "Did he talk to you
about Tony?"

"Tony!" Van Atta's treadmill buzzed like a hornet
for a moment. "If I never see that little geek again in
my life it will be too soon. He's been nothing but
trouble, trouble and expense."

"I was rather hoping to get some more use out of
him, myself," said Leo carefully. "Even if he's not
medically ready to go back on regular Outside work
shifts, I've got a lot of computer console work and
supervisory tasks I could delegate to him, if he was
here. If we could bring him up."

"Nonsense," snapped Van Atta. "You could much

more easily tap one of your other quaddie work gang leaders—Pramod, say—or pull any quaddie in the place. I don't care who, that's what I gave you the authorization for. We're going to start moving the little freaks *down* in just two weeks. It makes no sense to bring up one Minchenko wouldn't let out of the infirmary till then. And so I told him." He glared at Leo. "I don't want to hear one more word about Tony."

"Ah," said Leo. Damn. Clearly, he should have taken Minchenko aside before he'd muddied the waters with Van Atta. Too late now. It wasn't just the exercise that was making Van Atta red in the face. Leo wondered what all Minchenko had really said—doubtless pretty choice, it would have been a pleasure to hear. Too expensive a pleasure for the quaddies, though. Leo schooled his features to what he hoped would be read through his puffing and blowing as sympathy for Van Atta.

"How's the salvage planning going?" asked Van Atta after a while.

"Almost complete."

"Oh, really?" Van Atta brightened. "Well, that's something, at least."

"You'll be amazed at how totally the Habitat can be recycled," Leo promised with perfect truth. "So will the company brass."

"And fast?"

"Just as soon as we get the go-ahead. I've got it laid out like a war game." He closed his teeth on further double entendres. "You still planning the Grand Announcement to the rest of the staff at 1300 tomorrow?" Leo inquired casually. "In the main lecture module? I really want to be in on that, I have a few visual aids to present when you're done."

"Naw," said Van Atta.

"What?" Leo gulped. He missed a step, and the springs slammed him painfully down on one knee on the treadmill, padded against just such clumsiness. He struggled back to his feet.

"Did you hurt yourself?" said Van Atta. "You look funny. . . ."

"I'll be all right in a minute," He stood, leg muscles straining against the elastic pull, regaining his breath and equilibrium in the face of pain and panic. "I thought—that was how you were going to drop the shoe. Get everybody together, just go over the facts once."

"After Minchenko, I'm tired of arguing about it," said Van Atta. "I've told Yei to do it. She can call them into her office in small groups, and hand out the individual and department evacuation schedules at the same time. Much more efficient."

And so Leo and Silver's beautiful scheme for peacefully detaching the downsiders, hammered out through four secret planning sessions, was blown away on a breath. Wasted was the flattery, the oblique suggestion, that had gone into convincing Van Atta that it was his idea to gather, unusually, the entire Habitat downsider staff at once and make his announcement in a speech persuading them all they were being commended, not condemned. . . .

The shaped charges to cut the lecture module away from the Habitat at the touch of a button were all in place. The emergency breath masks to supply the nearly three hundred bodies with oxygen for the few hours necessary to push the module around the planet to the Transfer Station were carefully hidden within. The two pusher crews were drilled, their pushers fueled and ready.

Fool he had been, to lay plans that depended on

Van Atta following through on anything. . . . Leo felt suddenly sick.

It was going to have to be the second-choice plan, then, the emergency one they'd discussed and discarded as too risky, too potentially uncontrolled in its results. Numbly, he detached his springs and harness and hooked them back in their slots on the treadmill frame.

"That wasn't an hour," said Van Atta.

"I think I did something to my knee," lied Leo.

"I'm not surprised. Think I didn't know you've been skipping exercise sessions? Just don't try to sue GalacTech, 'cause we can prove personal neglect." Van Atta grinned and marched on virtuously.

Leo paused. "By the way, did you know that Rodeo Warehousing just mis-shipped the Habitat a hundred tons of gasoline? And they're charging it to us."

"What?"

As Leo turned away he had the small vindictive satisfaction of hearing Van Atta's treadmill stop and the snap of a too-hastily-detached harness rebounding to slap its wearer. "Ow!" Van Atta cried.

Leo did not look back.

Dr. Curry met Claire as she arrived for her appointment at the infirmary. "Oh, good, you're just on time."

Claire glanced up and down the corridor, and her eyes searched the treatment room into which Dr. Curry shoo'd her. "Where's Dr. Minchenko? I thought he'd be here."

Dr. Curry flushed faintly. "Dr. Minchenko is in his quarters. He won't be coming on duty."

"But I wanted to talk to him. . . ."

Dr. Curry cleared his throat. "Did they tell you what your appointment was for?"

"No . . . I supposed it was for more medication for my breasts."

"Ah, I see."

Claire waited a moment, but he did not expand further. He busied himself, laying out a tray of instruments by their velcro collars and placing them in the sterilizer, not meeting Claire's eyes. "Well, it's quite painless."

Once, she might have asked no questions, docilely submitting—she had undergone thousands of obscure medical tests starting even before she had been freed as an infant from the uterine replicator, the artificial womb that had gestated her in a now-closed section of this very infirmary. Once, she had been another person, before the downside disaster with Tony. For a little time thereafter she had hovered close to being no one at all. Now she felt strangely thrilled, as if she trembled on the edge of a new birth. Her first had been mechanical and painless, perhaps that was why it had failed to take root. . . .

"What—" she began to squeak. Too tiny a voice. She raised it, loud in her own ears. "What *is* this appointment for?"

"Just a small local abdominal procedure," said Dr. Curry airily. "It won't take long. You don't even have to get undressed, just roll up your shirt and push down your shorts a bit. I'll prep you. You have to be immobilized under the sterile-air-flow shield, in case a drop or two of blood gets on the loose."

You're not immobilizing me . . . "What is the procedure?"

"It won't hurt, and will do you no harm at all. Come on over, now." He smiled, and tapped the shield unit, which folded out from the wall.

"What?" repeated Claire, not moving.

"I can't discuss it. It's—classified. Sorry. You'll

have to ask—Mr. Van Atta, or Dr. Yei, or somebody.
Tell you what, I'll send you over to Dr. Yei right
after, and you can talk to her, all right?" He licked
his lips; his smile grew steadily more nervous.

"I wouldn't ask . . ." Claire groped after a phrase
she had heard a downsider use once, "I wouldn't ask
Bruce Van Atta for the time of day."

Dr. Curry looked quite startled. "Oh." And muttered, not quite under his breath, "I wondered why
you were second on the list."

"Who was first on the list?" asked Claire.

"Silver, but that engineering instructor has her on
some kind of assignment. Friend of yours, right?
You'll be able to tell her it doesn't hurt."

"I don't care—I don't give a *damn* if it hurts, I
want to know what it *is*." Her eyes narrowed, as the
connections clicked at last, then widened in outrage.
"The sterilizations," she breathed. "You're starting
the sterilizations!"

"How did you—you weren't supposed—I mean,
whatever makes you think that?" gulped Curry.

She dodged for the doorway. He was closer and
quicker, and sealed it in front of her nose. She
caromed off the closing panel.

"Now, Claire, calm down!" panted Curry, zigzag-
ging after her. "You'll only hurt yourself, totally unnecessarily. I can put you under a general anesthetic,
but it's better for you to use a local, and just lie still.
You do have to lie still. I have to do this, one way or
another—"

"Why do you *have* to do this?" cried Claire. "Did
Dr. Minchenko *have* to do this—or is that why he
isn't here? Who's making you, and how, that you
have to?"

"If Minchenko was here, I *wouldn't* have to,"
snapped Curry, infuriated. "He ducked out, and left

me holding the bag. Now come over here and position yourself under the steri-shield, and let me set up the scanners, or I'll have to get—get quite *firm* with you." He inhaled deeply, psyching himself up.

"Have to," Claire taunted, "have to, have to! It's amazing, some of the things downsiders think they have to do. But they're almost never the same things they think quaddies have to do. Why is that, do you suppose?"

His breath woofed out, and his lips tightened angrily. He plucked a hypodermic off his tray of instruments.

He laid it out in advance, Claire thought. *He's rehearsed this, in his mind—he made his mind up before I ever got here. . . .*

He launched himself over to where she hovered, and grabbed her left upper arm, stabbing the needle towards it in a swift silver arc. She grabbed his right wrist, slowing it to a straining standstill; so they were locked for a moment, muscles trembling, tumbling slowly in the air.

Then she brought up her lower arms to join her uppers. Curry gasped in surprise, and for breath, as she parted his arms wide, overpowering even his young male torso. He kicked, his knees thumping her, but with nothing to push against he couldn't drive them with enough force to really hurt.

She grinned in wild exhilaration, brought his arms in, out again at will. *I'm stronger! I'm stronger! I'm stronger than him and I never even knew it. . . .*

Carefully, she locked her power-gripping lower hands around his wrists, and freed her uppers. Both hands working together easily peeled his clutching fingers from the hypodermic. She held it up, and crooned, "This won't hurt a bit."

"No, no—"

He was wriggling too much for her inexperience to try for a swift venous injection, so she went for a deltoid muscle instead, and went on holding him until he grew woozy and weak, which took several minutes. After that, it was easy to immobilize him under the steri-shield.

She looked over his tray of instruments, and touched them wonderingly. "How far should I carry this turnabout, do you think?" she asked aloud.

He whimpered in his wooziness and twitched feebly against the soft restraints, panic in his eyes. Claire's eyes lit; she threw back her head and laughed, really laughed, for the first time in—how long? She couldn't remember.

She put her lips near his ear, and spoke clearly. "*I don't* have to."

She was still laughing softly when she sealed the doors to the treatment room behind her and flew down the corridor toward refuge.

Chapter 11

It had been a mistake to let Ti insist on docking to the Superjumper, Silver realized, as the crunch and shudder of their impact with the docking clamps reverberated through the pusher. Zara, hovering anxiously, emitted a tiny moan. Ti snarled wordlessly over his shoulder at her, returned his fraying attention to the controls.

No—*her* mistake, to let his downsider, male, legged authority override her own reason—she knew he wasn't rated for these pushers, he'd told her so himself. He was only the authority after they got inside the Superjumper.

No, she told herself firmly, *not even then.*

"Zara," she called, "take the controls."

"Dammit," Ti began, "if you'd just—"

"We need Ti too much on the comm channels to spare him for piloting," Silver inserted, hoping desperately Ti would not spurn this offered sop for his pride.

"Mm." Grudgingly, Ti let Zara shoulder him aside.

The flex tube docking ring wouldn't seal properly. A second docking, and all the hopeful jiggling the auto-waldos could supply, couldn't make the locking ring seal properly. Silver either feared she would die, or wished she could, she wasn't sure. All her palms sweated, and transferring the laser-solderer from one to another only made the grip clammier.

"See," said Ti to Zara, "you can't do any better."

Zara glared at him. "You bent one of the rings, you dipstick. You better hope it's theirs and not ours."

"That's 'dipshit,'" John, laboring back by the hatch trying to make it seal, corrected helpfully. "If you're going to use downsider terminology, get it right."

"Pusher R-26 calling GalacTech Superjumper D620," Ti quavered into the comm. "Von, we're going to have to disengage and come around to the other side. This isn't working."

"Go ahead, Ti," came the jump pilot's voice in return. "Are you sick? You don't sound so good. That was a miserable docking. Just what *is* this emergency, anyway?"

"I'll explain when we're aboard." Ti glanced up, got a confirming nod from Zara. "Disengaging now."

Their luck was better on the starboard hatch. *No,* Silver reminded herself again. *We make our own luck. And it's my responsibility to see it's good and not bad.*

Ti pushed through the flex tube first. The Jumpship's engineer was waiting for him on the other side. Silver could hear his angry voice, "Gulik, you bent our portside docking ring. You wireheads all think you're Mr. Twinkletoes when you're plugged into your sets, but on manual you are, without exception, the most ham-handed—" he broke off, his voice thinning out in a little hiss, as Silver flitted through the hatch and hovered, her laser-solderer pointed sturdily at his stomach. It actually took him a moment to notice the weapon. His eyes widened and his mouth opened as Siggy and Jon backed her up from behind.

"Take us to where the pilot is, Ti," said Silver. She hoped the fear that edged her voice made her sound angry and fierce, not pale and weak. All her strength seemed washed out of her, leaving her limp-stomached. She swallowed and took a tighter grip on the solderer.

"What the hell *is* this?" began the engineer, his voice a taut octave higher than before. He cleared his throat and brought it back down. "Who are you . . . people, anyway? Gulik, are they with you—?"

Ti shrugged and produced a sickly smile that was either very well acted, or real. "Not exactly. I'm kind of with them."

Siggy, reminded, pointed his solderer at Ti. Silver, when approving this ploy, had kept her inner thoughts about it most secret. Going in with Ti unarmed, apparently under the quaddies' guns, covered him in case of later capture and legal prosecution. Equally, it disguised the possibility of making his ersatz kidnapping real, should he decide to bolt back to the side of his legged companions at the last moment. Wheels within wheels; did all leaders have to think on multiple levels? It made her head hurt.

They filed quickly through the compact crew's section to Nav and Com. The Jump pilot sat enthroned in his padded chair, plugged into the massive crown of his control headset, a temporary, regal cyborg. His purple company coveralls were stitched with gaudy patches proudly proclaiming his rank and specialization. His eyes were closed, and he hummed tunelessly in time to the throbbing biofeedback from his ship.

He yelped in surprise as his headset detached and rose, cutting his communion with his machine, when Ti thumbed the disconnect control. "God, Ti, don't *do* things like that—you know better—" A second yelp at the sight of the quaddies was swallowed with a gulp. He smiled at Silver in complete bewilderment, his eyes, after one shocked pass over her anatomy, locked politely on her face. She wriggled the laser-solderer, to bring it to his attention.

"Get out of your chair," she ordered.

He shrank back into it. "Look, lady . . . uh . . . what *is* that?"

"Laser gun. Get out of your chair."

His eyes measured her, measured Ti, flicked to his engineer. His hand stole to his seat harness buckle, hesitated. His muscles tensed.

"Get out slowly," Silver added.

"Why?" he asked.

Stalling, Silver thought.

"These people want to borrow your ship," Ti explained.

"Hijackers!" breathed the engineer. He coiled, floating in his position near the airseal door. Jon's and Siggy's solderers swivelled toward him. "Mutants . . ."

"Get *out*," Silver repeated, her voice rising uncontrollably.

The pilot's face was drawn and thoughtful. His hands floated from his belt to rest in a parody of relaxation over his knees. "What if I don't?" he challenged softly.

She fancied she could feel control of the situation slipping from her to him, sucked up by his superior imitation of coolness. She glanced at Ti, but he was staying safely and firmly in his part of helpless—and unhelpful—victim, *lying low* as the downsiders phrased it.

A heartbeat passed, another, another. The pilot began to relax, visibly in his long exhalation, a smug light of triumph in his eyes. He had her number; he knew she could not fire. His hand went to his

belt buckle, and his legs curled under him, seeking
launch leverage.

She had rehearsed it in her mind so many times,
the actual event was almost an anticlimax. It had a
glassy clarity, as if she observed herself from a distance, or from another time, future or past. The
moment shaped the choice of target, something she
had turned over and over without decision before;
she sighted the solderer at a point just below his
knees because no valuable control surfaces lay behind them.

Pressing the button was surprisingly easy, the work
of one small muscle in her upper right thumb. The
beam was dull blue, not enough to even make her
blink, though a brief bright yellow flame flared at the
edge of the melted fabric of his supposedly non-
flammable coveralls, then winked out. Her nostrils
twitched with the stink of the burnt fabric, more
pungent than the smell of burnt flesh. Then the pilot
was bent over himself, screaming.

Ti was babbling, voice strained, "What d'ja do that
for? He was still strapped to his *chair*, Silver!" His
eyes were wells of astonishment. The engineer, after
a first convulsive movement, froze in a submissive
ball, eyes flickering from quaddie to quaddie. Siggy's
mouth hung open, Jon's was a tight line.

The pilot's screams frightened her, swelled up her
nerves to lance through her head. She pointed the
solderer at him again. "Stop that noise!" she demanded.

Amazingly, he stopped. His breath whistled past
his clenched teeth as he twisted his head to stare at
her through pain-slitted eyes. The centers of the
burns across his legs seemed to be cauterized, shad-
owed black and ambiguous—she was torn between
revulsion, and the curious desire to go take a closer

look at what she had done. The edges of the burns were swelling red, yellow plasma already seeping through but clinging to his skin, no need for a hand-vac. The injury did not seem to be immediately life-threatening.

"Siggy, unstrap him and get him out of that control chair," Silver ordered. For once, Siggy zipped to obey with no argument, not even a suggestion of how to do it better gleaned from his holodrama viewing.

In fact, the effect of her action on everyone present, not just their captives, was most gratifying. Everyone moved faster. *This could get addictive*, Silver thought. No arguments, no complaints—

Some complaints. "Was that necessary?" Ti asked, as the prisoners were bundled ahead of them through the corridor. "He was getting out of his seat for you . . ."

"He was going to try and jump me."

"You can't be sure of that."

"I didn't think I could hit him once he was moving."

"It's not like you had no choice—"

She turned toward him with a snap; he flinched away. "If we do not succeed in taking this ship, a thousand of my friends are going to die. I had a choice. I chose. I'd choose again. You got that?" *And you choose for everybody, Silver*, Leo's voice echoed in her memory.

Ti subsided instantly. "Yes, ma'am."

Yes, ma'am? Silver blinked, and pushed ahead of him to hide her confusion. Her hands were shaking in reaction now. She entered the life-pod first, ostensibly to yank all the communications equipment but for the emergency directional finder beeper, and to check for the first-aid kit—it was there, and complete—

also to be alone for a moment, away from the wide eyes of her companions.

Was this the pleasure in power Van Atta felt, when everyone gave way before him? It was obvious what firing the weapon had done to the defiant pilot; what had it done to her? For every action, an equal and opposite reaction. This was a somatic truth, visceral knowledge ingrained in every quaddie from birth, clear and demonstrable in every motion.

She exited the pod. A hoarse moan broke from the pilot's lips as his legs accidently bumped against the hatch, as they stuffed him and the engineer through into the life-pod, sealed it, and fired it away from the Jumpship.

Silver's agitation gave way to a cool pool of resolve, within her, even though her hands still trembled with distress for the pilot's pain. So. Quaddies were no different than downsiders after all. Any evil they could do, quaddies could do too. If they chose.

There. By placing the grow-tubes at this angle, with a six-hour rotation, they could get by with four fewer spectrum lights in the hydroponics module and still have enough lumens falling on the leaves to trigger flowering in fourteen days. Claire entered the command on her lap board computer and made the analog model cycle all the way through once on fast-forward, just to be sure. The new growth configuration would cut the power drain of the module by some twelve percent from her first estimate. Good: for until the Habitat reached its destination and they unfurled the delicate solar collectors again, power would be at a premium.

She shut off the lap board and sighed. That was the last of the planning tasks she could do while still locked up here in the Clubhouse. It was a good hiding place, but too quiet. Concentration had been horribly difficult, but having nothing to do, she discovered as the seconds crept on, was worse. She floated over to the cupboard and took a pack of raisins and ate them one at a time. When she finished the gluey silence closed back in.

She imagined holding Andy again, his warm little fingers clutching hers in mutual security, and wished for Silver to hurry up and send her signal. She pictured Tony, medically imprisoned downside, and hoped in anguish Silver might delay, that by some miracle they might yet regain him at the last minute. She didn't know whether to push or pull at the passing minutes, only that each one seemed to physically pelt her.

The airseal doors hissed, jolting her with anxiety. Was she discovered—? No, it was three quaddie girls, Emma, Patty, and Kara the infirmary aide.

"Is it time?" Claire asked hoarsely.

Kara shook her head.

"Why doesn't it start, what's keeping Silver . . ." Claire broke off. She could imagine all too many disastrous reasons for Silver's delay.

"She'd better signal soon," said Kara. "The hunt is up all over the Habitat for you. Mr. Wyzak, the Airsystems Maintenance supervisor, finally thought of looking behind the walls. They're over in the docking bay section now. Everybody on his crew is having the most terrific outbreak of clumsiness," a curved moon of a grin winked in her face, "but they'll be working this way eventually."

Emma gripped one of Kara's lower arms. "In that case, is this really the best place for *us* to hide?"

"It'll have to do, for now. I hope things break before Dr. Curry works all the way down his list, or it's going to get awfully crowded in here," said Kara.

"Is Dr. Curry recovered, then?" asked Claire, not certain if she wanted to hear a yes or a no. "Enough to do surgery? I'd hoped he'd be out longer."

Kara giggled. "Not exactly. He's kind of hanging there all squinty-eyed and puffy, just supervising while the nurse gives the injections. Or he would be, if they could find any of the girls to give injections to."

"Injections?"

"Abortifacient," Kara grimaced.

"Oh. A different list from mine, then." So, that was why Emma and Patty looked pale, as from a narrow escape.

Kara sighed. "Yeah. Well, we're all on one list or another, in the end, I guess." She slipped back out.

Claire was cheered by the company of the other two quaddies, even though it represented a growing danger of discovery not only of themselves but of their plans. How much more could go wrong before the Habitat's downsider staff started asking the right questions? Suppose the entire plot was discovered prematurely, following up the loose end she'd left? Should she have submitted docilely to Curry's procedure, just to keep the secret a little longer? Suppose "a little longer" was all it took to make the difference between success and disaster?

"Now what, I wonder?" said Emma in a thin voice.

"Just wait. Unless you brought something to do," said Claire.

Emma shook her head. "Kara just grabbed me off my work shift in Small Repairs about ten minutes ago. I didn't think to bring anything."

"She got me out of my sleep sack," Patty confirmed. A yawn escaped her despite the tension. "I'm so tired, these days . . ."

Emma rubbed her abdomen absently with her

lower palms in a circular motion familiar to Claire; so, the girls had already started childbirth training.

"I wonder how all this is going to go," sighed Emma. "How it will turn out. Where we'll all be in seven months . . ."

Hardly a figure chosen at random, Claire realized. "Away from Rodeo, anyway. Or dead."

"If we're dead, we won't have a problem," Patty said. "If not . . . Claire, how is labor? What's it *really* like?" Her eyes were urgent, seeking reassurance from Claire's expertise, as the sole initiate present in the maternal mysteries of the body.

Claire, understanding, responded, "It wasn't exactly comfortable, but it's nothing you can't handle. Dr. Minchenko says we have it a lot better than downsider women. We have a more flexible pelvis with a wider arch, and our pelvic floor is more elastic, on account of not having to fight the gravitational forces. He says that was his own design idea, like eliminating the hymen—whatever that was. Something painful, I gather."

"Ugh, poor things," said Emma. "I wonder if their babies ever get sucked from their bodies by the gravity?"

"I never heard of such a thing," said Claire doubtfully. "He did say they had trouble close to term with the weight of the baby cutting off circulation and squeezing their nerves and organs and things."

"I'm glad I wasn't born a downsider," said Emma. "At least not a female one. Think of the poor downsider mothers who have to worry about their helpers dropping their newborns." She shuddered.

"It's horrible, down there," Claire confirmed fervently, remembering. "It's worth risking anything, not to have to go there. Truly."

"But we'll be by ourselves, in seven months, that

is," said Patty. "You had help. You had Dr. Minchenko. Emma and me—we'll be all alone."

"No, you won't," said Claire. "What a nasty thought. Kara will be there—I'll come—we'll all help."

"Leo will be coming with us," Emma offered, trying to sound optimistic. "He's a downsider."

"I'm not sure that's exactly his field of expertise," said Claire honestly, trying to picture Leo as a medtech. He didn't care for hydraulic systems, he'd said. She went on more firmly, "Anyway, all the complicated stuff in Andy's birth mostly had to do with data collecting, because I was one of the first, and they were working out the procedures, Dr. Minchenko said. Just having the baby wasn't all that much. Dr. Minchenko didn't do it—really, I didn't do it, my body did. About all he did was hold the hand-vac. Messy, but straightforward." *If nothing goes wrong biologically*, she thought, and had the last-minute wit not to say aloud.

Patty still looked unhappy. "Yes, but birth is only the beginning. Working for GalacTech kept us busy, but we've been working three times as hard since this escape-thing came up. And you'd have to be a dim bulb not to see it's going to get harder later. There's no end in sight. How are we going to handle it all and babies too? I'm not sure I think much of this freedom-stuff. Leo talks it up, but freedom for who? Not me. I had more free time working for the company."

"You want to go report to Dr. Curry?" suggested Emma.

Patty shrugged uncomfortably. "No . . ."

"I don't think by freedom he means free time," said Claire thoughtfully. "More like survival. Like—like not having to work for people who have a right to shoot us if they want." A twinge of harsh memory edged her voice, and she softened it self-consciously. "We'll still have to work, but it will be for ourselves. And our children."

"Mostly our children," said Patty glumly.

"That's not all bad," remarked Emma.

Claire thought she caught a glimpse of the source of Patty's pessimism. "And next time—if you want a next time—*you* can choose who will father your baby. There won't be anybody around to tell you."

Patty brightened visibly. "That's true . . ."

Claire's reassurances seemed effective; the talk drifted to less threatening channels for a while. Much later, the airseal doors parted, and Pramod stuck his head in.

"We got Silver's signal," he said simply.

Claire sang out in joy; Patty and Emma hugged each other, whirling in air.

Pramod held out a cautionary hand. "Things haven't started yet. You've got to stay in here a while longer."

"No, why?" Emma cried.

"We're waiting for a special supply shuttle from downside. When it docks is the new signal for things to start happening."

Claire's heart thumped. "Tony—did they get Tony aboard?"

Pramod shook his head, his dark eyes sharing her pain. "No, fuel rods. Leo's really anxious about them. He's afraid that without them we might not have enough power to boost the Habitat all the way out to the wormhole."

"Oh—yes, of course." Claire folded back into herself.

"Stay in here, hang on, and ignore any emergency klaxons you may hear," said Pramod. His lower hands clenched together in a gesture of encouragement, and he withdrew.

Claire settled back to wait. She could have wept with the tension of it, but Patty and Emma didn't need the bad example.

Bruce Van Atta pressed a finger to one side of his nose, squeezing the nostril shut, and sniffed mightily, then switched sides and repeated the procedure. Damn free fall and its lack of proper sinus drainage, among its other discomforts. He could hardly wait to get back to Earth. Even dismal Rodeo would be an improvement. He wondered idly if he could whip up some excuse—go inspect the quaddie barracks being readied, perhaps. That could be stretched out to about five days, if he worked it right.

He drifted over and shored himself across one corner of Dr. Yei's pie-wedge-shaped office, sighting over her desk, his back to a flat inner wall and his feet braced where her magnet-board curved, thick with stuck-on papers and flimsies. Yei's lips tightened with annoyance, as she swivelled to face him. He hitched his feet to a comfortably crossed position, deliberately letting them muss her papers, outpsyching the psycher. She glanced back to her holovid display, declining to rise to the bait, and he mussed a few more. *Female wimp*, he thought. A relief, that they had only a few weeks left to work together, and he didn't have to jolly her up any more.

"So," he prodded, "how far along are we?"

"Well, I don't know how you're doing—in fact," she added rather venomously, "I don't even know what you're doing—"

Van Atta grinned in appreciation. So the worm could wriggle after all. Some administrators might have taken offense at the implied insubordination; he congratulated himself upon his sense of humor.

"—but so far I've finished orienting about half the staff to their new assignments."

"Anybody give you a hard time? I'll play bad guy, if necessary," he offered nobly, "and go lean on the non-cooperative."

"Everybody is naturally rather shocked," she replied, "however, I don't think your . . . direct intervention will be required."

"Good," he said jovially.

"I do think it would have been better to tell them all at once. This business of releasing the information in bits and dribbles invites just the sort of rumor-mongering that is least desirable."

"Yeah, well, it's too late now—"

His words were cut short by the startling hoot of an alarm klaxon, shrilling out over the intercom. Yei's holovid was abruptly overridden by the Central Systems emergency channel.

A hoarse male voice, a strained face—good God, it was Leo Graf—sprang from the display.

"Emergency, emergency," Graf called—where was he calling from?—"we are having a depressurization emergency. This is not a drill. All Habitat downsider staff should proceed at once to the designated safe area and remain there until the all-clear sounds—"

On the holovid, a computer-generated map sketched itself showing the shortest route from this terminal to the designated safe modules—module, Van Atta saw. Holy shit, the pressurization drop must be Habitat-wide. What the hell was going on?

"Emergency, emergency, this is not a drill," Graf repeated.

Yei too was staring bug-eyed at the map, looking more like a frog than ever. "How can that be? The sealing system is supposed to isolate the problem area from the rest—"

"I bet I know," spat Van Atta. "Graf's been mess-ing with the Habitat's structure, preparatory to salvage—I'll bet he, or his quaddies, just screwed something up royally. Unless it was that idiot Wyzak did something—come on!"

"Emergency, emergency," Graf's voice droned on, "this is not a drill. All Habitat downsider staff should proceed at once—son-of-a-*bitch*!" His head snapped around, winked out, leaving only the urgently puls-ing map on the display.

Van Atta beat Yei, whose eye was still caught by the map, out the door to her office and through the airseal doors at the end of the module that should have been sealed and weren't. The doors seemed to sag half-opened, controls dead, useless, as Van Atta and Yei joined a babbling stream of staffers speeding toward safety. Van Atta swallowed, cursing his sinuses, as one ear popped and the other, throbbing, failed to. Adrenalin-spurred anxiety shivered in his stomach.

Lecture Module C was already mobbed when they arrived, with downsiders in every state of dress and undress. One of the Nutrition staff had a case of frozen food clutched under her arm—Van Atta re-jected the notion that she had inside information about the duration of the emergency and decided she must have simply had it in her hands when the alarm sounded and not thought to drop it before she fled.

"Close the door!" howled a chorus of voices as his and Yei's group entered. A distinct breeze sighed past them, rising to a whistle cut to silence as the doors sealed.

Chaos and babble ruled in the crowded lecture module.

"What's going on?"

"Ask Wyzak."

"He's out there, surely, dealing with it."

"If not, he'd better *get* the hell out there—"

"Is everybody here?"

"Where are the quaddies? What about the quaddies?"

"They have their own safe area, this isn't big enough."

"Their gym, probably."

"I didn't catch any directions for them on the holovid, to the gym or anywhere else—"

"Try the comm."

"Half the channels are dead."

"Can't you even raise Central Systems?"

"Lady, I *am* Central Systems—"

"Shouldn't we have a head-count? Does anybody know exactly how many there are up on rotation right now?"

"Two hundred seventy-two, but how can you know which are missing because they're trapped and which are missing because they're out there dealing with it—"

"Let me at that damned comm unit—"

"CLOSE THE DOOR!" Van Atta himself joined the chorus this time, semi-involuntarily. The pressure differential was becoming more marked. He was glad he wasn't a latecomer. If this went on it would shortly become his duty to see the doors stayed closed at any cost, no matter who was pounding for admittance from the other side. He had a little list . . . Well, anybody who lacked the wit to respond quickly to emergency instructions shouldn't be on a space station. Survival of the fittest.

If they hadn't amassed the whole two hundred seventy-two by now, they were surely getting close. Van Atta pushed his way through the bobbing crowd toward the center of the module, stealing momentum from this or that person at the price of their own displacement. A few turned to object, saw who had nudged them, and bit short their complaints. Somebody had the cover off the comm unit and was peering into its guts in frustration, lacking delicate diagnostic tools doubtless dropped somewhere back in the Habitat.

"Can't you at least raise the quaddies' gym?" demanded a young woman. "I've got to know if my class made it there."

"Well, why didn't you go with 'em, then?" the would-be repairman snapped logically.

"One of the older quaddies took them. He told me to come here. I didn't think to argue with him, with that alarm howling in our ears—"

"No go." Grimacing, the man clicked the cover shut.

"Well, I'm going back and find out," said the young woman decisively.

"No, you're not," interrupted Van Atta. "There's too many people breathing in here to open the door and lose air unnecessarily. Not till we find out what's going on, how extensive this is, and how long it's likely to last."

The man tapped the holovid cover. "If this thing doesn't cut in, the only way we're going to find out anything is to send out somebody with a breath mask to go check."

"We'll give it a few more minutes." Damn that overweening fool Graf. What had he done? And where was he? In a breath mask somewhere, Van Atta trusted, or better yet a pressure suit—although if Graf had indeed caused this unholy mess, Van Atta wasn't sure he wished him a pressure suit. Let him have a breath mask, and a nasty case of the bends for just punishment. Idiot Graf.

So much for Graf's famous safety record. Blessings

in disguise, at least the engineer wouldn't be able to
jam that down his throat any more. A little humility
would be good for him.

And yet—the situation was so damned anomolous.
It shouldn't be possible to depressurize the whole
Habitat at once. There were back-ups on the back-
ups, interlocks, separated bays—any accident so
system-wide would take foresight and planning.

A little hiss escaped his teeth, and Van Atta locked
into himself in a sudden bubble of furious concentration, eyes widening. A planned accident—could it
be, could it possibly be . . . ?

Genius Graf. An accident, an accident, a *perfect*
accident, the very accident he'd most desired but
had never dared wish for aloud. Was that it? That
had to be it! Fatal disaster for the quaddies, now, at
the last moment when they were all together and it
could be accomplished at one stroke?

A dozen clues fell into place. Graf's insistence
upon handling all the details of the salvage planning
himself, his secretiveness, his anxiety for constant
updates on the evacuation schedule—his withdrawal
from social contacts that Yei had observed with disfa-
vor, obsessive work schedule, general air of a man
with a secret agenda driven to exhaustion—it was all
culminating in this.

Of course it was secret. Now that he had pene-
trated the plot himself, Van Atta could only concur.
The gratitude of the GalacTech hierarchy to Graf for
relieving them of the quaddie problem must appear
indirectly, in better assignments, quicker promo-
tions—he would have to think up some suitably
oblique way of transmitting it.

On the other hand—why share? Van Atta's lips
drew back in a vulpine grin. This was hardly a situation where Graf could demand credit where it was

due, after all. Graf had been subtle—but not subtle enough. There would have to be a sacrifice, for the sake of form, after the accident. All he had to do was keep his mouth shut, and . . . Van Atta had to wrench his attention back to his present surroundings.

"I've *got* to check on my quaddies!" The young woman was growing wild-eyed. She gave up on the comm unit and began to shove her way back toward the airseal doors.

"Yes," another man joined her, "and I've got to find Wyzak, he's still not here. He's bound to need help. I'll go with you—"

"No!" cried Van Atta urgently, almost adding *You'll spoil everything!* "You're to wait for the all-clear. I won't have a panic. We'll all just sit tight and wait for instructions."

The woman subsided, but the man said skeptically, "Instructions from whom?"

"Graf," said Van Atta. Yes, it was not too early to start making it clear to witnesses where the hands-on responsibility lay. He controlled his excitement-spurred rapid breathing, trying for an aura of steady calm. Though not too calm—he must appear as surprised as any—no, more surprised than any—when the full extent of the disaster became apparent.

He settled down to wait. Minutes dragged past. One last panting group of refugees made it through the airseal doors; the Habitat-wide rate of depressurization must be slowing. One of the administrators from inventory control—old habits die hard—presented him with an unsolicited head-count of those present.

He silently cursed the census-taker's initiative, even as he accepted the results with thanks. The proof that all were not present might compel him to action he did not desire to take.

Only eleven downsider staff members had not made it. *A necessary price to pay*, Van Atta assured himself nervously. Some were doubtless holed up in other pressurized pockets, or so he could maintain he had believed, later. Their fatal mistakes could be pinned on Graf.

A group by the airseal doors was making ready to bolt. Van Atta inhaled, and paused, momentarily uncertain how to stop them without giving away everything. But a cry of dismay went up from one woman—"All the air is out of the corridor now! We can't get through without pressure suits!" Van Atta exhaled in relief.

He made his way to one of the module's viewports; it framed a dull vista of unwinking stars. The port on the other side gave an oblique view back toward the Habitat. Movement caught his eye, and he mashed his nose to the cold glass in an attempt to make out the details.

The silvery flash of worksuits, bobbing over the outside surface of the Habitat. Refugees? Or a repair party? Could his first hypothesis of a real accident be correct after all? Not good, but in any case it was still Graf's baby.

But there were quaddies out there, dammit, quaddie survivors. He could see the arms. Graf had not made his stroke complete. Just two quaddie survivors, if one was male and the other female, would be as bad as a thousand, from Apmad's point of view. Perhaps the work party was all-male.

There was Graf himself, among the flitting figures! They carried an assortment of equipment. The wavering distortion of his transverse view through the port prevented him from making out just what. He twisted his neck, craning painfully. Then the work party was eclipsed by a curve of the Habitat. A pusher slid into, and out of, his view, arcing smoothly over the lecture module. More escapees? Quaddie or downsider?

"Hey," an excited voice from within the lecture module disrupted his frantic observations. "We're in luck, gang. This whole cupboard is filled with breath masks. There must be three hundred of 'em."

Van Atta swivelled his head to spot the cupboard in question. The last time he'd been in this module that storage had been filled with audiovisual equipment. Who the hell had made that switch, and why . . . ?

A bang reverberated through the module with a peculiar sharp resonance, like having one's head in a metal bucket when someone whacked it with a hammer. Hard. Shrieks and screams. The lights dimmed, then came up to about a quarter of their former brilliance. They were on the module's own emergency power. Power from the Habitat had been cut off.

Power wasn't all that had been cut off. Stunned, Van Atta saw the Habitat begin to turn slowly past his viewport. No, it wasn't the Habitat—it was the module that was moving. A generalized "Aaah!" went up from the mob within, as they began to drift toward one wall and pile up there against the gentle acceleration being imparted from without. Van Atta clung convulsively to the handholds by the viewport.

Realization washed over him almost physically, radiating hotly from his chest down his arms, his legs, pounding up through the top of his head as if to burst through his skull.

Betrayed! He was betrayed, betrayed completely and on every level. A space-suited figure with legs was waving a cheery farewell at the module from beside a gaping hole burned in the side of the Habitat. Van Atta shook with chagrin. *I'll get you, Graf! I'll get you, you double-crossing son-of-a-bitch! You and every one of those four-armed little creeps with you—*

"Calm down, man!" Dr. Yei was saying, having somehow snagged up by his viewport. "What is it?"

He realized he'd been mumbling aloud. He wiped saliva from the corners of his mouth and glared at Yei. "You—you—you *missed* it. You were supposed to be keeping track of everything that's going on with those little monsters, and you totally *missed* it—" He advanced on her, intending he knew not what, slipped from a handhold, swung and skidded down the wall. His blood beat so hard in his ears he was afraid he was having a coronary. He lay a moment with his eyes closed, gasping, temporarily overwhelmed by his emotions. *Control,* he told himself in a mortal fear of his imminent self-destruction. *Control, stay in control—and get Graf later. Get him, get them all. . . .*

Chapter 12

Leo unsuited to the wails of disturbed quaddies.

"What do you mean, we didn't get them all?" he asked, his elation draining away. He had so hoped that his troubles—or at least the downsider parts of them—would be over with the ignition of the jet cord cutting off Lecture Module C.

"Four of the area supervisors are locked in the vegetable cooler with breath masks and won't come out," reported Sinda from Nutrition.

"And the three crewmen from the shuttle that just docked tried to make it back to their ship," said a yellow-shirted quaddie from Docks & Locks. "We trapped them between two airseal doors, but they've been working on the mechanism and we don't think we can hold them much longer."

"Mr. Wyzak and two of the life-support systems supervisors are, um, tied up in Central Systems. To the wall hand grips," reported another quaddie in yellow, adding nervously, "Mr. Wyzak sure is mad."

"Three of the creche mothers refused to leave their kids," said an older quaddie girl in pink. "They're all still in the gym with the rest of the little ones. They're pretty upset. Nobody's told them what's going on yet, at least not when I'd left."

"And, um, there's one other person," added red-clad Bobbi from Leo's own welding and joining work gang in a faint tone. "We're not quite sure what to do about him . . ."

"Immobilize him, to start," began Leo wearily. "We'll just have to arrange a life pod to take the stragglers."

"That may not be so easy," said Bobbi.

"You outnumber him, take ten—take twenty—you can be as careful as you like—is he armed?"

"Not exactly," admitted Bobbi, seeming to find her lower fingernails objects of new fascination. The quaddie equivalent of foot-shuffling, Leo realized.

"Graf!" boomed an authoritative voice, as the airseals at the end of the worksuit locker room slid open. Dr. Minchenko launched himself across the module to thump to a halt beside Leo, and gave the locker an extra bang with his fist for emphasis. One could not, after all, stomp in free fall. The unused breath mask trailing from his hand bounced and quivered. "What the hell is going on here? There's no bleeding pressurization emergency—" He inhaled vigorously, as if to prove his point.

The quaddie girl Kara in the white T-shirt and shorts of Medical trailed him, looking mortified. "Sorry, Leo," she apologized. "I couldn't get him to go."

"Am I to run off to some closet while all my quaddies asphyxiate?" Minchenko demanded indignantly of her. "What do you take me for, girl?"

"Most everybody else did," she offered hesitantly.

"Cowards—scoundrels—*idiots*," he sputtered.

"They followed their computerized emergency instructions," said Leo. "Why didn't you?"

Minchenko glared at him. "Because the whole thing stank. A Habitat-wide pressurization loss should be almost impossible. A whole chain of interlocking accidents would have to occur."

"Such chains do occur, though," said Leo, speaking from wide experience. "They're practically my speciality."

"Just so," purred Minchenko, lidding his eyes. "And that vermin Van Atta billed you as his pet engineer when he brought you in. Frankly, I thought—ahem!" he looked only mildly embarrassed, "that you might be his triggerman. The accident seemed so suspiciously convenient just now, from his point of view. Knowing Van Atta, that was practically the first thing I thought of."

"Thanks," snarled Leo.

"I knew Van Atta—I didn't know you." Minchenko paused, and added more mildly, "I still don't. What do you think you're doing?"

"Isn't it obvious?"

"Not entirely, no. Oh, certainly, you can hold out in the Habitat for a few months, cut off from Rodeo—perhaps years, barring counterattacks, if you were conservative and clever enough—but what then? There is no public opinion to come to your rescue here, no audience to grandstand for. It's half-baked, Graf. You've made no provisions for reaching help—"

"We're not asking for help. The quaddies are going to rescue themselves."

"How?" Minchenko's tone scoffed, though his eyes were alight.

"Jump the Habitat. Then keep going."

Even Minchenko was silenced momentarily. "Oh . . ."

Leo finished struggling into his red coveralls, and found the tool he wanted. He pointed the laser-solderer firmly at Minchenko's midsection. It did not appear to be a task he could safely delegate to the quaddies. "And you," he said stiffly, "can go to the

Transfer Station in the life pod with the rest of the downsiders. Let's go."

Minchenko barely glanced at the solderer. His lips curled with contempt for the weapon and, Leo felt, its wielder. "Don't be more of an idiot than you can help, Graf. I know they foxed that cretin Curry, so there are still at least fifteen pregnant quaddie girls out there. Not counting the results of unauthorized experiments, which judging from the way the level is dropping in that box of condoms in the unlocked drawer in my office, are becoming significant."

Kara started in guilty dismay, and Minchenko added aside to her, "Why do you think I pointed them out to you, dear? Be that as it may, Graf," he fixed Leo with a stern eye, "if you throw me off what do you plan to do if one of them presents at labor with placenta praevia? Or a post-partum prolapsed uterus? Or any other medical emergency that requires more than a band-aid?"

"Well . . . but . . ." Leo was taken aback. He wasn't quite sure what placenta praevia was, but somehow he didn't think it was medical gobbledy-gook for a hangnail. Nor that a precise explanation of the term would do anything to ease the ominous anxiety it engendered in him. Was it something likely to occur, given the alterations of quaddie anatomy? "There is no choice. To stay here is death for every quaddie. To go is a chance—not a guarantee—of life."

"But you need me," argued Minchenko.

"You have to—what?" Leo's tongue stumbled.

"You need me. You can't throw me off." Minchenko's eyes flicked infinitesimally to the solderer.

"Well, huh," Leo choked, "I can't kidnap you, either."

"Who's asking you to?"

"You are, evidently . . ." he cleared his throat. "Look, I don't think you understand. I'm taking this Habitat out, and we're not coming back, not ever. We're going out as far as we can go, beyond every inhabited world. It's a one-way ticket."

"I'm relieved. At first I thought you were going to try something stupid."

Leo found his emotions churning, a mixture of suspicion, jealousy?—and a sharp rising anticipation— what a *relief* it would be, not to have to carry it all alone. . . . "You sure?"

"They're *my* quaddies . . ." Minchenko's hands clenched, opened. "Daryl's and mine. I don't think you half understand what a job we did. What a *good* job, developing these people. They're finely adapted to their environment. Superior in every way. Thirty-five years' work—am I to let some total stranger drag them off across the galaxy to who-knows-what fate? Besides, GalacTech was going to retire me next year."

"You'll lose your pension," Leo pointed out. "Maybe your freedom—possibly your life."

Minchenko snorted. "Not much of that left."

Not true, Leo thought. The bioscientist possessed enormous life, over three-quarters of a century of accumulation. When this man died, a universe of specialized knowledge would be extinguished. Angels would weep for the loss. Unless— "Could you train quaddie doctors?"

"It's a forgone conclusion *you* couldn't." Minchenko ran his hands through his clipped white hair in a gesture part exasperation, part pleading.

Leo glanced around at the anxiously hovering quaddies, listening in—listening in while men with legs decided their fate, again. Not right . . . the words popped out of his mouth before reasoned caution could stop them. "What do you kids think?"

A ragged but immediate chorus of assent for Minchenko—relief in their eyes, too. Minchenko's familiar authority would clearly be an immense comfort to them, as they travelled farther into the unknown. Leo was suddenly put in mind of the way the universe had changed to a stranger place the day his father had died. *Just because we're adults doesn't automatically mean we can save you . . .* But this was a discovery each quaddie would have to make in their own time. He took a deep breath. "All right . . ." How could one suddenly feel a hundred kilos lighter when already weightless? Placenta praevia, God.

Minchenko did not react with immediate pleasure. "There's just one thing," he began, arranging his features in a humble smile quite horribly out of place on his face.

What's he sweating for now? Leo wondered, suspicions renewed. "What?"

"Madame Minchenko."

"Who?"

"My wife. I have to get her."

"I didn't—realize you were married. Where is she?"

"Downside. On Rodeo."

"Hell . . ." Leo suppressed an urge to start tearing out the remains of his hair.

Pramod, listening, reminded, "Tony's down there too."

"I know, I know—and I promised Claire—I don't know how we're going to work this . . ."

Minchenko was waiting, his expression intense—not a man used to begging. Only his eyes pleaded. Leo was moved. "We'll try. We'll try. That's all I can promise."

Minchenko nodded, dignified.

"How's Madame Minchenko going to feel about all this, anyway?"

"She's loathed Rodeo for twenty-five years," Minchenko promised—somewhat airily, Leo thought. "She'll be delighted to get away." Minchenko didn't add *I hope* aloud, but Leo heard it anyway.

"All right. Well, we've still got to round up these stragglers and get rid of them. . . ." Leo wondered wistfully if it was possible to drop dead painlessly from an anxiety attack. He led his little troop from the locker room.

Claire flew from hand-grip to hand-grip along the branching corridors, done with patience at last. Her heart sang with anticipation. The airseal doors to the raucous gym were crowded with quaddies, and she had to restrain herself from forcibly elbowing them out of her way. One of her old dormitory mates, in the pink T-shirt and shorts of creche duty, recognized her with a grin and reached out with a lower hand to pull her through the mob.

"The littlest ones are by Door C," said her dorm mate. "I've been expecting you . . ." After a quick visual check to be sure her flight plan didn't violently intersect anyone else's taking a similar shortcut, her dorm mate helped her launch herself in that direction by the most direct route, across the diameter of the big chamber.

The buxom figure in pink coveralls Claire sought was practically buried in a swarm of excited, frightened, chattering, crying five-year-olds. Claire felt a twinge of real guilt, that it had been judged too dangerous to their secrecy to warn the younger quaddies in advance of the great changes about to sweep over them. *The little ones didn't get a vote, either,* she thought.

Andy was tethered to Mama Nilla, weeping miserably. Mama Nilla was desperately trying to pacify him with a squeeze bottle of formula with one hand while holding a reddening gauze pad to the forehead of a crying five-year-old with the other. Two or three more clung for comfort to her legs as she tried to verbally direct the efforts of a sixth to help a seventh who had torn open a package of protein chips too wide and accidently allowed the contents to spill into the air. Through it all her calm familiar drawl was only slightly more compressed than usual, until she saw Claire approaching. "Oh, dear," she said in a weak voice.

"Andy!" Claire cried.

His head swivelled toward her, and he launched himself away from Mama Nilla with frantic swimming motions, only to fetch up at the end of his tether and rebound back to the creche mother's side. At this point he began screaming in true earnest. As if by resonance, the bleeding boy started crying harder too.

Claire braked by the wall and closed in on them.

"Claire, honey, I'm sorry," said Mama Nilla, twitching her hips around to eclipse Andy, "but I can't let you have him. Mr. Van Atta said he'd fire me on the spot, twenty years or no twenty years—and God knows who they'd get then—there's so few I can really trust to have their heads screwed on right—" Andy interrupted her by launching himself again; he batted the proffered bottle violently out of her hand and it spun away, a few drops of formula adding tangentially to the general environmental degradation. Claire's hands reached for him.

"—I can't, I really can't—oh, hell, *take* him!" It was the first time Claire had ever heard Mamma Nilla swear. She unhooked the tether and her freed left side was instantly set upon by the waiting five-year-olds.

Andy's screams faded at once to a muffled weeping, as his little hands clamped her fiercely. Claire folded him to her with all four arms no less fiercely. He rooted in her shirt—uselessly, she realized. Just holding him might be enough for her, but the reverse was not necessarily true. She nuzzled in his scant hair, delighting in the clean baby smell of him, tender sculptured ears, translucent skin, fine eyelashes, every part of his wriggling body. She wiped his nose happily with the edge of her blue shirt.

"It's Claire," she overheard one of the five-year-olds explaining knowlegeably to another. "She's a real mommy." She glanced up to catch them gravely inspecting her; they giggled. She grinned back. A seven-year-old from an adjoining group had retrieved the bottle, and hung about watching Andy with interest.

The cut on the little quaddie's forehead having clotted enough, Mama Nilla was at last able to carry on a conversation. "You don't happen to know where Mr. Van Atta is, do you?" she asked Claire worriedly.

"Gone," said Claire joyously, "gone forever! *We're* taking over."

Mama Nilla blinked. "Claire, they won't let you . . ."

"We have help." She nodded across the gym, where Leo in his red coveralls caught her eye—he must have just arrived. With him was another legged figure in white coveralls. What was Dr. Minchenko still doing here? A sudden fear twinged through her. Had they failed to clear the Habitat of downsiders after all? For the first time it occurred to her to question Mama Nilla's presence. "Why didn't you go to your safe zone?" Claire asked her.

"Don't be silly, dear. Oh, Dr. Minchenko!" Mama Nilla waved to him. "Over here!"

The two downsider men, lacking the free-flying

confidence of the quaddies, crossed the chamber via a rope net hung across a farther arc, and made their way toward Mama Nilla's group.

"I've got one here who needs some biotic glue," Mama Nilla, hugging the cut quaddie, said to Dr. Minchenko as soon as he drew near enough to hear. "What's going on? Is it safe to take them back to the creche modules yet?"

"It's safe," replied Leo, "but you're going to have to come with me, Ms. Villanova."

"I don't leave my kids till my relief arrives," said Mama Nilla tartly, "and nine-tenths of the department seems to have evaporated, including my department head."

Leo frowned. "Have you had your briefing from Dr. Yei yet?"

"No . . ."

"They were saving the best for last," said Dr. Minchenko grimly, "for obvious reasons." He turned to the creche mother. "GalacTech has just terminated the Cay Project, Liz. Without even consulting me!" Bluntly, he outlined the termination scenario for her. "I was writing up protests, but Graf here beat me to it. Rather more effectively, I suspect. The inmates are taking over the asylum. He thinks he can convert the Habitat into a colony ship. I think . . . I choose to believe he can."

"You mean you're responsible for this mess?" Mama Nilla glared at Leo, and looked around, clearly stunned. "I thought Claire was babbling . . ." The other two downsider creche mothers had come over during the explanation, and hung in the air looking equally nonplussed. "GalacTech's not *giving* you the Habitat . . . are they?" Mama Nilla asked Leo faintly.

"No, Ms. Villanova," said Leo patiently. "We are stealing it. Now, I wouldn't ask you to get involved in anything illegal, so if you'll just follow me to the life pod—"

Mama Nilla stared around the gym. A few groups of youngsters were already being herded out by some older quaddies. "But these kids can't handle all these kids!"

"They're going to have to," said Leo.

"No, no—I don't think you have the foggiest idea how labor-intensive this department is!"

"He doesn't," confirmed Dr. Minchenko, rubbing his lips thoughtfully with a forefinger.

"There's *no choice*," said Leo through his teeth. "Now kids, let go of Ms. Villanova," he addressed the quaddies clutching her. "She has to leave."

"No!" said the one wrapped around her left knee. "She's gotta read our stories after lunch, she *promised*." The one with the cut began crying again. Another one tugged her left sleeve and whispered loudly, "Mama Nilla! I gotta go to the toilet!"

Leo ran his hands through his hair, unclenched them with a visible effort. "I need to be suited up and Outside *right now*, lady, I don't have *time* to argue. All of you," his glare took in the other two creche mothers, "move it!"

Mama Nilla's eyes glinted. She held out her left arm with the quaddie attached, blue eyes peering frightenedly at Leo around Mama Nilla's sturdy bicep. "Are you going to take this little girl to the bathroom, then?"

The quaddie girl and Leo stared at each other in equal horror. "Certainly not," the engineer choked. He looked around "Another quaddie will. Claire . . . ?"

After a barracuda-like investigation, Andy chose this moment to begin wailing protests at the lack of expected milk from his mother's breasts. Claire tried to soothe him, patting his back; she felt like crying herself for his disappointment.

"I don't suppose," Dr. Minchenko interjected mildly, "that you would care to come along with us, Liz? There would be no going back, of course."

"Us?" Mama Nilla regarded him sharply. "Are you going along with this nonsense?"

"I rather think so."

"That's all right, then." She nodded.

"But you can't—" Leo began.

"Graf," Dr. Minchenko said, "did your little depressurization drama just now give these ladies any reason to think they were still going to have air to breathe if they stayed with their quaddies?"

"It shouldn't have," said Leo.

"I didn't even think about it," said one of the creche mothers, looking suddenly dismayed.

"I did," said the other, frowning at Leo.

"I knew there were emergency air supplies in the gym module," said Mama Nilla, "it's in the regular drill, after all. The whole department ought to have come here."

"I diverted 'em," said Leo shortly.

"The whole department should have told you to go screw yourself," Mama Nilla added evenly. "Allow me to speak for the absent." She smiled icily at the engineer.

One of the creche mothers addressed Mama Nilla in distress. "But I can't come with you. My husband works downside!"

"Nobody's asking you to!" roared Leo.

The other creche mother, ignoring him, added to Mama Nilla, "I'm sorry. I'm sorry, Liz, I just can't. It's just too much."

"Yes, exactly." Leo's hand hesitated over a lump in his coveralls, abandoned it, and switched to trying to herd them all along with broad arm-waving gestures.

"It's all right girls, I understand," Mama Nilla

soothed their evident anxiety. "I'll stay and hold the fort, I guess. Got nobody waiting for this old body, after all," she laughed. It was a little forced.

"Will you take over the department, then?" Dr. Minchenko confirmed with Mama Nilla. "Keep it going any way you can—come to me when you can't."

She nodded, looking withdrawn, as if the bottomless complexity of the task before her was just beginning to dawn.

Dr. Minchenko took charge of the quaddie boy with the still-oozing cut on his forehead; Leo at last successfully pried loose the other two downsider women, saying, "Come *on*. I have to go empty the vegetable cooler next."

"With all this going on, what is he doing spending time cleaning out a refrigerator?" Mama Nilla muttered under her breath. "Madness . . ."

"Mama Nilla, I gotta go *now*," the little quaddie wrapped all her arms tightly around her torso by way of emphasis, and Mama Nilla perforce broke away.

Andy was still wailing his indignant disappointment in intermittent bursts.

"Hey, little fellow," Dr. Minchenko paused to address him, "that's no way to talk to your mama. . . ."

"No milk," explained Claire. Glumly, feeling dreadfully inadequate, she offered him the bottle, which he batted away. When she attempted to detach him momentarily in order to dive after it, he wrapped himself around her arm and screamed frantically. One of the five-year-olds twisted up and put all four of his hands over his ears, pointedly.

"Come with us to the infirmary," said Dr. Minchenko with an understanding smile. "I think I have something that will fix that problem. Unless you want to wean him now, which I don't recommend."

"Oh, please," said Claire hopefully.

"It will take a couple of days to get your systems interlocked again," he warned, "the biofeedback lag time being what it is. But I haven't had a chance to examine you two since I came up anyway . . ."

Claire floated after him with gratitude. Even Andy stopped crying.

Pramod hadn't been joking about the clamps, Leo thought with a sigh, as he studied the fused lump of metal before him. He punched up the specs on the computer board floating beside him, a bit slowly and clumsily with his pressure-gloved hands. This particular insulated pipe conducted sewage. Unglamorous, but a mistake here could be just as much a disaster as any other.

And a lot messier, Leo thought with a grim grin. He glanced up at Bobbi and Pramod hovering at the ready beside him in their silvery worksuits; five other quaddie work teams were visible along the Habitat's surface, and a pusher jockeyed into position nearby. Rodeo's sunlit crescent wheeled in the background. Well, they must certainly be the galaxy's most expensive plumbers.

The mess of variously-coded pipes and tubing before him formed the umbilical connections between one module and the next, shielded by an outer casing from microdust pitting and other hazards. The task at hand was to re-align the modules in uniform longitudinal bundles to withstand acceleration. Each bundle, strapped together like the cargo pods, would form a sturdy, self-supporting, balanced mass, at least in terms of the relatively low thrusts Leo was contemplating. Just like driving a team of yoked hippopotamuses. But re-aligning the modules entailed re-aligning all their connections, and there were lots and lots and *lots* of connections.

A movement caught the corner of Leo's eye. Pramod's helmet followed the tilt of Leo's.

"There they go," Pramod remarked. Both triumph and regret mingled in his voice.

The life pod with the last remnant of downsiders aboard fled silently into the void, a flash of light winking off a port even as it shrank from sight around Rodeo's curvature. That was it, then, for the legged ones, bar himself, Dr. Minchenko, Mama Nilla, and a slightly demented young supervisor waving a spanner they'd pried out of a duct who declared his violent love for a quaddie girl in Airsystems Maintenance and refused to be budged. If he came to his senses by the time they reached Orient IV, Leo decided, they could drop him off. Meantime it was a choice between shooting him or putting him to work. Leo had eyed the spanner, and put him to work.

Time. The seconds seemed to wriggle over Leo's skin like bugs, beneath his suit. The remnant group of evicted downsiders must soon catch up with the bewildered first batch and start comparing notes. It wouldn't be long after that, Leo judged, that Galac-Tech must start making its counter-moves. It didn't take an engineer to see a thousand ways in which the Habitat was vulnerable. The only option left to the quaddies now was speedy flight.

Phlegmatic calm, Leo reminded himself, was the key to getting out of this alive. Remember that. He turned his attention back to the job at hand. "All right, Bobbi, Pramod, let's do it. Get ready with the emergency shut-offs on both ends, and we'll get this monster horsed around . . ."

Chapter 13

His fellow refugees gave way before him as Bruce Van Atta stormed out of the boarding tube and into the passenger arrival lounge of Rodeo Shuttleport Three. He had to pause a moment, hands braced on his knees, to overcome a wave of dizziness induced by his abrupt return to planetside gravity. Dizziness and rage.

For several hours during the ride around Rodeo orbit in the cut-off lecture module Van Atta had been horribly certain that Graf was intending to murder them all, despite the contrary evidence of the breath masks. If this was war, Graf would never make a good soldier. *Even I know better than to humiliate a man like this, and then leave him alive. You'll be sorry you double-crossed me, Graf; sorrier still you didn't kill me when you had the chance.* He restrained his rage with an effort.

Van Atta had ordered himself aboard the first available shuttle down from a Transfer Station overburdened by the surprise arrival of almost three hundred unexpected bodies. He had not slept in the twenty hours since the detached lecture module's airlock had, with agonizing glitches and delays, finally been married to that of a Station personnel carrier. He and the other Cay Habitat employees had disembarked in disorganized batches from their cramped prison-mobile and been ferried to the Tranfer Station, where yet more time had been wasted.

Information. It had been almost a full day since they had been evicted from the Cay Habitat. He must have information. He boarded a slide tube and headed for Shuttleport Three's administration building, with its communications center. Dr. Yei pattered after him, wimping about something; he paid little attention.

He caught sight of his own wavering reflection in the plexiplastic walls of the tube as he was carried along above the shuttleport tarmac. Haggard. He straightened, and sucked in his gut. It would not do to appear before other administrators looking beaten or weak. The weak went under.

He gazed through his pale image and across the shuttleport laid out below. On the far side of the tarmac at the monorail terminal cargo pods were already starting to pile up. Ah, yes: the damned quaddies were a link in that chain, too. A weak link, a broken link, soon to be replaced.

He arrived at the communications center at the same moment as Shuttleport Three's chief administrator, Chalopin. She was trailed by her Security captain, what's-his-name, oh, yes, that idiot Bannerji.

"What the hell is going on here?" Chalopin snapped without preamble. "An accident? Why haven't you requested assistance? They told us to hold all flights—we've got a major production run backed up halfway to the refinery."

"Keep holding it, then. Or call the Transfer Station. Moving your cargo is not my department."

"Oh, yes it is! Orbital cargo marshalling has been under Cay Project aegis for a year."

"*Ex*-perimentally." He frowned, stung. "It may be my department, but it's not my biggest worry right now. Look, lady, I got a full-scale crisis here." He turned to one of the comm controllers. "Can you punch me through to the Cay Habitat at all?"

"They're not answering our calls," said the comm controller doubtfully. "Almost all of the regular telemetry has been cut off."

"Anything. Telescopic sighting, anything."

"I might be able to get a visual off one of the comsats," said the controller. He turned to his panel, muttering. In a few minutes his screen coughed up a distant flat view of the Cay Habitat as seen from synchronous orbit. He stepped up the magnification.

"What are they *doing*?" asked Chalopin, staring.

Van Atta stared too. What insane vandalism was this? The Habitat resembled a complex three-dimensional puzzle pulled apart by an idle child. Detached modules seemed spilled carelessly, floating at all angles in space. Tiny silver figures jetted among them. The solar power panels had mysteriously shrunk to a quarter of their normal area. Was Graf embarked on some nutty scheme for fortifying the Habitat against counterattack, perhaps? Well, it would do him no good, Van Atta swore silently.

"Are they . . . preparing for a siege or something?" Dr. Yei asked aloud, evidently following a similar line of thought. "Surely they must realize how futile it would be . . ."

"Who knows what that damn fool Graf thinks?" Van Atta growled. "The man's run mad. There are a dozen ways we can stand off at a distance and knock that installation to bits even without military supplies. Or just wait and starve them out. They've trapped themselves. He's not just crazy, he's stupid."

"Maybe," said Yei doubtfully, "they mean to just go on quietly living up there, in orbit. Why not?"

"The hell you say. I'm going to hook them out of there, and double-quick, too. Somehow . . . No bunch of miserable mutants are going to get away with sabotage on *this* scale. Sabotage—theft—terrorism . . ."

"They are not mutants," began Yei, "they are genetically-engineered childr—"

"Mr. Van Atta, sir?" piped up another comm controller. "I have an urgent memo for you listed on my all-points. Can you take it here?" Yei, cut off, spread her hands in frustration.

"Now what?" Van Atta muttered, seating himself before the comm unit.

"It's a recorded message from the manager of the cargo marshalling station out at Jumppoint. I'll put it on-line," said the tech.

The vaguely familiar face of the Jump point station manager wavered into focus before Van Atta. Van Atta had met him perhaps once, early in his stint here. The small Jumppoint station was manned from the Orient IV side, and was under Orient IV's operations division, not Rodeo's. Its employees were regular Union downsiders and did not normally have contact with Rodeo, nor with the quaddies once destined to replace them.

The station manager looked harried. He gabbled through the preliminary ID's, then came abruptly to the meat of his matter; "What the hell is going on with you people, anyway? A crew of mutant freaks just came out of nowhere, kidnapped a Jump pilot, shot another, and hijacked a GalacTech cargo Superjumper. But instead of jumping *out*, they've headed back with it toward Rodeo. When we notified Rodeo Security, they indicated the mutants probably belonged to you. Are there more out there? Are they running wild or something? I want answers, dammit. I've got a pilot in the infirmary, a terrorized engineer, and a crew on the verge of panic." From the look on his face the station manager was on the verge of panic himself. "Jumppoint Station out!"

"How old is this memo?" said Van Atta rather blankly.

"About," the comm tech checked his monitor, "twelve hours, sir."

"Does he think the hijackers are quaddies? Why wasn't I informed—" Van Atta's eye fell on Bannerji, standing blandly at attention by Chapolin's elbow, "why wasn't I informed of this at once by Security?"

"At the time the incident was first reported, you were unavailable," said the Security captain, devoid of expression. "Since then we've been tracking the D-620, and it's continued to boost straight toward Rodeo. It doesn't answer our calls."

"What are you doing about it?"

"We're monitoring the situation. I have not yet received orders to do anything about it."

"Why not? Where's Norris?" Norris was Operations manager for the entire Rodeo local space area; he ought to be on this thing. True, the Cay Project was not in his chain of command proper, as Van Atta reported directly to company Ops.

"Dr. Norris," said Chalopin, "is attending a materials development conference on Earth. In his absence, I am acting Operations manager. Captain Bannerji and I have discussed the possibility of his taking his men and the Shuttleport Three Security and Rescue shuttle and attempting to board the hijacked ship. We're still not sure who these people are or what they want, but they appear to have taken a hostage, compelling caution on our part. So we've let them continue to decrease their range while we *attempt* to gain more information about them. This," she eyed him beadily, "brings us to you, Mr. Van

Atta. Is this incident somehow connected to your crisis at the Cay Habitat?"

"I don't see how—" Van Atta began, and broke off, because suddenly he did see how. "Son-of-a-bitch . . ." he whispered.

"Lord Krishna," Dr. Yei said, and wheeled to stare again at the live vid of the Habitat half-dismantled in orbit far above them. "It can't be . . ."

"Graf's crazy. He's crazy, the man's a flaming megalomaniac. He can't *do* this—" The engineering parameters paraded inexorably through Van Atta's mind. Mass—power—distance—yes, a pared-down Habitat, a percentage of its less-essential components dropped, might just barely be torqued by a Superjumper into wormhole space, if it could be wrestled into position at the distant jump point. The whole damn thing . . . "They're hijacking the whole damn thing!" Van Atta cried aloud.

Yei wrung her hands, half-circling the vid. "They'll never manage. They're barely more than children! He'll lead them to their deaths! It's criminal!"

Captain Bannerji and the shuttleport administrator glanced at each other. Bannerji pursed his lips and opened his hand to her, as if to say, *Ladies first*.

"Do you think the two incidents are connected, then?" Chalopin pressed.

Van Atta too paced back and forth, as if he could so coax an angle from flat view of the Habitat. ". . . the whole damn thing!"

Yei answered for him, "Yes, we think so."

Van Atta paced on. "Hell, and they've got it apart already! We aren't going to have time to starve 'em out. Got to stop 'em some other way."

"The Cay Project workers were very upset at the abrupt termination of the Project," Yei explained. "They found out about it prematurely. They were afraid of being remaindered downside, being unaccustomed to gravity. I never had a chance to introduce the idea gradually. I think they may actually be trying to—run away, somehow."

Captain Bannerji's eyes widened. He leaned across the console on one hand and stared into the vid. "Consider the lowly snail," he muttered, "who carries its house on its back. On cold rainy days when it goes for a walk, it never has to backtrack. . . ."

Van Atta put an extra half meter of distance between himself and the suddenly poetic Security captain.

"Weapons," Van Atta said. "What kind of weapons does Security have on tap?"

"Stunners," answered Bannerji, straightening up and studying his right thumbnail. Was there a flash of mockery in his eyes? No, he wouldn't dare.

"I mean on your shuttle," said Van Atta irritably. "Ship-mounted weapons. Teeth. You can't make a threat without teeth."

"There are two medium-power ship-mounted laser units. Last time we used them was—let me see—to burn through a log snag that had backed up flood waters threatening an exploration camp."

"Yes, well, it's more than *they* have, anyway," said Van Atta excitedly. "We can attack the Habitat—or the Superjumper—either, really. The main thing is to keep them from connecting with each other. Yes, get the Jumpship first. Without it the Habitat is a sitting target we can polish off at our leisure. Is your security shuttle fueled up and ready to go, Bannerji?"

Dr. Yei had paled. "Hold on! Who's talking about attacking anything? We haven't even made verbal contact yet. If the hijackers are indeed quaddies, I'm sure I could persuade them to listen to reason—"

"It's too late for reason. This situation calls for *action*." Van Atta's humiliation burned hot in his stomach, fueled by fear. When the company brass found out how totally he had lost control—well, he'd better be firmly back in control by then.

"Yes, but . . ." Yei licked her lips, "it's all very well to threaten, but the actual use of force is dangerous—maybe destructive—hadn't you better get some kind of authorization first? If something went horribly wrong, you wouldn't want to be left holding the bag, surely."

Van Atta paused. "It would take too much time," he objected at last. "Maybe a day, to reach District HQ on Orient IV and return. And if they decided it was too hot and bounced it all the way to Apmad on Earth, it could be several days before we got a reply."

"But it's going to be several days, isn't it?" said Yei, watching him intently. "Even if they succeed in fitting the Habitat to the Superjumper, they aren't going to be able to swing it around and boost it like a fast courier. It would never stand the strain, it would use too much fuel—there's lots of time yet. Wouldn't it be better to get authorization, to be safe? Then, if anything went wrong—it wouldn't be *your* fault."

"Well . . ." Van Atta slowed still further. How typical of Yei's wishy-washy, wimpy indecision. He could almost hear her, in his head; *Now, let's all sit down and discuss this like reasonable people. . . .* He loathed letting her push his buttons; still, she had a valid point: cover-your-ass was a fundamental rule for survival even of the fittest.

"Well . . . no, dammit! One thing I can damn well guarantee is that GalacTech is going to want this whole fiasco kept quiet. The last thing they'll want is a lot of rumors flying around about their pet mutants running wild. Better for all of us if this is handled strictly inside Rodeo local space." He turned to

Bannerji. "That's the first priority, then—you and your men have got to get that Jumpship back, or at least disable it."

"That," remarked Bannerji to the air, "would be vandalism. Besides, as has been pointed out before—Shuttleport Three Security is not in your chain of command, Mr. Van Atta." He glanced significantly at his boss, who stood listening and pulling worriedly on a strand of hair escaped from her sleek coiffure.

"True," she agreed. "The Habitat may be your problem, Mr. Van Atta, but this Jumpship hijacking is clearly under my jurisdiction, regardless of their connections. And there's still a cargo shuttle docked up there that's mine, too, though the Transfer Station reported they picked up its crew from a life pod."

Van Atta stood fuming, blocked. Blocked by the damned women. It had been Chalopin's buttons Yei had been aiming for, he realized suddenly, and she'd scored a hit, too. "That's it, then," he said through his teeth at last. "We'll bounce it to HQ. And then we'll see who's in charge here."

Dr. Yei closed her eyes briefly, as if in relief. At a word from Chalopin a comm tech began readying his system for the relay of a scrambled emergency message to District, to be radioed at the speed of light to the wormhole station, recorded and Jumped through on the next available transport, and radio-relayed again to its destination.

"In the meantime," said Van Atta to Chalopin, "what are you going to do about *your*," he drew the word out sarcastically, "hijacking?"

"Proceed with caution," she replied levelly. "We believe there is a hostage involved, after all."

"We're not sure if all the GalacTech staff is off the Habitat yet, either," put in Dr. Yei.

Van Atta growled, unable to contradict her. But if

there were still downsiders being held aboard, senior management must surely realize the need for a swift and vigorous response. He must call the Transfer Station next and get the final head count. If all these dithering idiots were going to force him to sit on his hands for the next several days, he could at least lay his plans for action when he was unleashed.

And he was certain he would be unleashed, sooner or later. He had not failed to read Apmad's underlying horror of the mutant quaddies. When word of this mess finally arrived on her desk it would goose her three meters straight up in the air, hostages or no hostages— Van Atta's eyes narrowed. "Hey," he said suddenly, "we're not as helpless as you think. Two can play that game—*I* have a hostage too!"

"You do?" said Dr. Yei, puzzled. Then her hand went to her throat.

"Damn straight. And to think I almost forgot. That four-armed geek Tony is down here!"

Tony was Graf's teacher's pet—and that little cunt Claire's favorite prick, and *she* was surely a ringleader—if she couldn't swing this to his advantage, he was dead in the head. He spun on his heel. "Come on, Yei! Those little suckers are going to answer our calls now!"

Jump pilots might swear their ships were beautiful, but really, Leo thought as the D-620 heaved silently into view, the Superjumper looked like nothing so much as a mutant mechanical squid. A pod-like section at the front end contained the control room and crew quarters, protected from the material hazards encountered during acceleration by an oblate laminated shield and from the hazards of radiation by an invisible magnetic cone. Arcing out behind trailed four enormously long, mutually braced arms. Two housed normal space thrusters, two housed the heart of the ship's purpose, the Necklin field generator rods that spun the ship through wormhole space during a jump. Between the four arms was a huge empty space normally occupied by cargo pods. The bizarre ship would look more sensible when that space was filled with Habitat modules, Leo decided. At that point he would even break down and call it beautiful himself.

With a jerk of his chin Leo called up a vid of his worksuit's power and supply levels, displayed on the inside of his faceplate. He would have just time to see the first module bundle pushed into place and attached before being forced to take a break and restock his suit. Not that he hadn't been ready for a break hours ago. He blinked sand and water from his itching, no-doubt-bloodshot eyes, wishing he could rub them, and sucked another mouthful of hot coffee from his drink tube. He wanted fresh coffee, too. The stuff he was drinking now had been out here as long as he had, and was growing just as chemically vile, opaque and greenish.

The D-620 sidled near the Habitat, matching velocities precisely, and shut down its engines. The flight lights blinked out and the parking lights, signalling that it was safe to approach, flicked on. Banks of floods suddenly illuminated the vast cargo space, as if to say, *Welcome aboard*.

Leo's gaze strayed to the crew's section, dwarfed by the arcing arms. From the corner of his eye he saw a personnel pod peel away from the Superjumper's starboard side and ferry off toward the Habitat modules. Somebody heading home—Silver? Ti? He had to talk to Ti as soon as possible. A previously unrealized knot unwound in his stomach. *Silver's back safe*. He caught himself up; *everybody* was back. But not safe yet. He activated his suit jets and caught up with his quaddie crew.

Thirty minutes later Leo's heart eased as the first module bundle slid smoothly into place in the D-620's embrace. In a minor nightmare, undispelled by checking and re-checking his figures, he'd envisioned something Not Fitting, followed by endless delays for correction. The fact that they'd heard nothing from downside yet apart from repeated pleas for communication did not reassure him much. GalacTech management on Rodeo had to respond eventually, and there wasn't a thing he could do to counter that response until it shaped itself. Rodeo's apparent paralysis couldn't last much longer.

Meanwhile, it was half past breaktime. Maybe Dr. Minchenko could be persuaded to disgorge something for his throbbing head, to replace the eight hours sleep he wasn't going to get. Leo punched up his work gang leaders' channel on his suit comm.

"Bobbi, take over as foreman. I'm going Inside. Pramod, bring in your team as soon as that last strap is bolted down. Bobbi, be sure that second module bundle is tied in solid before you adjust and seal all the end airlocks, right?"

"Yes, Leo. I'm on it." Bobbi waved acknowledgement from the far end of the module bundle with a lower arm.

As Leo turned away, one of the one-man minipushers that had helped tug the module bundle into place detached itself and rotated, preparing to thrust away and help the next bundle already being aligned beyond the Superjumper. One of its attitude jets puffed, then, even as Leo watched, emitted a sudden intense blue stream. Its rotation picked up speed.

That's uncontrolled! Leo thought, his eyes widening. In the bare moment it took him to call up the right channel on his suit comm, the rotation became a spin. The pusher jetted off wildly, missing colliding with a worksuited quaddie by a scant meter. As Leo watched in horror it caromed off a nacelle on one of the Superjumper's Necklin rod arms and tumbled into space beyond.

The comm channel from the pusher emitted a wordless scream. Leo bounced channels. "Vatel!" he called the quaddie manning the nearest other little pusher. "Go after her!"

The second pusher rotated and sped past him; he saw the flash of one of Vatel's gloved hands visually acknowledging the order through the pusher's wide-angle front viewport. Leo restrained a heart-wrenching urge to jet after them himself. Damn little he could do in a power-depleted worksuit. It was up to Vatel.

Had it been human—or quaddie—error, or a mechanical defect that had caused the accident? Well, he would be able to tell quickly enough once the pusher was retrieved. *If the pusher was retrieved* . . . He squelched that thought. Instead he jetted over to the Necklin rod nacelle.

The nacelle housing was deeply dented where the pusher had collided with it. Leo tried to reassure himself. *It's only a housing. It's put there just to protect the guts from accidents like this, right?* Hissing in dismay, he pulled himself around to shine his worksuit light into the man-high dark aperture at one end of the housing.

Oh, God.

The vortex mirror was cracked. Over three meters wide at its elliptical lip, mathematically shaped and polished to angstrom-unit precision, it was an integral control surface of the Jump system, reflecting, bleeding or amplifying the Necklin field generated by the main rods at the will of the pilot. Not just cracked—shattered in a starry burst, cold titanium deformed past its limits. Leo moaned.

A second light shone in past him. Leo glanced around to find Pramod at his shoulder.

"Is that as bad as it looks?" Pramod's voice choked over the suit comm.

"Yes," sighed Leo.

"You can't—do a welded repair on those, can you?" Pramod's voice was rising. "What are we going to do?"

Fatigue and fear, the worst possible combination— Leo kept his own tired voice flat. "My suit supply-level readout says we're going to go Inside and take a break right now. After that we'll see."

To Leo's immense relief, by the time he had un-suited Vatel had retrieved the errant pusher and brought it back to dock at its Habitat module. They unloaded a frightened, bruised quaddie pilot.

"It locked on, I couldn't get it off," she wept. "What did I hit? Did I hit somebody? I didn't *want* to dump the fuel, it was the only way I could think of to kill the jet. I'm sorry I wasted it. I couldn't shut it off . . ."

She was, Leo guessed, all of fourteen years old. "How long have you been on work shift?" he demanded.

"Since we started," she sniffed. She was shaking, all four of her hands trembling, as she hung in air sideways to him. He resisted an urge to straighten her "up."

"Good God, child, that's over 26 hours straight. Go take a break. Eat something and go sleep."

She looked at him in bewilderment. "But the dorm units are all cut off and bundled with the creches. I can't get there from here."

"Is that why . . . ? Look, three-fourths of the Habitat is inaccessible right now. Stake out a corner of the suit locker room or anywhere you can find." He gazed at her tears in bafflement a moment, then added, "It's *allowed.*" She clearly wanted her own familiar sleep sack, which Leo was in no position to supply.

"All by myself?" she said in a very small voice.

She'd probably never slept with less than seven other kids in the room in her life, Leo reflected. He took a deep, controlling breath—he would *not* start screaming at her, no matter how wonderfully it would relieve his own feelings—how had he gotten sucked into this children's crusade, anyway? He could not at the moment recall.

"Come along." He took her by the hand off to the locker room, found a laundry bag to hook to the wall, and helped stuff her into it along with a packaged sandwich. Her face peered from the opening, making him feel for a weird moment like a man in process of drowning a sack of kittens.

"There." He forced a smile. "All better, huh?"

"Thank you, Leo," she sniffed. "I'm sorry about the pusher. And the fuel."

"We'll take care of it." He winked heroically. "Get some sleep, huh? There'll still be plenty of work to do when you wake up, you're not going to miss anything. Uh . . . nighty-night."

" 'Night . . ."

In the corridor he rubbed his hands over his face. "*Nng . . .*"

Three-fourths of the Habitat inaccessible? It was more like nine-tenths by now. And all the module bundles were running on emergency power, waiting to be reattached to the main power supply as they were loaded into the Superjumper. It was vital to the safety and comfort of those trapped aboard various sub-units that the Habitat be fully reconfigured and made operational as swiftly as possible.

Not to mention everyone's having to start to learn their way around a new maze. Multiple compromises had driven the design—creche units, for example, could go in an interior bundle; docks and locks had to be positioned facing out into space; some garbage vents were unavoidably cut off, power mods had to be positioned just *so*, the nutrition units, now serving some three thousand meals a day, required certain kinds of access to storage. . . . Getting everyone's routines readjusted was going to be an unholy mess for a while, even assuming all the module bundles were loaded in right-side-up and attached head-end-round when Leo wasn't personally supervising—or even when he *was* watching, Leo admitted to himself. His face was numb.

And now the kicker-question—should they continue loading at all onto a Superjumper that was, just possibly, fatally disabled? The vortex mirror, God. Why couldn't she have rammed one of the normal space thruster arms? Why couldn't she have run over Leo himself?

"Leo!" called a familiar male voice.

Floating down the corridor, his arms crossed angrily, came the jump pilot, Ti Gulik. Silver starfished from hand-grip to hand-grip behind him, trailed by Pramod. Gulik grabbed a grip and swung to a halt beside Leo. Leo's gaze crossed Silver's in a frustratingly brief and silent *Hello!* before the jump pilot pinned him to the wall.

"What have your damned quaddies done to my Necklin rods?" sputtered Ti. "We go to all this trouble to catch this ship, bring it here, and practically the first thing you do is start smashing it up—I barely got it parked!" His voice faded "Please—tell me that little mutant," he waved at Pramod, "got it wrong . . . ?"

Leo cleared his throat. "One of the pusher attitude jets apparently got stuck in an 'on' position, throwing the pusher into an uncontrollable spin. The term 'unpreventable accident' is not in my vocabulary, but it certainly wasn't the quaddie's fault."

"Huh," said Ti. "Well, at least you're not trying to pin it on the pilot . . . but what was the damage, really?"

"The rod itself wasn't hit—"

Ti let out a relieved breath.

"—but the portside titanium vortex mirror was smashed."

Ti's breath became a howl in a minor key. "That's just as bad!"

"Calm down! Maybe not quite as bad. I have one or two ideas yet. I wanted to talk to you anyway. When we took over the Habitat, there was a freight shuttle in dock."

Ti eyed him suspiciously. "Lucky you. So?"

"Planning, not luck. Something Silver doesn't know yet—" Leo caught her eye; she braced herself visibly, soberly intent upon his words, "we weren't able to get Tony back before we took over the Habitat. He's still in hospital downside on Rodeo."

"Oh, no," Silver whispered. "Is there any way—?"

Leo rubbed his aching forehead. "Maybe. I'm not sure it's good military thinking—the precedent had to do with sheep, I believe—but I don't think I could live with myself if we didn't at least try to get him back. Dr. Minchenko has also promised to go with us if we can somehow pick up Madame Minchenko. She's downside too."

"Dr. Minchenko stayed?" Silver clapped her hands, clearly thrilled. "Oh, good."

"Only if we retrieve the Madame," Leo cautioned. "So that's two reasons to chance a downside foray. We have a shuttle, we have a pilot—"

"Oh, no," began Ti, "now, wait a minute—"

"—and we desperately need a spare part. If we can locate a vortex mirror in a Rodeo warehouse—"

"You won't," Ti cut in firmly. "Jumpship repairs are handled solely by the District orbital yards at Orient IV. Everything's warehoused on that end. I know 'cause we had a problem once and had to wait four days for a repair crew to arrive from there. Rodeo's got nothing to do with Superjumpers, nothing." He crossed his arms.

"I was afraid of that," said Leo lowly. "Well, there's one other possibility. We could try to fabricate a new one, here on the spot."

Ti looked like a man sucking on a lemon. "Graf, you don't weld those things together out of scrap iron. I know damn well they make 'em all in one piece—something about joins impeding the field flow—and that sucker's three meters wide at the top end! The thing they stamp them out with weighs multi tons. And the precision required—it would take you six months to put a project like that together!"

Leo gulped, and held up both hands, fingers spread. Had he been a quaddie he might have been tempted to double the estimate, but, "Ten hours," he said. "Sure, I'd like to have six months. Downside. In a foundry. With a monster alloy-steel press die machined to the millimicron, just like the big boys. And mass water-cooling, and a team of assistants, and unlimited funding—I'd be all set up to make ten thousand units. But we don't need ten thousand units. There *is* another way. A quick-and-dirty one-shot, but one shot's all we're going to have time for. But I can't be up *here*, refabricating a vortex mirror, and down *there*, rescuing Tony, both at the same time. The quaddies can't go. I need you, Ti. I'd have needed you to pilot the shuttle in any case. Now I'll just need you to do a little more."

"Look, you," Ti began. "Theory was, I was going to get out of this with a whole skin 'cause GalacTech would think I was kidnapped, and had Jumped you out with a gun to my head. A nice, simple, believable scenario. This is getting too damned complicated. Even if I could pull off a stunt like that, they're not going to believe I did it under duress. What would keep me from flying downside—and just turning myself in? That's the sort of questions they'll be asking, you can bet your ass. No, dammit. Not for love nor money."

"I know," Leo growled. "We've offered both." Ti glared at him, but ducked his head to evade Silver's eyes.

A thin young voice was echoing down the corridor. "Leo? Leo . . . !"

"Here!" Leo answered. What now . . . ?

One of the younger quaddies swung into sight and darted toward them. "Leo! We've been looking all over for you. Come quick!"

"What is it?"

"An urgent message. On the comm. From downside."

"We're not answering their messages. Total blackout, remember? The less information we give them, the longer it's going to take them to figure out what to do about us."

"But it's Tony!"

Leo's guts knotted, and he lurched after the messenger. Silver, pale, and the others followed hot behind.

* * *

The holovid solidified, showing a hospital bed. Tony was braced against the raised backrest, looking directly into the vid. He wore T-shirt and shorts, a white bandage around his left lower bicep, a thick stiffness to his torso hinting at wrappings beneath. His face was furrowed, flushed over a pale underlay. His blue eyes shifted nervously, white-rimmed like a frightened pony's, to the right of his bed where Bruce Van Atta stood.

"Took you long enough to answer your call, Graf," Van Atta said, smirking unpleasantly.

Leo swallowed hard. "Hullo, Tony. We haven't forgotten you, up here. Claire and Andy are all right, and back together—"

"You're here to listen, Graf, not talk," Van Atta interrupted. He fiddled with a control. "There, I've just cut your audio, so you can save your breath. All right, Tony," Van Atta prodded the quaddie with a silver-colored rod—what was it? Leo wondered fearfully—"say your piece."

Tony's gaze shifted back, to the silent vid image Leo guessed, and his eyes widened urgently. He took a deep breath and began gabbling, "Whatever you're doing, Leo, keep doing it. Never mind about me. Get Claire away—get Andy away—"

The holovid blacked out abruptly, although the audio channel remained open a moment longer. It emitted a strange spatting noise, a scream, and Van Atta swearing "Hold still, you little shit!" before the sound cut off too.

Leo found himself gripping one of Silver's hands.

"Claire was on her way over," Silver said lowly, "to be in on this call."

Leo's eyes met hers. "I think you'd better go divert her."

Silver nodded grim understanding. "Right." She swung away.

The vid came back up. Tony was huddled silently in the far corner of the bed, head down, hands over his face. Van Atta stood glaring, rocking furiously on his heels.

"The kid's a slow learner, evidently," Van Atta snarled to Leo. "I'll make it short and clear, Graf. You may hold hostages, but if you so much as touch 'em, you can be swung in any court in the galaxy. *I've* got a hostage I can do anything I want to, legally. And if you don't think I will, just try me. Now, we're going to be sending a Security shuttle up there in a little while to restore order. And you *will* cooperate with it." He held up the silvery rod, pressed something; Leo saw an electric spark spit from its tip. "This is a simple device, but I can get real creative with it, if you force me to. Don't force me to, Leo."

"Nobody's forcing you to—" Leo began.

"Ah," Van Atta interrupted, "just a minute . . ." he touched his holovid control, "now talk so's I can hear you. And it had better be something I want to hear."

"Nobody here can force you to do anything," Leo grated. "Whatever you do, you do of your own free will. We don't have any hostages. What we have is three volunteers, who chose to stay for—for their consciences' sake, I guess."

"If Minchenko's one of them, you'd better watch your back, Leo. Conscience hell, he wants to hang onto his own little empire. You're a fool, Graf. Here—" he made a motion off-vid, "come talk to him in his own language, Yei."

Dr. Yei stepped stiffly into view, met Leo's eyes and moistened her lips. "Mr. Graf, please, stop this madness. What you are trying to do is incredibly dangerous, for all concerned—" Van Atta illustrated

this by waving the electric prod over her head with a
sour grin; she glanced at him in irritation, but said
nothing and plowed on grimly, "Surrender now, and
the damage can at least be minimized. Please. For
everyone's sake. You have the power to stop this."

Leo was silent for a moment, then leaned forward.
"Dr. Yei, I'm forty-five thousand kilometers up. You're
there in the same room . . . *you* stop him." He
flicked the holovid off, and floated in numb silence.

"Is that wise?" choked Ti uncertainly.

Leo shook his head. "Don't know. But without an
audience, there's no reason to carry on a show, surely."

"Was that acting? How far will that guy really go?"

"In the past I've known him to have a pretty
uncontrolled temper, when he got wound up. An
appeal to his self-interest usually unwound him. But
as you've realized yourself, the, um career rewards
in this mess are minimal. I don't know how far he'll
go. I don't think even he knows."

After a long pause Ti said, "Do you, ah—still need
a shuttle pilot, Leo?"

Chapter 14

Silver clutched the arms of the shuttle co-pilot's seat tightly in mixed exhilaration and fear. Her lower hands curled over the seat's front edge, seeking purchase. Deceleration and gravity yanked at her. She spared a hand to double-check the latch of the shoulder-harness snugging her in as the shuttle altered its attitude to nose-down and the ground heaved into view. Red desert mountains, rocky and forbidding, wrinkled and buckled below them, passing faster and faster as they dropped closer.

Ti sat beside her in the commander's chair, his hands and feet barely moving the controls in tiny, constant corrections, eyes flicking from readout to readout and then to the real horizon, totally absorbed. The atmosphere roared over the shuttle's skin and the craft rocked violently in some passing wind shear. Silver began to see why Leo, despite his expressed anguish at the risk to them all of losing Ti downside, had not substituted Zara or one of the other pusher pilots in Ti's stead. Even barring the foot pedals, landing on a planet was definitely a discipline apart from jetting about in free fall, especially in a vehicle nearly the size of a Habitat module.

"There's the dry lake bed," Ti nodded forward,

addressing her without taking his eyes from his work. "Right on the horizon."

"Will it be—very much harder than landing on a shuttleport runway?" Silver asked in worry.

"No problem," Ti smiled. "If anything, it's easier. It's a big puddle—it's one of our emergency alternate landing sites anyway. Just avoid the gullies at the north end, and we're home free."

"Oh," said Silver, reassured. "I hadn't realized you'd landed out here before."

"Well, I haven't, actually," Ti murmured, "not having had an emergency yet. . . ." He sat up more intently, taking a tighter grip on the controls, and Silver decided perhaps she would not distract him with further conversation just now.

She peeked around the edge of her seat at Dr. Minchenko, holding down the engineer's station behind them, to see how he was taking all this. His return smile was sardonic, as if to tease her for her anxiety, but she noticed his hand checking his seat straps, too.

The ground rushed up from below. Silver was almost sorry they had not, after all, waited for the cover of night to make this landing. At least she wouldn't have been able to see her death coming. She could, of course, close her eyes. She closed her eyes, but opened them again almost immediately. Why miss the last experience of one's life? She was sorry Leo had never made a pass at her. He must suffer from stress accumulation too, surely. Faster and faster . . .

The shuttle bumped, bounced, banged, rocked, and roared out over the flat cracked surface. She was sorry *she* had never made a pass at Leo. Clearly, you could die while waiting for other people to start your life for you. Her seat harness cut across her breasts as deceleration sucked her forward and the rumbling vibration rattled her teeth.

"Not quite as smooth as a runway," Ti shouted, grinning and sparing her a bright glance at last. "But good enough for company work . . ."

All right, so nobody else was gibbering in terror, maybe this was the way a landing was supposed to be. They rolled to a quite demure stop in the middle of nowhere. Toothed carmine mountains ringed an empty horizon. Silence fell.

"Well," said Ti, "here we are. . . ." He released his harness with a snap and turned to Dr. Minchenko, struggling up out of the engineer's seat. "Now what? Where is she?"

"If you would be good enough," said Dr. Minchenko, "to provide us with an exterior scan . . ."

A view of the horizon scrolled slowly several times through a monitor, as the minutes ticked by in Silver's brain. The gravity, Silver discovered, was not nearly so awful as Claire had described it. It was much like the time spent under acceleration on the way to the wormhole, only very still and without vibration, or like at the Transfer Station only stronger. It would have helped if the design of the seat had matched the design of her body.

"What if Rodeo Traffic Control saw us land?" she said. "What if GalacTech gets here first?"

"It's more frightening to think Traffic Control might have missed us," said Ti. "As for who gets here first—well, Dr. Minchenko?"

"Mm," he said glumly. Then he brightened, leaned forward and froze the scan, and put his finger on a small smudge in the screen, perhaps 15 kilometers distant.

"Dust devil?" said Ti, plainly trying to control his hopes.

The smudge focused. "Land rover," said Dr. Minchenko, smiling in satisfaction. "Oh, *good* girl."

The smudge grew into a boiling vortex of orange dust spun up behind a speeding land rover. Five minutes later the vehicle braked to a halt beside the shuttle's forward hatchway. The figure under the dusty bubble canopy paused to adjust a breath mask, then the bubble swung up and the side ramp swung down.

Dr. Minchenko adjusted his own breath mask firmly over his nose and, followed by Ti, rushed down the shuttle stairs to assist the frail, silver-haired woman who was struggling with an assortment of odd-shaped packages. She gave them all up to the men with evident gladness but for a thick black case shaped rather like a spoon which she clutched to her bosom in much the same way, Silver thought, as Claire clutched Andy. Dr. Minchenko shepherded his lady anxiously upward toward the airlock—her knees moved stiffly, on the stairs—and through, where they could at last pull down their masks and speak clearly.

"Are you all right, Warren?" Madame Minchenko asked.

"Perfectly," he assured her.

"I could bring almost nothing—I scarcely knew what to choose."

"Think of the vast amounts of money we shall save on shipping charges, then."

Silver was fascinated by the way gravity gave form to Madame Minchenko's dress. It was a warm, dark fabric with a silver belt at the waist, and hung in soft folds about her booted ankles. The skirt swirled as Madame Minchenko stepped, echoing her agitation.

"It's utter madness. We're too old to become refugees. I had to leave my harpsichord!"

Dr. Minchenko patted her sympathetically on the

shoulder. "It wouldn't work in free fall anyway. The little pluckers fall back into place by gravity." His voice cracked with urgency, "But they're trying to kill my quaddies, Ivy!"

"Yes, yes, I understand . . ." Madame Minchenko twitched a somewhat strained and absent smile at Silver, who hung one-handed from a strap listening. "You must be Silver?"

"Yes, Madame Minchenko," said Silver breathlessly in her most-politest voice. This woman was quite the most aged downsider Silver had ever seen, bar Dr. Minchenko and Dr. Cay himself.

"We must go now, to get Tony," Dr. Minchenko said. "We'll be back as quick as we can drive. Silver will help you, she's very good. Hold the ship!"

The two men hustled back out, and within moments the land rover was boiling off across the barren landscape.

Silver and Madame Minchenko were left regarding each other.

"Well," said Madame Minchenko.

"I'm sorry you had to leave all your things," said Silver diffidently.

"H'm. Well, I can't say I'm sorry to be leaving here." Madame Minchenko's glance around the shuttle's cargo bay took in Rodeo by implication.

They shuffled forward to the pilot's compartment and sat; the monitor scanned the monotonous horizon. Madame Minchenko still clutched her giant spoon suitcase in her lap. Silver hitched herself around in her wrong-shaped seat and tried to imagine what it would be like to be married to someone for more than twice the length of her own life. Had Madame Minchenko been young once? Surely Dr. Minchenko had been old forever.

"However did you come to be married to Dr. Minchenko?" Silver asked.

"Sometimes I wonder," Madame Minchenko murmured dryly, half to herself.

"Were you a nurse, or a lab tech?"

She looked up with a little smile. "No, dear, I was never a bioscientist. Thank God." Her hand caressed the black case. "I'm a musician. Of sorts."

Silver perked with interest. "Synthavids? Do you program? We've had some synthavids in our library, the company library that is."

The corner of Madame Minchenko's mouth twisted up in a half-smile. "There's nothing synthetic in what I do. I'm a registered historian-performer. I keep old skills alive—think of me as a live museum exhibit, somewhat in need of dusting—only a few spider webs clinging to my elbow. . . ." She unlatched her case and opened it to Silver's inspection. Burnished reddish wood, satin-smooth, caught and played back the colored lights of the pilot's compartment. Madame Minchenko lifted the instrument and tucked it under her chin. "It's a violin."

"I've seen pictures of them," Silver offered. "Is it real?"

Madame Minchenko smiled, and drew her bow across the strings in a quick succession of notes. The music ran up and down like—like quaddie children in the gym, was the only simile Silver could think of. The volume was astounding.

"Where do those wires on top attach to the speakers?" Silver inquired, pushing up on her lower hands and craning her neck.

"There are no speakers. The sound all comes from the wood."

"But it filled the compartment!"

Madame Minchenko's smile became almost fierce. "*This* instrument could fill an entire concert hall."

"Do you . . . play concerts?"

"Once, when I was very young—your age, maybe . . . I went to a school that taught such skills. The only school for music on my planet. A colonial world, you see, not much time for the arts. There was a competition—the winner was to travel to Earth, and have a recording career. Which he subsequently did. But the recording company underwriting the affair was only interested in the very best. *I* came in second. There is room for so very few . . ." her voice faded in a sigh. "I was left with a pleasing personal accomplishment that no one wanted to listen to. Not when they had only to plug in a disc to hear not just the best from my world, but the best in the galaxy. Fortunately, I met Warren about then. My permanent patron and audience of one. Probably as well I wasn't trying to make a career of it, we moved so often in those days, when he was finishing school and starting work with GalacTech. I've done some teaching here and there, to interested antiquarians . . ." She tilted her head at Silver. "And did they teach you any music, with all the things they've been teaching you up on that satellite?"

"We learned some songs when we were little," said Silver shyly. "And then there were the flute-toots. But they didn't last long."

"Flute-toots?"

"Little plastic things you blew in. *They* were real. One of the creche-mothers brought them up when I was about, oh, eight. But then they sort of got all over the place, and people were complaining about the, um, tooting. So she had to take them all back."

"I see. Warren never mentioned the flute-toots."

Madame Minchenko's eyebrows quirked. "Ah . . . what sort of songs?"

"Oh. . ." Silver drew breath, and sang, "Roy G. Biv, Roy G. Biv, he's the color quaddie that the spectrum gives; Red-orange-yellow, green and blue, indigo, violet, all for you—" she broke off, flushing. Her voice sounded so wavery and weak, compared to that astonishing violin.

"I see," said Madame Minchenko in a strangely choked voice. Her eyes danced, though, so Silver didn't think she was offended. "Oh, Warren," she sighed, "the things you have to answer for . . ."

"May I," Silver began, and stopped. Surely she would not be permitted to touch that lavish antique. What if she forgot to hold onto it for a moment and the gravity pulled it from her hands?

"Try it?" Madame Minchenko finished her thought. "Why not? We appear to have a little time to kill, here."

"I'm afraid—"

"Tut. Oh, I used to protect this one. It sat unplayed for years, locked up in climate-controlled vaults . . . dead. Then of late I began to wonder what I was saving it for. Here, now. Raise your chin, so; tuck, so," Madame Minchenko curled Silver's fingers around the violin's neck. "What nice long fingers you have, dear. And, er . . . what a *lot* of them. I wonder . . ."

"What?" asked Silver as Madame Minchenko trailed off.

"Hm? Oh. I was just having a mental picture of a quaddie in free fall with a twelve-string guitar. If you weren't squashed into a chair as you are now you could bring that lower hand up . . ."

It was a trick of the light, perhaps, of Rodeo's westering sun sinking toward the sawtoothed horizon and sending its red beams through the cabin windows, but Madame Minchenko's eyes seemed to gleam. "Now arch your fingers, so . . ."

Fire.

The first problem had been to find enough pure scrap titanium around the Habitat to add to the mass of the ruined vortex mirror to allow for the inevitable losses during refabrication. A forty-percent extra mass margin would have been enough for Leo to feel comfortable with.

There ought to have been titanium storage tanks for nasty corrosive liquids—a single, say, hundred-liter tank would have done the trick—conduits, valves, something. For the first desperate hour of scrounging Leo was convinced his plan would come to grief right there in Step One. Then he found it in, of all places, Nutrition; a cooler full of titanium storage canisters massing a good half-kilo apiece. Their varied contents were hastily dumped into every substitute container Leo and his quaddie raiders could find. "Clean-up," Leo had called guiltily over his shoulder to the appalled quaddie girl now running Nutrition, "is left as an exercise for the student."

The second problem had been to find a place to work. Pramod had pointed out one of the abandoned Habitat modules, a cylinder some four meters in diameter. It was the work of another two hours to tear holes in the side for entry and pack one end of it with all the conductive scrap metal mass they could find. The mass was then surfaced with more abandoned Habitat module skin, pounded out and rendered as nearly glass-smooth as they could make it in a shallow concave bowl of carefully calculated arc that spanned the diameter of the module.

Now their mass of scrap titanium hung weightless in the center of the module. The broken-up pieces of the vortex mirror and the flattened-out food canisters were all bound together by a spool of pure titanium wire some brilliant quaddie child had produced for them out of Stores. The dense grey metal glittered and glowed in their work-lights and the reflection from a shaft of hard-edged sunlight falling through one of their entry holes.

Leo glanced around the chamber one last time. Four worksuited quaddies each manned a laser unit braced around the walls, bracketing the titanium mass. Leo's measuring instruments floated tethered to his belt, ready to his pressure-gloved hands. It was time. Leo touched his helmet control, darkening his faceplate.

"Commence firing," said Leo into his suit comm.

Four beams of laser light lanced out in unison, pouring into the scrap. For the first few minutes, nothing appeared to be happening. Then it began to glow, dark red, bright red, yellow, white—then, visibly, one of the ex-food canisters began to sag, flowing into the jumble. The quaddies continued to pour in the energy.

The mass was beginning to drift slightly, one of Leo's readouts told him, although the effect was not yet visible to the naked eye. "Unit Four, power-up about ten percent," Leo instructed. One of the quaddies flashed a lower palm in acknowledgement and touched his control box. The drift stopped. Good, his bracketing was working. Leo had had a horrid vision of the molten mass of metal drifting off into the side wall, or worse, fatally brushing into somebody, but the very beams that melted it seemed enough to control its motion, at least in the absence of stronger sources of momentum.

Now the melt was obvious, the metal becoming a white glowing blob of liquid floating in the vacuum, struggling toward the shape of a perfect sphere. *Boy, is that stuff ever going to be pure when we're done,* Leo reflected with satisfaction.

He checked his monitoring devices. Now they were coming up on a moment of critical judgment; when to stop? They must pour in enough energy to achieve an absolutely uniform melt, no funny lumps left in the middle of the gravy. But not too much; even though it was not visible to the eye Leo knew there was metal vapor pouring off that bubble now, part of his calculated loss.

More importantly, looking ahead to the next step— every kilocalorie they dumbed into that titanium mass was going to have to be brought back out. Planetside, the shape he was trying to get would have been formed against a copper mold, with lots and lots of water to carry away the heat at the desired rate, in this case rapidly; single-crystal splat-cooling, it was called. Well, at least he'd figured out how to achieve the splat part of it. . . .

"Cease firing," Leo ordered.

And there it hung, their sphere of molten metal, blue-white with the violent heat energy contained within it, perfect. Leo checked and re-checked its centered position, and had laser number two give it one more half-second blast not for melt but for momentum's sake.

"All right," said Leo into his suit comm. "Now let's get everything out of this module that's going out, and double-check everything that's staying. Last thing we need now is for somebody to drop his wrench in the soup pot, right?"

Leo joined the quaddies in shoving their equipment unceremoniously out the holes torn in the side of the module. Two of his laser operators went with it, two stayed with Leo. Leo checked centering again, and then they all strapped themselves to the walls.

Leo switched channels in his suit comm. "Ready, Zara?" he called.

"Ready, Leo," the quaddie pilot responded from her pusher, now attached to the gutted module's stern.

"Now remember, slow and gentle does it. But firm. Pretend your pusher is a scalpel, and you're just about to operate on one of your friends or something."

"Right, Leo." There was a grin in her voice. *Don't swagger, girl,* Leo prayed inwardly.

"Go when you're ready."

"Going. Hang on up there!"

There was at first no perceivable change. Then Leo's harness straps began to tug gently at him. It was the Habitat module, not the molten ball of titanium, that was moving, Leo reminded himself. The metal did not drift; it was the back wall that moved forward and engulfed it.

It was working, by God it was working! The metal bubble touched the back wall, spread out, and settled into its shallow bowl mold.

"Increase acceleration by the first increment," Leo called into his comm. The pusher powered up, and the molten titanium circle spread, its edges growing toward the desired diameter some three meters wide, already losing its bright glow. Creating a titanium blank of controlled thickness, ready (after cooling) for explosive molding into its final subtle form.

"Steady on. That does it!"

Splat-cooling? Well, not exactly. Leo was uncomfortably aware that they were probably not going to achieve a perfect internal single-crystal freeze. But it would be good, good enough—as long as it was good enough that they didn't have to melt it down and start all over again, that was the most Leo dared pray for. They might, barely, have time to make one of these suckers. Not two. And when *was* the threatened response from Rodeo arriving? Soon, surely.

He wondered briefly what the new gravity technology was going to do to fabrication problems in space like this. Revolutionize seemed too mild a term, certainly. *Too bad we didn't have some now*, he thought. Still—he grinned, concealed within his helmet—they were doing all right.

He pointed his temperature gauge at the back wall. The piece was cooling almost as rapidly as he had hoped. They were still due for a couple of hours of driving around until it had dumped enough heat to remove from the wall and handle without danger of deformation.

"All right, Bobbi, I'm leaving you and Zara in charge here," Leo said. "It's looking good. When the temperature drops to about five hundred degrees centigrade, bring it on back. We'll try to be ready for the final cooling and the second phase of the shaping."

Carefully, trying not to add excess vibration to the walls, Leo loosed his harness and climbed to the exit hole. From this distance he had a fine view of the D-620, now more than half loaded, and Rodeo beyond. Better go now, before the view became more distant than his suit jets could close.

He activated his jets and zipped quickly away from the side of the still-gently-accelerating module-and-pusher unit. It chugged off, looking a drunken, jury-rigged wreck indeed, concealing hope in its heart.

Leo aimed toward the Habitat, and Phase II of his Jumpships-Repaired-While-U-Wait scheme.

It was sunset on the dry lake bed. Silver gazed

anxiously into the monitor in the shuttle control cabin as it swept the horizon, brightening and darkening each time the red ball of the sun rolled past.

"They can't possibly be back for at least another hour," Madame Minchenko, watching her, pointed out, "in the best case."

"That's not who I'm looking for," answered Silver.

"Hm." Madame Minchenko drummed her long, age-sculptured fingers on the console, unlatched and tilted back the co-pilot's seat, and stared thoughtfully at the cabin roof. "No, I suppose not. Still—if GalacTech traffic control saw you land and sent out a jetcopter to investigate, they should have been here before now. Perhaps they missed your landing after all."

"Perhaps they're just not very organized," suggested Silver, "and they'll be along any minute."

Madame Minchenko sighed. "All too likely." She regarded Silver, pursing her lips. "And what are you supposed to do in that case?"

"I have a weapon." Silver touched the laser-solderer, lying seductively on the console before the pilot-commander's seat in which she sprawled. "But I'd rather not shoot anybody else. Not if I can help it."

"Anybody *else*?" There was a shade more respect in Madame Minchenko's voice.

Shooting people was such a *stupid* activity, why should everybody—anybody!—be so impressed? Silver wondered irritably. You would think she had done something truly great, like discover a new treatment for black stem-rot. Her mouth tightened.

Then her lips parted, and she leaned forward to stare into the monitor. "Oh, oh. Here comes a ground car."

"Not our boys already, surely," said Madame

Minchenko in some unease. "Has something gone wrong, I wonder?"

"It's not your land rover." Silver fiddled with the resolution. The slanting sunlight poured through the dust, turning it into a glowing red smokescreen. "I think . . . it's a GalacTech Security groundcar."

"Oh, dear." Madame Minchenko sat up straight. "Now what?"

"We don't open the hatches, anyway. No matter what."

In a few minutes the groundcar pulled up about fifty meters from the shuttle. An antenna rose from its roof and quivered demandingly. Silver switched on the comm—it was so irritating, not to have the full use of her lower arms—and called up a menu of the comm channels from the computer. The shuttle seemed to have access to an inordinate number of them. Security audio was 9999. She tuned them in.

"—by God! Hey, you in there—answer!"

"Yes, what do you want?" said Silver.

There was a spluttery pause. "Why didn't you answer?"

"I didn't know you were calling me," Silver answered logically.

"Yeah, well—this freight shuttle is the property of GalacTech."

"So am I. So what?"

"Eh . . . ? Look, lady, this is Sergeant Fors of GalacTech Security. You have to disembark and turn this shuttle over to us."

A voice in the background, not quite sufficiently muffled, inquired, "Hey, Bern—d'you think we'll get the ten percent bonus for recovering stolen property on *this* one?"

"Dream on," growled another voice. "Nobody's gonna give *us* a quarter million."

Madame Minchenko held up a hand, and leaned forward to cut in, quavering, "Young man, this is Ivy Minchenko. My husband, Dr. Minchenko, has commandeered this craft in order to respond to an urgent medical emergency. Not only is this his right, it's his legally compelled duty—and *you* are required by GalacTech regulation to assist, not hinder him."

A somewhat baffled growl greeted this. "I'm required to take this shuttle back. Those are my orders. Nobody told me anything about any medical emergency."

"Well, I'm telling you!"

The background voice again, ". . . it's just a couple of women. Come on!"

The sergeant: "Are you going to open the hatch, lady?"

Silver did not respond. Madame Minchenko raised an inquiring eyebrow, and Silver shook her head silently. Madame Minchenko sighed and nodded.

The sergeant repeated his demands, his voice fraying—he stopped just short, Silver felt, of degenerating into obscenities. After a minute or two he broke off.

After a few more minutes the doors of the ground car winged up and the three men, now wearing breath masks, clambered out to stamp over and stare up at the hatches of the shuttle high over their heads. They returned to the groundcar, got in—it circled. Going away? Silver hoped against hope. No, it came up and parked again under the forward shuttle hatch. Two of the men rummaged in the back for tools, then climbed to the car's roof.

"They've got some kind of cutting things," said Silver in alarm. "They must be going to try to cut their way in."

Banging reverberated through the shuttle.

Madame Minchenko nodded toward the laser-solderer. "Is it time for that?" she asked fearfully.

Silver shook her head unhappily. "No. Not again. Besides, I can't let them damage the ship either—it's got to stay spaceworthy or we can't get home."

She had watched Ti. . . . She inhaled deeply and reached for the shuttle controls. The foot pedals were hopelessly awkward to grope for, she would have to get along without them. Right engine, activate; left engine, activate—a purr ran through the ship. Brakes—there, surely. She pulled the lever gently to the "release" position. Nothing happened.

Then the shuttle lurched forward. Frightened at the abrupt motion, Silver hit the brake lever again and the ship rocked to a halt. She searched the outside monitors wildly. Where—?

The shuttle's starboard airfoil had swept over the roof of the Security groundcar, missing it by half a meter. Silver realized with a guilty shudder that she should have checked its height before she began to move. She might have torn the wing right off, with ghastly chaining consequences to them all.

The Security guards were nowhere to be seen—no, there they were, scattered out onto the dry lake bed. One picked himself up out of the dirt and started back toward the groundcar. Now what? If she parked, or even rolled some distance and parked, they would only try again. It couldn't take too many more attempts till they got smart and shot out the shuttle's tires or otherwise immobilized it. A dangerously unstable stand-off.

Silver sucked on her lower lip. Then, leaning forward awkwardly in a seat never designed for quaddies, she released the brakes partway and powered up the port engine. The shuttle shuddered a few meters farther forward, skidding and yawing. Behind them, the monitor showed the groundcar half obscured by orange dust kicked by the exhaust, its image wavering in the heat of it.

She set the brakes as hard as they would go and powered up the port engine yet more. Its purr became a whine—she dared not bring it to the howling pitch Ti had used during landing, who knew what would happen then?

The groundcar's plastic canopy cracked in a crazed starburst and began to sag. If Leo had been right in his description of that hydrocarbon fuel they used downside here for their vehicles, in just a second more she ought to get. . .

A yellow fireball engulfed the groundcar, momentarily brighter than the setting sun. Pieces flew off in all directions, arcing and bouncing fantastically in the gravity field. A glance at her monitors showed Silver the Security men now all running in the other direction.

Silver powered down the port engine, released the brakes, and let the shuttle roll forward across the hard-baked mud. Fortunately, the old lake bed was quite uniform, so she didn't have to worry about the fine points of shuttle operation such as steering.

One of the Security men ran after them for a minute or two, waving his arms, but he fell behind quickly. She let the shuttle roll on for a couple of kilometers, braked again, and shut the engines off.

"Well," she sighed, "that takes care of *them*."

"It certainly does," said Madame Minchenko faintly, adjusting the monitor magnification for a last glance behind. A column of black smoke and a dying orange glow in the distant gathering dusk marked their former parking place.

"I hope all their breath masks were well filled," Silver added.

"Oh, dear," said Madame Minchenko. "Perhaps we ought to go back and . . . do something. Surely they'll have the sense to stay with their car and wait for help, though, and not try to walk off into the desert. The company safety vids always emphasize that. 'Stay with your vehicle and wait for Search and Rescue.'"

"Aren't they supposed to *be* Search and Rescue?" Silver studied the tiny images in the monitor. "Not much vehicle left. But they all three seem to be staying there. Well . . ." she shook her head. "It's too dangerous for us to try and pick them up. But when Ti and the doctor get back with Tony, maybe the security guards could have your land rover to go home in. If, um, nobody else gets here first."

"Oh," said Madame Minchenko, "that's true. Good idea. I feel much better." She peered reflectively into the monitor. "Poor fellows."

Ice.

Leo watched from the sealed control booth overlooking the Habitat freight bay as four worksuited quaddies eased the intact vortex mirror taken from the D-620's second Necklin rod through the hatch from Outside. The mirror was an awkward object to handle, in effect an enormous shallow titanium funnel, three meters in diameter and a centimeter thick at its broad lip, mathematically curved and thickening to about two centimeters at the central, closed dip. A lovely curve, but definitely non-standard, a fact Leo's re-fabrication ploy must needs cope with.

The undamaged mirror was jockeyed into place, nested into a squiggle of freezer coils. The spacesuited quaddies exited. From the control booth, Leo sealed the Outside hatch and set the air to pump back into the loading bay. In his anxiety Leo literally popped out of the control booth, with a *whoosh* of air from the remaining pressure differential, and had to work his jaw to clear his ears.

The only freezer coils big enough to be adequate to the task had been found by Bobbi in a moment of inspiration, once more in Nutrition. The quaddie girl running the department had moaned when she saw Leo and his work gang approach again. They had ruthlessly ripped the guts out of her biggest freezer compartment and carried them off to their work space, in the largest available docking module now installed as part of the D-620. Less than a quarter of the final Habitat re-assembly was left to go, Leo estimated, despite the fact that he'd pulled a dozen of the best workers onto this project.

In a few minutes three of his quaddies joined Leo in the freight bay. Leo checked them over. They were bundled up in extra T-shirts and shorts and long-sleeved coveralls left by the evicted downsiders, with the legs wrapped tight to their lower arms and secured by elastic bands. They had scrounged enough gloves to go around; good, Leo had been worried about frostbite with all those exposed fingers. His breath smoked in the chilled air.

"All right, Pramod, we're ready to roll. Bring up the water hoses."

Pramod unrolled several lengths of tubing and gave them to the waiting quaddies; another quaddie ran a final check of their connections to the nearest water spigot. Leo switched on the freezer coils and took a hose.

"All right, kids, watch me and I'll show you the trick of it. You must bleed the water slowly onto the cold surfaces, avoiding splash into the air; at the same time you must keep it going constantly enough so that your hoses don't freeze up. If you feel your fingers going numb, take a short break in the next chamber. We don't need any injuries out of this."

Leo turned to the backside of the vortex mirror, nestled among but not touching the freezer coils. The mirror had been in the shade for the last several hours Outside, and was good and cold now. He thumbed his valve and let a silvery blob of water flow onto the mirror's surface. It spread out in swift feathers of ice. He tried some drops on the coils; they froze even faster.

"All right, just like that. Start building up the ice mold around the mirror. Make it as solid as you can, no air pockets. Don't forget to place the little tube to let the air evacuate from the die chamber, later."

"How thick should it be?" asked Pramod, following suit with his hose and watching in fascination as the ice formed.

"At least one meter. At a minimum the mass of the ice must be equal to the mass of the metal. Since we've only got one shot at this, we'll go for at least twice the mass of the metal. We aren't going to be able to recover any of this water, unfortunately. I want to double-check our water reserves, because two meters thick would certainly be better, if we can spare it."

"However did you think of this?" asked Pramod in an awed tone.

Leo snorted, as he realized Pramod had the impression that he was making this entire engineering procedure up out of his head in the heat of the moment. "I didn't invent it. I read about it. It's an old method they used to use for preliminary test designs, before fractal theory was perfected and computer simulations improved to today's standards."

"Oh." Pramod sounded rather disappointed.

Leo grinned. "If you ever have to make a choice

between learning and inspiration, boy, choose learning. It works more of the time."

I hope. Critically, Leo drew back and watched his quaddies work. Pramod had two hoses, one in each set of hands, and was rapidly alternating between them, blob after blob of water flowing onto the coils and the mirror, the ice already starting to thicken visibly. So far he hadn't lost a drop. Leo heaved a weary sigh of relief; it seemed he could safely delegate this part of the task. He gave Pramod a high sign, and left the bay to pursue a part of the job he dared not delegate to anyone else.

Leo got lost twice, threading his way through the Habitat to Toxic Stores, and he'd designed the reconfiguration himself. It was no wonder he passed so many bewildered-looking quaddies on the way. Everyone seemed frantically busy; on the principle of misery-loves-company, Leo could only approve.

Toxic Stores was a chill module sharing no connections whatsoever with the rest of the Habitat but a triple-chambered and always-closed airlock of thick steel. Leo entered to meet one of his own welding and joining gang quaddies still assigned to Habitat reconfiguration on his way out.

"How's it going, Agba?" Leo asked him.

"Pretty good." Agba looked tired. His tan face and skin were marked with red lines, telltales of recent and prolonged time in his worksuit. "Those stupid frozen clamps were really slowing us up, but we're just about to the end of them. How's your thing going?"

"All right so far. I came in to prepare the explosive, we're that far along. Do you remember where the devil in all this—" the module's curved walls were packed with supplies, "we keep the slurry explosive?"

"It *was* over there," Agba pointed.

"Good—" Leo's stomach shrank suddenly. "What do you mean, *was?*" *He only means it's been moved,* Leo suggested hopefully to himself.

"Well, we've been using it up at a pretty good clip, blowing open clamps."

"Blowing them open? I thought you were cutting them off."

"We were, but then Tabbi figured out how to pack a small charge that cracked them apart on the line of the vacuum fuse. About half the time they're reusable. The other half they're no more ruined than if we'd cut 'em." Agba looked quite proud of himself.

"You haven't used it *all* for that, surely!"

"Well, there was a little spillage. Outside, of course," Agba, misapprehending, added in response to Leo's horrified look. He held out a sealed half-liter flask to Leo's inspection. "This is the last of it. I figure it will just about finish the job."

"Nng!" Leo's snatching hands closed around the bottle and clutched it to his stomach like a man smothering a grenade. "I need that! I have to have it!" *I have to have ten times that much!* his thought howled silently.

"Oh," said Agba. "Sorry." He gave Leo a look of limpid innocence. "Does this mean we have to go back to cutting clamps?"

"Yes," squeaked Leo. "Go," he added. Yes, before he exploded himself.

Agba, with an uncertain smile, ducked back out the airlock. It sealed, leaving Leo alone a moment to hyperventilate in peace.

Think, man, think, Leo told himself. *Don't panic.* There was something, some elusive fact or factor in the back of his mind, trying to tell him this wasn't the end, but he could not at present recall . . . Unfortunately, a careful mental review of his calculations, keeping track on his fingers (oh, to be a quaddie!) only confirmed his initial fear.

The explosive fabrication of the titanium blank into the complex shape of the vortex mirror required, besides an assortment of spacers, rings, and clamps, three main parts; the ice die, the metal blank, and the explosive to marry the two. Shotgun wedding indeed. And what is the most important leg of a three-legged stool? The one that is missing, of course. And he'd thought the slurry explosive was going to be the *easy* part . . .

Forlorn, Leo began systematically going around the Toxic Stores module, checking its contents. An extra flask of slurry explosive *might* have been misplaced somewhere. Alas, the quaddies were all too conscientious in their inventory control. Each bin contained only what its label proclaimed, no more, no less. Agba had even updated the label on the bin just now; *Contents, Slurry Explosive Type B-2, one-half liter flasks. Quantity, 0.*

About this time Leo stumbled, literally, over a barrel of gasoline. No, some six barrels of the damn stuff, which had somehow washed up here, now strapped firmly to the walls. God knew where the rest of the hundred tons had gone. Leo wished it all in Hell, where it might at least be of some conceivable use. He would gladly trade the whole hundred tons of it for four aspirins. A hundred tons of gasoline, of which—

Leo blinked, and let out an "aaah" of exultation.

Of which a liter or so, mixed with tetranitro methane, would make an even *more* powerful explosive.

He would have to look it up, to be sure—he would

have to look up the exact proportions in any case—but he was certain he had remembered aright. Learning *and* inspiration, that was the best combination of all. Tetranitro methane was used as an emergency oxygen source in several Habitat and pusher systems. It yielded more O_2 per cc than liquid oxygen, without the temperature and pressure problems of storage, in a highly refined version of the early tetranitro methane candles which, when burned, gave *off* oxygen. Now—oh, God—if only the TNM hadn't all been used by somebody, to—to blow up balloons for quaddie children or some damn thing—they *had* been losing air during the Habitat reconfiguration . . .

Pausing only to put the flask back in its bin and arrange a sign on the barrels reading, in large red print, THIS IS LEO GRAF'S GASOLINE. IF ANYONE ELSE TOUCHES IT HE WILL BREAK ALL THEIR ARMS, he raced out of the Toxic Stores module and away to find the nearest working library computer terminal.

Chapter 15

Twilight lingered on the dry lake bed, the luminous bowl of the sky darkening gradually through a deep turquoise to a star-flecked indigo. Silver found her attention constantly distracted from horizon-scan by the entrancing color changes of the planetary atmosphere seen through the ports. What subtle variety downsiders enjoyed: bands of purple, orange, lemon, green, blue, with cobalt feathers of water vapor melting in the western sky. It was with some regret that Silver switched the scan to infra-red. Its computer-enhanced colors gave clarity to her vision, but seemed crude and garish after the real thing.

At last came the sight her heart desired: a land rover, bouncing over the distant hilly pass and skidding down the last rocky slopes, then peeling out over the lake bed at maximum acceleration. Madame Minchenko hurried out of the pilot's compartment to let down the hatch stairs as the land rover roared to a halt beside the shuttle.

Silver clapped all her hands with delight as she saw Ti thump up the ramp, burdened with Tony clinging piggy-back just as Leo had carted her at the Transfer Station. *They got him! They got him!* Dr. Minchenko followed close behind.

There was a short argument back at the airlock, Doctor and Madame Minchenko's muffled voices, then Dr. Minchenko galloped back down the stairs to crack a cold flare and stick it to the land rover's roof. It gave off a brilliant green glare. Good, the stranded security guards should have no trouble seeing that beacon, Silver decided with some relief.

Silver scrambled back across to the co-pilot's seat as Ti staggered into the pilot's compartment, dumped Tony into the engineer's seat, and vaulted into the command chair. He yanked his breath mask down around his neck with one hand while switching on controls with the other. "Hey, who's been messing with my ship . . . ?"

Silver turned and pulled herself up to look over the top of her seat at Tony, who had rid himself of his own breath mask and was trying to get his seat straps in order. "You made it!" she grinned.

He grinned back. " 'ust bar-ry. 'Er right behin' us." His blue eyes, Silver realized, were huge with pain as well as excitement, his lips swollen.

"What happened to you—?" Silver turned to Ti. "What happened to Tony?"

"That shit Van Atta burned him in the mouth with his damn cattle prod, or whatever the hell that thing was he had," said Ti grimly, his hands dancing over the controls. The engines came alive, lights flickered, and the shuttle began to roll. Ti hit his intercom. "Dr. Minchenko? You folks strapped down back there yet?"

"Just a moment—" came Dr. Minchenko's reply. "There. Yes, go!"

"Did you have any trouble?" asked Silver, sliding back into her seat and groping for her own straps as the shuttle taxied.

"Not at first. We got to the hospital all right,

walked right in with no problem. I thought sure the
nurses were going to question our taking Tony, but
evidently they all think Minchenko is God, there.
We just blasted right through and were on our way
out, with me playing donkey—that's all I am, just
transportation, y'know?—when who should we meet,
going out the door, but that son-of-a-bitch Van Atta
coming in."

Silver gasped.

"We tripped him up—Dr. Minchenko wanted to
stop and beat the shit out of him, on account of
Tony's mouth, but he would have had to delegate
the most of it to me—he *is* an old man, little though
he wants to admit it—I dragged him out to the land
rover. I last heard Van Atta running off screaming
for a security jetcopter. He's surely found one by
now . . ." Ti scanned the monitors nervously. "Yes.
Damn. There," he pointed. A colorized flare swooped
over the mountains, marking the following 'copter's
position in the monitor. "Well, they can't catch us
now."

The shuttle rocked in a wide circle, then halted;
the engines' pitch rose from purr to whine to scream.
Its white landing lights tunneled the darkness in
front of them. Ti released the brakes and the ship
sprang forward, gobbling up the light, with a terrifying noisy rumble that ceased abruptly as they rotated
into the air. The acceleration shoved them all back in
their seats.

"What the *hell* does that idiot think he's doing?" Ti
muttered through his teeth as the jetcopter grew
rapidly in the tracking monitor. "Try to play chicken
with *me*, will you . . . ?"

It was swiftly apparent that was exactly the jetcopter's intent. It arced toward them, diving as they
rose, evidently with some idea of forcing them down.

Ti's mouth thinned to a white line, his eyes blazing, and he powered his ship up further. Silver gritted her teeth, but kept her eyes open.

They passed close enough to see the 'copter out the ports, whipping in a strobe-like flash through their lights. In the blink Silver could see faces through the bubble canopy, frozen white blurs with dark round holes of eyes and mouths, but for one individual, possibly the pilot, who had his hands pressed over his eyes.

Then there was nothing between them and the silver stars.

Fire and ice.

Leo rechecked the tightness of every C-clamp personally, then jetted back a few meters in his worksuit to give his efforts one last visual inspection. They floated in space a safe kilometer's distance from the D-620-Habitat configuration, which hung huge and complete now above Rodeo's arc. Anyway, it looked complete on the outside, as long as you didn't know too much about the hysterical last-minute tie-downs still going on within.

The ice die, when finished, had turned out over three meters wide and nearly two meters thick. Its outer surface was irregular; it might have been a tumbling bit of space debris from some gas giant's ice ring. Its secret inner side precisely duplicated the smooth curve of the vortex mirror that had molded it.

The evacuated inner chamber was capped by layers. First, the titanium blank; next, a layer of pure gasoline for a spacer—a handy second use Leo had found for it: unlike other possible liquids it would not freeze at the ice's present temperature—then the thin plastic divider circle, then his precious TNM-gasoline explosive, then a cap of scrap Habitat skin, then the bars and clamps—all in all, quite a birthday cake. Time to light the candle and make his wish come true, before the ice die began to sublimate in the sunlight.

Leo turned to motion his quaddie helpers to get behind the protective barrier of one of the abandoned Habitat modules floating nearby. Another quaddie, he saw, was just jetting over from the D-620-Habitat configuration. Leo waited a moment, to give him or her time to come up and get behind their shelter. Not a messenger, surely, he had his suit comm for that. . . .

"Hai, Leo," said Tony's voice thickly through the suit comm. "Sorry I'm lae' for work—d'you leave any for me?"

"Tony!"

It wasn't easy, trying to embrace someone through a worksuit, but Leo did his best. "Hey, hey, you're just in time for the best part, boy!" said Leo excitedly. "I saw the shuttle dock a bit ago." Yes, and a horrid turn it had given him for a moment, thinking it was Van Atta's threatened Security force at last, until he'd correctly identified it as theirs. "Didn't think Dr. Minchenko'd let you go anywhere but the infirmary. Is Silver all right? Shouldn't you be resting?"

"She's fine. Dr. Minchenko had a lot t' do, 'n Claire 'n Andy's asleep—I looked in—didn't want to wake the baby."

"You sure you're feeling all right, son? Your voice sounds funny."

"Hurt mah mout'. S'all right."

"Ah." Briefly, Leo explained the task in progress. "You've arrived for the grand finale."

Leo jockeyed his suit around until he could just see over the abandoned module. "What we've got out there, in that box on top—the cherry-bomb on the icing, as it were—is a charge capacitor with a couple thousand volts stored in it. Leads down into a filament placed in the liquid explosive—I used an incandescent light bulb filament with the polyglass envelope knocked off—that thing sticking up is an electric eye swiped from a door control. When we hit it with a burst from this optical laser, it closes the switch—"

"And the 'lectricity sets the ex'losive off?"

"Not exactly. The high voltage pouring through the filament literally explodes the wire, and it's the shock wave from the exploding wire that sets off the TNM and gasoline. Which blows the titanium blank out until it hits the ice die and transfers its momentum, whereupon the titanium stops and the ice, ah, carries the momentum away. Quite spectacularly, which is why we're behind this module . . ." he turned to check his quaddie crew. "Everybody ready?"

"If you can stick your head up and watch, why can't we?" complained Pramod.

"I have to have line-of-sight for the laser," said Leo primly.

Leo aimed the optical laser carefully, and paused a moment for the anxiety rush. So many things could go wrong—he'd checked and re-checked—but there comes a time when one must let all the doubts go and commit to action. He gave himself up to God and pressed the button.

A brilliant, soundless flash, a cloud of boiling vapor, and the ice die exploded, shards flying off in all directions. The effect was utterly enchanting. With an effort Leo tore his gaze away and ducked hastily back behind the module. The afterimage danced across his retinas, teal green and magenta. His pressure-gloved hand, resting against the module's skin, transmitted sharp vibrations as a few high-speed ice cubes pelted against the other side and ricocheted off into space.

Leo remained hunkered a moment, staring rather blankly at Rodeo. "*Now* I'm afraid to look."

Pramod jetted around the module. "It's all in one piece, anyway. It's tumbling—hard to see the exact shape."

Leo inhaled. "Let's go catch it, kids. And see what we've got."

It was the work of a few minutes to capture the work piece. Leo refused to let himself call it "the vortex mirror" just yet—it might still turn out to be scrap metal. The quaddies ran their various scanners over the curving grey surface.

"I can't find any cracks, Leo," said Pramod breathlessly. "It's a few millimeters over-thick in spots, but nowhere too thin."

"Thick we can take care of during the final laser-polish. Thin we can't remedy. I'll take thick," said Leo.

Bobbi waved her optical laser, crossing and re-crossing the curved surface, numbers blurring in her digital readout. "It's in spec! Leo, it's within spec! We did it!"

Leo's innards were melting wax. He breathed a long and very tired sigh of happiness. "All right, kids, let's take it Indoors. Back to the—the—darn it, we can't keep calling it the 'D-620-and Habitat-Reconfiguation'."

"Ah sure can't," agreed Tony.

"So what are we going to name it?" An assortment of possibilities flitted through Leo's mind—*the Ark*—*the Freedom Star*—*Graf's Folly*. . . .

"Home," said Tony simply after a moment. "Let's go home, Leo."

"Home." Leo rolled the name in his mouth. It tasted good. It tasted very good. Pramod nodded, and one of Bobbi's upper hands touched her helmet in salute of the choice.

Leo blinked. Some irritating vapor in his suit's air was making his eyes water, no doubt, and tightening his chest. "Yeah. Let's take our vortex mirror home, gang."

Bruce Van Atta paused in the corridor outside Chalopin's office at Shuttleport Three, to catch his breath and control his trembling. He had a stitch in his side, too. He wouldn't be the least surprised if he were developing an ulcer out of all this. The fiasco out on the dry lake bed had been infuriating. To pave the way, and then have fumbling subordinates totally fail him—utterly infuriating.

Sheer chance, that having returned to his own downside quarters for a much-needed shower and some sleep, he'd awakened to take a piss and called Shuttleport Three to check progress. They might not even have told him about the shuttle landing otherwise! Anticipating Graf's next move, he had flung on his clothes and rushed to the hospital—if he'd been moments sooner, he might have trapped Minchenko within.

He had already chewed out the jetcopter pilot, reamed his ass for his cowardice in failing to force down the launching shuttle, for his dilatory failure to arrive at the lake bed faster. The red-faced pilot had clamped his jaw and his fists and said nothing, doubtless properly ashamed of himself. But the real failure lay higher up—on the other side of these very office doors. He jabbed the control, and they slid aside.

Chalopin, her security captain Bannerji, and Dr. Yei had their heads together around Chalopin's computer vid display. Captain Bannerji had his finger on it, and was saying to Yei, ". . . can get in here. But how *much* resistance, d'you think?"

"You'll surely frighten them very much," said Yei.

"Hm. I'm not crazy about asking my men to go up with stunners against desperate folk with much more lethal weapons. What *is* the real status of those so-called hostages?"

"Thanks to you," snarled Van Atta, "the hostage ratio is now five to zero. They got away with Tony, damn them. Why didn't you put a 27-hour guard on that quaddie like I told you? We should have put a guard on Madame Minchenko, too."

Chalopin's head came up, and she gave him an expressionless stare. "Mr. Van Atta, you seem to be laboring under some misconceptions about the size of my security forces here. I have only ten men, to cover three shifts, seven days a week."

"Plus ten each from each of the other two shuttle-ports. That's thirty. Properly armed, they'd be a substantial strike force."

"I've already borrowed six men from the other two 'ports to cover our own routine, while my entire force is devoted to this emergency."

"Why haven't you stripped them all?"

"Mr. Van Atta, Rodeo Ops is a big company—but a very small town. There are not ten thousand employees here altogether, plus an equal number of dependents not also employed by GalacTech. My Security is a police force, not a military one. They have to cover their own duties, double for emergency squad and search and rescue, and be ready to assist Fire Control."

"Dammit—I drove a wedge for you with Tony. Why didn't you follow up immediately and board the Habitat?"

"I had a force of eight ready to go up to orbit," said Chalopin tartly, "upon your assurance of cooperation from your quaddies. We were not, however, able to get any confirmation of that cooperation from the Habitat itself. They went right back to maintaining comm silence. Then we spotted our freight shuttle returning, so we diverted the forces to capture it—first a ground car, and then, as you yourself came howling in here demanding not two hours ago, a jetcopter."

"Well, get them back together and get them into orbit, dammit!"

"For one thing, *you* left three of them out on the lake bed," remarked Captain Bannerji. "Sergeant Fors just reported in—says their groundcar was disabled. They're returning in Dr. Minchenko's abandoned land rover. It'll be at least another hour before they're back. For another, as Dr. Yei has several times pointed out, we have not yet received authorization to use any kind of deadly force."

"Surely you've got some kind of hot pursuit clause," argued Van Atta. "*That,*" he pointed upward, indicating the events now going on in Rodeo orbit, "is grand theft in progress at the very least. And don't forget, a GalacTech employee has already been shot by them!"

"I haven't overlooked that fact," murmured Bannerji.

"But," Dr. Yei put in, "having asked HQ for authorization to use force, we are now obliged to wait for their reply. What, after all, if they deny the request?"

Van Atta frowned at her, his eyes narrowing. "I knew we should never have asked. You maneuvered us into that, damn you. They'd have swallowed any fait accompli we presented, and been glad of it.

Now . . ." he shook his head in frustration. "Anyway, you're overlooking other sources of personnel. The Habitat staff itself can be used to follow up the opening Security drives into the Habitat."

"They're scattered all over Rodeo by now," Dr. Yei remarked, "back to their downside leave quarters, most of them."

Bannerji cringed visibly. "And do you have any idea the kind of legal liability that situation would present to Security?"

"So deputize 'em—"

A beeping from Chalopin's desk console interrupted Van Atta; a comm tech's face appeared in the vid.

"Administrator Chalopin? Comm Center here. You asked us to advise you of any change in the status of the Habitat or the D-620. They, um—appear to be preparing to leave orbit."

"Put it on up here," Chalopin ordered.

The comm tech produced the flat view from the satellite again. He upped the magnification, and the Habitat-D-620 configuration half-filled the vid. The D-620's two normal-space thruster arms had been augmented by four of the big thruster units the quaddies used to break cargo bundles out of orbit. Even as Van Atta watched in horror, the array of engines flared into life. Stirring a glittering wake of space trash, the monstrous vehicle began to move.

Dr. Yei stood staring open-mouthed, her hands clapped to her chest, her eyes glistening strangely. Van Atta felt like weeping with rage himself.

"You see—" he pointed, his voice cracking, "you see what all this interminable dithering has resulted in? They're getting *away!*"

"Oh, not yet," purred Dr. Yei. "It will be at least a couple of days before they can possibly arrive at the wormhole. There is no just cause for panic." She blinked at Van Atta, went on in an almost hypnotically cloying voice, "You are extremely fatigued, of course, as are we all. Fatigue invites mistakes in judgment. You should rest—get some sleep. . . ."

His hands twitched; he burned to strangle her on the spot. The shuttleport administrator and that idiot Bannerji were nodding, reasonable agreement. A choked growl steamed from Van Atta's throat. "Every minute you wait is going to complicate our logistics—increase the range—increase the risk—"

They all had the same bland stare on their faces. Van Atta didn't need his nose rubbed in it—he could recognize concerted non-cooperation when he smelled it. Damn, damn, damn! He glowered suspiciously at Yei. But his hands were tied, his authority undercut by her sweet reason. If Yei and all her ilk had their way, nobody would ever shoot anybody, and chaos would rule the universe.

He snarled inarticulately, wheeled on his heel, and stalked out.

Claire woke without yet opening her eyes, snugged in her sleep sack. The exhaustion that had drenched her at the end of last shift was slow to ebb from her limbs. She could not hear Andy stirring yet; good, a brief respite before diaper change. In ten minutes she would wake him, and they would exchange services; he relieving her tingling breasts of milk, the milk relieving his hungry tummy—moms need babes, she thought sleepily, as much as babes need moms, an interlocking design, two individuals sharing one biological system . . . so the quaddies shared the technological system of the Habitat, each dependent on all the others. . . .

Dependent on her work, too. What was next?

Germination boxes, grow tubes—no, she could not yank grow tubes around today, today was Acceleration Day—her eyes sprang open. And widened in joy.

"Tony!" she breathed. "How long have you been here?"

"Been watching you abou' fifteen minutes. You sleep pretty. Can I come in?" He hung in air, dressed again in his familiar, comfortable red T-shirt and shorts, watching her in the half-light of her chamber. "Gotta tie down anyway, acceleration's about to start."

"Already . . . ?" She wriggled aside and made room for him, entwining all their arms, touching his face and the alarming bandage still wrapping his torso. "Are you all right?"

"All right now," he sighed happily. "Lying there, in that hospital—well, I didn't expect anyone to come after me. Horrible risk to you—not worth it!" He nuzzled her hair.

"We talked about it, the risk. But we couldn't leave you. Us quaddies—we've got to stick together." She was fully awake now, reveling in his physical reality, muscled hands, bright eyes, fuzzy blond brows. "Losing you would have diminished us, Leo said, and not just genetically. We have to be a people now, not just Claire and Tony and Silver and Siggy—and Andy—I guess it's what Leo calls 'synergistic.' We're something synergistic now."

A strange vibration purred through the walls of her chamber. She hitched around to scoop Andy out of his sleep restraints beside her, and fold him to her with her upper hands while still holding Tony's lowers with her lowers, under the sleep sack's cover. Andy squeaked, lips smacking, and fell back to sleep. Slowly, gently, her shoulderblades began to press against the wall.

"We're on our way," she whispered. "It's starting. . . ."

"It's holding together," Tony observed in wonder. They clung to each other. "Wanted to be with you, at this moment. . . ."

She let the acceleration have her, laying her head against the wall, cushioning Andy on her chest. Something went *clunk* in her cupboard; she'd check it later.

"This is the way to travel," sighed Tony. "Beats stowing away. . . ."

"It's going to be strange, without GalacTech," said Claire after a while. "Just us quaddies . . . what will Andy's world be like, I wonder?"

"That'll be up to us, I guess," said Tony soberly. "That's almost scarier than downsiders with guns, y'know? Freedom. Huh." He shook his head. "Not like I'd pictured it."

Yei's suggested sleep was out of the question. Morosely, Van Atta returned not to his living quarters, but to his own downside office. He had not checked in there for a couple of weeks. It was about midnight now, Shuttleport Three time; his downside secretary was off-shift. It suited his foul humor to sulk alone.

After about twenty minutes spent muttering to himself in the dim light, he decided to scan his accumulated electronic mail. His usual office routine had gone to pot these last few weeks anyway, and of course the events of the last two days had blown it entirely to hell. Perhaps a dose of boring routine would calm him enough to consider sleep after all.

Obsolete memos, out-of-date requests for instructions, irrelevant progress reports—the quaddie downside barracks, he noted with a grim snort, was advertised as ready for occupancy at fifteen percent over budget. If he could catch any quaddies to put in them. Instructions from HQ viz wrapping up the Cay Project, unsolicited advice upon salvage and disposal of its various parts . . .

Van Atta stopped abruptly, and backed up two screens on his vid. What had that said again?

Item: Post-fetal experimental tissue cultures. Quantity: 1000. Disposition: cremation by IGS Standard Biolab Rules.

He checked the source of the order. No, it hadn't come through Apmad's office, as he'd first guessed. It came from General Accounting & Inventory Control, part of a long computer-generated list including a variety of lab stores. The order was signed by a human, though, some unknown middle manager in the GA&IC back on Earth.

"By damn," Van Atta swore softly, "I don't think this twit even knows what quaddies *are*." The order had been signed some weeks before.

He read the opening paragraph again. *The Project Chief will oversee the termination of this project with all due speed. The quick release of personnel for other assignments is particularly desirable. You are authorized to make whatever temporary requisitions of material or personnel from adjacent divisions you require to complete this termination by 6/1.*

After another minute his lips drew back in a furious grin. Carefully, he pulled the precious message disc from the machine, pocketed it, and left to go find Chalopin. He hoped he might rout her out of bed.

Chapter 16

"Aren't you about done out there yet?" Ti's taut voice crackled through Leo's worksuit comm.

"One last weld, Ti," Leo answered. "Check that alignment one more time, Tony."

Tony waved a gloved hand in acknowledgement and ran the optical laser check up the line that the electron beam welder would shortly follow. "You're clear, Pramod," he called, and moved aside.

The welder advanced in its tracks across the workpiece, stitching a flange for the last clamp to hold the new vortex mirror in place in its housing. A light on the beam welder's top flashed from red to green, it shut itself off, and Pramod moved in to detach it. Bobbi floated up immediately behind to check the weld with a sonic scan. "It's good, Leo. It'll hold."

"All right. Clear the stuff out and bring the mirror in."

His quaddies moved fast. Within minutes the vortex mirror was fitted into its insulated clamps, its alignment checked. "All right, gang. Let's move back and let Ti run the smoke test."

"Smoke test?" Ti's voice came over the comm. "What's that? I thought you wanted a ten-percent power-up."

"It's an ancient and honorable term for the final step in any engineering project," Leo explained. "Turn it on, see if it smokes."

"I should have guessed," Ti choked. "How very scientific."

"Use is always the ultimate test. But power-up slowly, eh? Gently does it. We've got a delicate lady here."

"You've said that about eight or ten times, Leo. Is that sucker in spec or out?"

"In. On the surface, anyway. But the internal crystalline structure of the titanium—well, it just isn't as controlled as it would have been in a normal fabrication."

"Is it *in* spec or *out*? I'm not going to Jump a thousand people to their deaths, dammit. Especially if I'm included."

"In, in," Leo spoke through his teeth. "But just—don't horse it around, huh? For the sake of my blood pressure, if nothing else."

Ti muttered something; it might have been, *Screw your blood pressure*, but Leo wasn't sure. He didn't ask for a repeat.

Leo and his quaddie work gang gathered their equipment and jetted a safe distance from the Necklin rod arm. They hung a hundred meters or so above Home. The light of Rodeo's sun was pale and sharp here within an hour of the wormhole Jump point; more than a bright star, but far less than the nuclear furnace that had warmed the Habitat in Rodeo orbit.

Leo seized the moment to gaze upon their cobbled-together colony ship from this rare exterior vantage. Over a hundred modules had finally been bundled together along the ship's axis, all carrying on—more or less—their previous functions. Damned if the design didn't look almost intended, in a lunatic-functional sort of way. It reminded Leo a bit of the thrilling ugliness of the early space probes of the Twentieth and Twenty-first Centuries.

Miraculously, it had held together under two days' steady acceleration and deceleration. Inevitably items here and there Inside had been found to have been overlooked. The younger quaddies had crawled about bravely, cleaning up; Nutrition had managed to get everyone fed something, though the menu was a trifle random; thanks to yeoman efforts on the part of the young airsystems maintenance supervisor who had stayed on and his quaddie work gang, they no longer had to cease accelerating periodically for the plumbing to work. For a while Leo had been convinced the potty stops were going to be the death of them all, not that he hadn't grabbed the opportunities himself for the final touching-up on their vortex mirror.

"See any smoke?" Ti's voice inquired in his ear.

"Nope."

"That's it, then. You people better get your asses Inside. And as soon as you've got everything nailed down, Leo, I'd appreciate it if you'd come up to Nav and Com."

Something in the timbre of Ti's voice chilled Leo. "Oh? What's up?"

"There's a Security shuttle closing on us from Rodeo. Your old buddy Van Atta's aboard, and ordering us to halt and desist. I don't think there's much time left."

"You're still maintaining comm silence, I trust?"

"Oh, yeah, sure. But that doesn't prevent me from listening, eh? There's a lot of chatter from the Jump Station—but that doesn't worry me as much as what's coming up from behind. I, um . . . don't think Van Atta handles frustration too well."

"On edge, is he?"

"Over the edge, I think. Those Security shuttles are armed, y'know. And a lot faster than this monster in normal space. Just 'cause their lasers are classed as 'light weaponry' doesn't mean it's exactly healthy to stand around in front of 'em. I'd just as soon Jump *before* they got in range."

"I read you." Leo waved his work gang toward the entry hatch to the worksuit locker module.

So it was coming at last. Leo had devised a dozen defenses in his mind, upended beam welders, explosive mines, for the long-anticipated physical confrontation with GalacTech employees trying to retake the Habitat. But all his time had been gobbled up by the vortex mirror, and as a result only the most instant of weapons, such as the beam welders, were now available, and even they would have no use Indoors in a boarding battle. He could just picture one missing its target and slicing through a wall into an adjoining creche module. Hand-to-hand in free fall the quaddies might have some advantage; weapons cancelled that, being more dangerous to the defenders than the attackers. It all depended on what kind of attack Van Atta launched. And Leo hated depending on Van Atta.

Van Atta swore into the comm one last time, then dealt the OFF key an angry blow. He had run out of fresh invective hours before, and was conscious of repeating himself. He turned from the comm console and glowered around the Security shuttle's control compartment.

The pilot and co-pilot, up front, were busy about their work. Bannerji, commanding the force, and Dr. Yei—and how had she inserted herself into this expedition, anyway?—were strapped to their acceleration couches, Yei in the engineer's seat, Bannerji holding down the weapons console across the aisle from Van Atta.

"That's it, then," snapped Van Atta. "Are we in range for the lasers yet?"

Bannerji checked a readout. "Not quite."

"Please," said Dr. Yei, "let me try to talk to them just once more—"

"If they're half as sick of the sound of your voice as I am, they're not going to answer," growled Van Atta. "You've spent hours talking to them. Face it— they're not *listening* any more, Yei. So much for psychology."

The Security sergeant, Fors, stuck his head through from the rear compartment where he rode with his twenty-six fellow GalacTech guards. "What's the word, Captain Bannerji? Should we suit up for boarding yet?"

Bannerji quirked an eyebrow at Van Atta. "Well, Mr. Van Atta? Which plan is it to be? It appears we're going to have to cross off all the scenarios that started with their surrendering."

"You got that shit straight." Van Atta brooded at the comm, which emitted only a grey empty hiss on its vid. "As soon as we're in range, start firing on 'em, then. Disable the Necklin rod arms first, then the normal space thrusters if you can. Then we blast a hole in the side, march in, and mop up."

Sergeant Fors cleared his throat. "You did say there were a *thousand* of those mutants aboard, didn't you, Mr. Van Atta? What about the plan of skipping the boarding part and just taking the whole vessel in tow, back to wherever you want it? Aren't the odds a little, um, lopsided for boarding?"

"Complain to Chalopin, she's the one who balked at drafting help from outside Security proper. But the odds aren't what they appear. The quaddies are creampuffs. Half of them are children under twelve, for God's sake. Just go in, and stun anything that moves. How many five-year-old girls do you figure you're equal to, Fors?"

"I don't know, sir," Fors blinked. "I never pictured myself fighting five-year-old girls."

Bannerji drummed his fingers on his weapons console and glanced at Yei. "Is that girl with the baby aboard, the ones I almost shot that day in the warehouse, Dr. Yei?"

"Claire? Yes," she replied levelly.

"Ah." Bannerji glanced away from her intent gaze, and shifted in his seat.

"Let's hope your aim is better this time, Bannerji," said Van Atta.

Bannerji rotated a computer schematic of a Superjumper in his vid, running calculations. "You realize," he said slowly, "that the real event is going to have some uncontrolled factors—the probability is good that we're going to end up punching some extra holes in the inhabited modules while we're going for the Necklin rods."

"That's all right," said Van Atta. Bannerji's lips screwed up doubtfully. "Look, Bannerji," added Van Atta impatiently, "the quaddies are—ah, have made themselves expendable by turning criminal. It's no different than shooting a thief fleeing from any other kind of robbery or break-in. Besides, you can't make an omelette without breaking eggs."

Dr. Yei ran her hands hard over her face. "Lord Krishna," she groaned. She favored Van Atta with a tight, peculiar smile. "I've been wondering when you were going to say that. I should have put a side bet on it—run a pool—"

Van Atta bristled defensively. "If you had done

your job right," he returned no less tightly, "we wouldn't be here now breaking eggs. We could have boiled them in their shells back on Rodeo at the very least. In fact I intend to point out to management later, believe me. But I don't have to argue with you any more. For everything I intend to do, I have a proper authorization."

"Which you have not shown to me."

"Chalopin and Captain Bannerji saw it. If I have my way you'll get a termination out of this, Yei."

She said nothing, but acknowledged the threat with a brief ironic tilt of her head. She leaned back in her chair and crossed her arms, apparently silenced at last. *Thank God*, Van Atta added to himself.

"Get suited up, Fors," he told the Security sergeant.

Nav and Com in the D-620 was a crowded chamber. Ti ruled from his control chair, enthroned beneath his headset; Silver manned the comm; and Leo—held down the post of chief engineer, he supposed. The chain of command became rather blurred at this point. Perhaps his title ought to be Official Ship's Worrier. His guts churned and his throat tightened as all lines of action approached their intersection at the point of no return.

"The Security shuttle has stopped broadcasting," Silver reported.

"That's a relief," said Ti. "You can turn the sound back up, now."

"Not a relief," denied Leo. "If they've stopped talking, they may be getting ready to open fire." And it was too late, too close to Jump point to put a beam welder and crew Outside to fire back.

Ti's mouth twisted in dismay. He closed his eyes; the D-620 seemed to tilt, lumbering under acceleration. "We're almost in position to Jump," he said.

Leo eyed a monitor. "They're almost in range to fire." He paused a moment, then added, "They *are* in range to fire."

Ti made a squeaking noise, and pulled his headset down. "Powering-up the Necklin field—"

"*Gently,*" yelped Leo. "My vortex mirror—"

Silver's hand sought Leo's. He was overwhelmed by a desire to apologize, to Silver, to the quaddies, to God, he didn't know who. *I got you into this . . . I'm sorry . . .*

"If you open a channel, Silver," said Leo desperately, his head swimming in panic—all those children— "We could still surrender—"

"Never," said Silver. Her grip tightened on his hand, and her blue eyes met his. "And I choose for all, not just for myself. We go."

Leo ground his teeth, and nodded shortly. The seconds thudded in his brain, syncopated with the hammering of his heart. The Security shuttle grew in the monitor.

"Why don't they fire now?" asked Silver.

"Fire," ordered Van Atta.

Bannerji's bright computer schematics drew toward alignment, numbers flickering, lights converging. Dr. Yei, Van Atta noticed, was no longer in her seat. Probably hiding out in the toilet chamber. This dose of real life and real consequences was doubtless too much for her. *Just like one of those wimp politicians,* Van Atta thought scathingly, *who talks people into disaster and disappears when the shooting starts. . . .*

"Fire *now,*" he repeated to Bannerji, as the computer blinked readiness, locked onto its target.

Bannerji's hand moved toward the firing switch, hesitated. "Do you have a work order for this?" he asked suddenly.

"Do I have a *what*?" said Van Atta.

"A work order. It occurs to me that, technically, this could be considered an act of hazardous waste disposal. It takes a work order signed by the originator of the request—that's you—my supervisor—that's Administrator Chalopin—and the company Hazardous Waste Management Officer."

"Chalopin has turned you over to me. That makes it official, mister!"

"But not complete. The Hazardous Waste Management Officer is Laurie Gompf, and she's back on Rodeo. You don't have *her* authorization. The work-order is incomplete. Sorry, sir." Bannerji vacated the weapons console and plunked himself down in the empty engineer's seat, crossing his arms. "It's as much as my job is worth to complete an act of hazardous waste disposal without a proper order. The Environmental Impact Assessment has to be attached, too."

"This is mutiny!" yelled Van Atta.

"No, it isn't," Bannerji disagreed cordially. "This isn't the military."

Van Atta glared red-faced at Bannerji, who studied his fingernails. With an oath, Van Atta flung himself into the weapons console seat and reset the aim. He might have known—anything you wanted done right you had to do yourself—he hesitated, the engineering parameters of the D-class Superjumpers racing through his mind. Where on that complex structure might a hit not merely disable the rods, but cause the main thrusters to blow entirely?

Cremation, indeed. And the deaths of the four or five downsiders aboard could, at need, be blamed on Bannerji—*I did my best, ma'am*—if he'd done his job as I'd first requested. . . .

The schematic spun in the vid display. There must

be a point in the structure—yes. There and there. If he could knock out both *that* control nexus and *those* coolant lines, he could start an uncontrolled reaction that would result in—promotion, probably, after the dust had settled. Apmad would kiss him. Just like a heroic doctor, singlehandedly stopping a plague of genetic abomination from spreading across the galaxy . . .

The target schematic pulled toward alignment again. Van Atta's sweating palm closed around the firing switch. In a moment—just a moment—

"What are you doing with *that*, Dr. Yei?" asked Bannerji's voice in startlement.

"Applying psychology."

The back of Van Atta's head seemed to explode with a sickening crack. He pitched forward, cutting his chin on the console, bumping the keypads, turning his firing program to confetti-colored hash in the vid. He saw stars *inside* the shuttle, blurring purple and green spots—gasping, he straightened back up.

"Dr. Yei," Bannerji objected, "if you're trying to knock a man out you've got to hit him a *lot* harder than that."

Yei recoiled fearfully as Van Atta surged up out of his seat. "I didn't want to risk killing him. . . ."

"Why not?" muttered Bannerji under his breath.

Furiously, Van Atta's hands closed around Yei's wrist. He yanked the metal wrench from her grasp. "You can't do anything right, can you?" he snarled.

She was gasping and weeping. Fors, space-suited but still minus his helmet, stuck his head through again from the rear compartment. "What the hell is going on up here?"

Van Atta shoved Yei toward him. Bannerji, squirming uncomfortably in his seat, was clearly not to be trusted. "Hold onto this crazy bitch. She just tried to kill me with a wrench."

"Oh? She told *me* she needed it to adjust a seat attitude," remarked Fors. "Or—*did* she say 'seat'?" But he held Yei's arms. Her struggle, as ever, was weak and futile.

With a hiss, Van Atta heaved himself back into the weapons console seat and called up the targeting program again. He reset it, and switched on the view from the exterior scanners. The D-620-Habitat configuration stood out vividly in the vid, the cold and distant sunlight silver-gilding its structure. The schematics converged, caging it.

The D-620 wavered, rotated, and vanished.

The lasers fired, lances of light striking into empty space.

Van Atta howled, beating his fists on the console, blood droplets flicking from his chin. "They got *out*. They got *out*. They got *out*—"

Yei giggled.

Leo hung limply in his seat restraints, laughter bubbling in his throat. "We made it!"

Ti swung his headset up and sat no less limply, his face white and lined—Jumps drained pilots. Leo felt as if he'd just been twisted inside out himself, squeaking, but the nausea passed quickly.

"Your mirror was in spec, Leo," Ti said faintly.

"Yes. I'd been afraid it might explode, during the stresses of the Jump."

Ti eyed him indignantly. "That's not what you *said*. I thought you were the hot-shot testing engineer."

"Look, I'd never made one of those things before," Leo protested. "You never *know*. You only make the best possible guesses." He sat up, trying to gather his scattered wits. "We're here. We made it. But what's going on Outside, was there any damage to the Habitat—Silver, see what you can get on the comm."

She too was pale. "My goodness," she blinked. "So that was a Jump. Sort of like six hours of Dr. Yei's truth serum all squeezed into a second. Ugh. Are we going to be doing this a lot?"

"I certainly hope so," said Leo. He unstrapped himself and floated over to assist her.

Space around the wormhole was empty and serene— Leo's secret paranoid vision of Jumping into waiting military fire was not to be, he noted gladly. But wait, a ship was approaching them—not a commercial vessel, something dangerous and official-looking. . . .

"It's some sort of police ship from Orient IV," Silver guessed. "Are we in trouble?"

"Undoubtedly," Dr. Minchenko's voice cut in as he floated into Nav and Com. "GalacTech will certainly not take this lying down. You will do us all a favor, Graf, if you let me do the talking just now." He elbowed both Silver and Leo aside, taking over the comm. "The Minister of Health of Orient IV happens to be a professional colleague of mine. While his is not a position of great political power, it is a channel of communication to the highest levels of government. If I can get through to him we will be in a much better position than if we try to deal with some low level police sergeant, or worse, military officer." Minchenko's eyes glinted. "There is no love lost between GalacTech and Orient IV at the moment. Whatever GalacTech's charges, we can counter— tax fraud—oh, the possibilities. . . ."

"What do we do while you're talking?" asked Ti.

"Keep boosting," advised Minchenko.

"It's not over, is it?" Silver said quietly to Leo, as they floated out of Minchenko's way. "Somehow, I thought our troubles would be over if only we could get away from Mr. Van Atta."

Leo shook his head. A jubilant grin still kept crooking up the corner of his mouth. He took one of her upper hands. "Our troubles would have been over if Brucie-baby had scored a hit. Or if the vortex mirror had blown up in the middle of the Jump, or if—don't be afraid of troubles, Silver. They're a sign of life. We'll deal with them together—tomorrow."

She breathed a long sigh, the tension draining from her face, her body, her arms. An answering smile at last lighted her eyes, making them bright like stars. She turned her face expectantly toward his.

He found himself grinning quite foolishly, for a man pushing forty. He tried to twitch his face into more dignified lines. There was a pause.

"Leo," said Silver in a tone of sudden insight, "are you *shy?*"

"Who, me?" said Leo.

The blue stars squeezed for a moment into quite predatory glitters. She kissed him. Leo, indignant at her accusation, kissed her back more thoroughly. Now it was her turn to grin foolishly. A lifetime with the quaddies, Leo reflected, could be all right. . . .

They turned their faces to the new sun.

MILES VORKOSIGAN/NAISMITH: HIS UNIVERSE AND TIMES

Chronology	Events	Chronicle
Approx. 200 years before Miles's birth	Quaddies are created by genetic engineering.	*Falling Free*
During Beta-Barrayaran War	Cordelia Naismith meets Lord Aral Vorkosigan while on opposite sides of a war. Despite difficulties, they fall in love and are married.	*Shards of Honor*
The Vordarian Pretendership	While Cordelia is pregnant, an attempt to assassinate Aral by poison gas fails, but Cordelia is affected; Miles Vorkosigan is born with bones that will always be brittle and other medical problems. His growth will be stunted.	*Barrayar*
Miles is 17	Miles fails to pass physical test to get into the Service Academy. On a trip, necessities force him to improvise the Free Dendarii Mercenaries into existence; he has	*The Warrior's Apprentice*

Chronology	Events	Chronicle
	unintended but unavoidable adventures for four months. Leaves the Dendarii in Ky Tung's competent hands and takes Elli Quinn to Beta for rebuilding of her damaged face; returns to Barrayar to thwart plot against his father. Emperor pulls strings to get Miles into the Academy.	
Miles is 20	Ensign Miles graduates and immediately has to take on one of the duties of the Barrayaran nobility and act as detective and judge in a murder case. Shortly afterwards, his first military assignment ends with his arrest. Miles has to rejoin the Dendarii to rescue the young Barrayaran emperor. Emperor accepts Dendarii as his personal secret service force.	"The Mountains of Mourning" in *Borders of Infinity* *The Vor Game*
Miles is 22	Miles and his cousin Ivan attend a Cetagandan state funeral and are caught up in Cetagandan internal politics.	*Cetaganda*

Chronology	Events	Chronicle
	Miles sends Commander Elli Quinn, who's been given a new face on Beta, on a solo mission to Kline Station.	*Ethan of Athos*
Miles is 23	Now a Barrayaran Lieutenant, Miles goes with the Dendarii to smuggle a scientist out of Jackson's Whole. Miles's fragile leg bones have been replaced by synthetics.	"Labyrinth" in *Borders of Infinity*
Miles is 24	Miles plots from within a Cetagandan prison camp on Dagoola IV to free the prisoners. The Dendarii fleet is pursued by the Cetagandans and finally reaches Earth for repairs. Miles has to juggle both his identities at once, raise money for repairs, and defeat a plot to replace him with a double. Ky Tung stays on Earth. Commander Elli Quinn is now Miles's right-hand officer. Miles and the Dendarii depart for Sector IV on a rescue mission.	"The Borders of Infinity" in *Borders of Infinity* *Brothers in Arms*

Chronology	Events	Chronicle
Miles is 25	Hospitalized after previous mission, Miles's broken arms are replaced by synthetic bones. With Simon Illyan, Miles undoes yet another plot against his father while flat on his back.	*Borders of Infinity*
Miles is 28	Miles meets his clone brother Mark again, this time on Jackson's Whole.	*Mirror Dance*
Miles is 29	Miles hits thirty; thirty hits back.	*Memory*
Miles is 30	Emperor Gregor dispatches Miles to Komarr to investigate a space accident, where he finds old politics and new technology make a deadly mix.	*Komarr*

MORE PRAISE FOR
LOIS MCMASTER BUJOLD

What the readers say:

"My copy of *Shards of Honor* is falling apart I've reread it so often.... I'll read whatever you write. You've certainly proved yourself a grand storyteller."

—Liesl Kolbe, Colorado Springs, CO

"I experience the stories of Miles Vorkosigan as almost viscerally uplifting.... But certainly, even the weightiest theme would have less impact than a cinder on snow were it not for a rousing good story, and good storytelling with it. This is the second thing I want to thank you for.... I suppose if you boiled down all I've said to its simplest expression, it would be that I immensely enjoy and admire your work. I submit that, as literature, your work raises the overall level of the science fiction genre, and spiritually, your work cannot avoid positively influencing all who read it."

—Glen Stonebraker, Gaithersburg, MD

"'The Mountains of Mourning' [in *Borders of Infinity*] was one of the best-crafted, and simply best, works I'd ever read. When I finished it, I immediately turned back to the beginning and read it again, and I can't remember the last time I did that."   —Betsy Bizot, Lisle, IL

"I can only hope that you will continue to write, so that I can continue to read (and of course buy) your books, for they make me laugh and cry and think ... rare indeed."   —Steven Knott, Major, USAF

What Do You Say?

<u>*Send me these books!*</u>

Shards of Honor	72087-2	$5.99	☐
Barrayar	72083-X	$5.99	☐
Cordelia's Honor (trade)	87749-6	$15.00	☐
The Warrior's Apprentice	72066-X	$5.99	☐
The Vor Game	72014-7	$5.99	☐
Young Miles (trade)	87782-8	$15.00	☐
Cetaganda (hardcover)	87701-1	$21.00	☐
Cetaganda (paperback)	87744-5	$5.99	☐
Ethan of Athos	65604-X	$5.99	☐
Borders of Infinity	72093-7	$5.99	☐
Brothers in Arms	69799-4	$5.99	☐
Mirror Dance (paperback)	87646-5	$6.99	☐
Memory (paperback)	87845-X	$6.99	☐
The Spirit Ring (paperback)	72188-7	$5.99	☐

LOIS MCMASTER BUJOLD

Only from Baen Books

visit our website at www.baen.com